I0824448

Wretch

Also by Eric LaRocca

Things Have Gotten Worse Since We Last Spoke and Other Misfortunes

The Trees Grew Because I Bled There: Collected Stories

Everything the Darkness Eats

This Skin Was Once Mine and Other Disturbances

At Dark, I Become Loathsome

We Are Always Tender with Our Dead (Burnt Sparrow, 1)

Wretch

or, The Unbecoming of Porcelain Khaw

Eric LaRocca

LONDON NEW YORK TORONTO
AMSTERDAM/ANTWERP NEW DELHI SYDNEY/MELBOURNE

1230 AVENUE OF THE AMERICAS, NEW YORK, NEW YORK 10020

This book is a work of fiction. Any references to historical events, real people, or real places are used fictitiously. Other names, characters, places, and events are products of the author's imagination, and any resemblance to actual events or places or persons, living or dead, is entirely coincidental.

First Saga Press hardcover edition March 2026

SAGA PRESS and colophon are trademarks of Simon & Schuster, LLC

Interior design by Kathryn A. Kenney-Peterson

Manufactured in the United States of America

1 3 5 7 9 10 8 6 4 2

Library of Congress Cataloging-in-Publication Data has been applied for.

ISBN 978-1-6680-7009-3
ISBN 978-1-6680-7011-6 (ebook)

For Clive and all the exquisite suffering

Nothing else wounds so deeply and irreparably. Nothing else robs us of hope so much as being unloved by one we love.

—Clive Barker

Reverse Haunting

Every living thing—no matter how small, no matter how hollow and crude—is a kind of mirror. We recognize all the painful, abhorrent parts of ourselves by seeing them reflected in others.

There's a remarkable carnage—a swift kind of cruelty, a haughty sort of viciousness—thrumming beneath the blighted, rotting sinew of the world. I feel it in the air, in the stone steps, in the frame of the small redbrick house with the roof tiled in dark gray shingles that I stand in front of. *Why have I come here?* I wonder to myself, as the door pulls back and a man appears there in a suit so sharp it could cut. He eyes me up and down, quietly eviscerating my willpower. I want only to be a loyal subject, to become a kind of servant the way all women must submit themselves before men, to be possessed.

There are a number of ways a human—a frail thing, a miserable waif—can be possessed. It doesn't just mean by spirits. A human can be owned, just like any other object of desire. I've often struggled to come to terms with such a barbed and perilous thought. There's usually such empowering talk of autonomy and volition when it comes to humanity, and how we must break free from the poor circumstances that bind us. *But is any of it actually true?* I often think of ourselves as trapped inside small enclosures that others have built for us, for the showmanship of our suffering—to make certain we realize that we are not free, and we will never be liberated. Because it's a dangerous thing to be free—to be wild and unfettered, like a show horse that will not be restrained. Sometimes it's wonderful to simply *belong* to another person, to dwell in the safety, the warmth of their presence. Other times, it's a cruel and savage mockery—some sort of mean-spirited cosmic joke told at our expense.

From the way this man glares at me with such cruel intention, I can tell for certain he's expecting to annihilate me with a mere flick of his wrist. If he could simply command the tide of blood swelling inside me to finally burst, I know that he would. If he could undo the resistance I've threaded into every fiber of my hair, he'd be a far more content man.

"You're earlier than we agreed," he says, craning his neck outside and glancing around with a curious look to make sure that I haven't been followed to the house.

I glance at my phone screen for the time. "Only ten minutes."

He swipes the phone from me, tossing it in a small wooden box, and then fastens a latch to lock it. I can tell he's annoyed. His correspondence with me had been overwhelmingly curt and impersonal, almost as though I were talking to something that was trying to imitate a human being but could never comprehend the complexities, the nuances of existing as such. I often thought of him on the other end of the computer screen—a luminous waif bathed in a soft silver glow—and twisting himself, carefully disfiguring himself to be as humanlike as possible. *Perhaps he's already expired.* Yes, perhaps he's a frightened or lovelorn spirit, and I'm idling in the presence of someone who once was but is unquestionably no more. Part of me relishes the idea of him prevailing as some sort of spectral presence, an unfathomable thing incapable of understanding humanity any longer.

While I stand there at the threshold, I cannot help but wonder to myself if he has ever heard of something called a reverse haunting. After all, there are certainly poisonous ways in which the living can torment and exhaust the dead. Indeed, there are different ways for us to haunt them. He might be surprised to know that not every living thing is careful and affectionate with those who have passed on. I suppose it's fair to argue that things that are dead want nothing from the living. A dead plant does not know enough to yearn for a drop of water, a mountain spring that might save it. The rotting corpse of a once-beloved pet does not ache for momentary relief from the leash that strangled them. Such consolations, such pities would be inadequate for them now. They are unmistakably and unequivocally without life. Dead things have no needs, no immediate desires. Not like things that are alive. If you're living, you make good use of your wants, your needs. It's simple to be filled with longing, with an insatiable hunger for something you cannot and will never completely possess.

Perhaps ghosts only exist because we want them to. We will them into existence with our hunger, our need to know if there's life beyond the dark curtain of death, beyond where the dim lights reach. There are times when I've wondered if I've actually seen a ghost in the dark corners of a room. I imagine I see black, spindle-thin arms sprouting from a round torso as dark as soot. I wish to see a kind, gentle face greeting me from the far edge of my room—the place where I'm afraid to go because it feels so familiar and yet so forbidden at the same time. Perhaps the thing I see there is smiling. But the grin is withered-looking, almost like the horrible thing were trying to replicate a semblance of joy, of humanity, when such a reproduction is not at all possible right now. Because even though ghosts were once living things, it's so easy to lose touch with your sense of humanity, your true perception of self. The ghosts that I imagine suffering in the room with me don't seem to know how to be human. They're awkward and clumsy when they stir, peeling themselves from the wall paint where they frequently laze. They have difficulty speaking to me or even uttering simple words like "cat" or "tree."

I ache to witness these spirits—to know them, to call them mine and possess them in a way I cannot properly articulate. Even a ghost can be owned. Can you imagine if we could barter with them as if they were a kind of currency? Perhaps these spirits will not make themselves known to me because they know I'd abuse them; I'd manipulate them into doing things that might make them pale. The truth is this: *I* wish to haunt *them*—the insistent presence in the dimly lit corner with teeth gnashing, eyeballs widening, hands curling to fists, hair prickling and standing on end. I'm the pain of this world, and they are the fortunate ones without hunger, without craving, without injury. When I imagine how they come to me, then I linger in their company like the distant sound of thunder heard from a room without doors or windows. My very presence is a haunting, and I want them to know this. But why do I insist on reaching out to them? Why can't I simply allow these poor, unfortunate phantoms to rest in peace, to be eaten by maggots, to be devoured by the cruel, unforgiving ache of time? Instead, do I call to them because of my own wants and longings? I can say with some certainty that no dead thing ever wanted to return to this world. Dead things don't require such needs. *But the living do.* I certainly do.

"You've brought the item we agreed upon?" he asks me, his tone firming with a suspicion that I've arrived unprepared, unrehearsed.

I swallow hard, and my throat itches with a horrible burning sensation.

I unfold the golden clasp securing my handbag, and I pull out the small, framed photograph of my dead husband I was advised to bring. The photograph's frame is wooden, but somewhat expensive-looking. Not because it appears as though it might be an antique, but rather because it's neatly polished and heavy to hold. For some inexplicable reason, I've always considered an object's weight to be equal to its worth. The heavier an item, the more costly. For a moment, I wonder if human souls are considered similarly. Perhaps the heftier the soul, the more penance to be taken by the final collector. I imagine my soul to be burdened with the immeasurable weight of longing, of hoping and yearning for something to happen—something wonderful, something truly miraculous. Perhaps that's what spoils a person's spirit in the end. Perhaps idling in despair and yearning for what can never be is what causes the soul to ferment, to rot, to become diseased like the skin of a leper.

With some reluctance, I pass the framed photograph to him. I observe him while he studies the photograph with such attention, such dedication and care. I know for certain he's looking for a flaw, for a sign that I've misunderstood the assignment, for a telltale notice that I've delivered something unreasonable to him for the ritual. *Women are permanently incapable of understanding,* he must think. Although it's probably objectionable to assign him certain thoughts without actually knowing what he's thinking, it can't be helped, especially because of the loathsome way in which he regards me. I wonder if he looks at me the way he most likely addresses all women in need who come to him—a horrible disruption, a force that has disturbed him needlessly for the sake of a pittance of comfort. *But don't I deserve comfort?* I think to ask him. *Isn't life so cruel and so callous that I've earned a modicum of comfort?* Unfortunately, I'm left to wonder if he'd agree.

"The first item you mailed us was unsatisfactory," he says to me. "You're certain this item holds more emotional value?"

My stomach twists a little. I wonder if he thinks I'm trying to trick him. I must look so suspicious with the way my eyes dart around the room, the panicky way I breathe, the awful way my hands tremble.

"Yes," I tell him. "I promise."

"It's smaller than I thought it might be," he says, his lower lip curling a little with visible disdain.

I stammer, unsure how to respond at first. Of course, I knew that the item I was asked to bring here was supposed to be valuable. Not only costly, but sentimentally precious as well. I know for certain it's too late to change things now. I've already fucked up once along the way. I certainly won't recover from another slipup.

"It's the most meaningful thing I have from my husband," I say.

For a moment, I gaze at the photograph with such longing, such unreserved affection, for the middle-aged man permanently captured there—his gray suit, his full head of dark hair brushed to one side, the gentle way he rests one of his hands in his lap and the other on his knee while he sits casually in a leather armchair in front of a large bookcase stuffed to the gills with antique-looking hardcovers. My husband, Laird, was many things to many different people. I suppose that's true of everyone. But when I think of him, I can't help but think of him enjoying a glass of scotch while listening to one of his records play in his private library. I took that photograph of him ten years ago, and, to this day, it's one of the clearest, most soul-defining memories I share with him even though he's no longer here to appreciate it. Of course, he'd curse how maudlin I've become now that he's gone. He'd chastise me for building a memorial in his honor—articles of well-worn clothing, different household items he used regularly like combs, toothbrushes, empty bottles of his favorite shampoo. Naturally, there were many different things I could have delivered to my host for the ritual to work, for our private ceremony to take root; however, I think so fondly of the memory of taking that particular photograph. I recall how I took a few pictures before I fell into his arms, and we made love right there while one of Gershwin's records played for us.

"I suppose it will do," he says to me, handing me the photograph again and luring me farther and farther into the house.

I glance around at my surroundings and notice how all the walls are empty. There are no pictures hanging, no glimpses into the lives that might dwell here. There are no items for decoration to be enjoyed or studied. The entire house looks like a blank slate, a place that has no identity and that, more importantly, wishes to claim no identity. After all, to claim an identity is to be godlike in some way. I was once told in the strictest confidence that a god's name must never be known or written down. To name something is to possess ownership over the very thing. It feels as though this house cannot wish to possess its inhabitants in any way, to claim its guests the way a mother might claim ownership over her own flesh and blood. After all, a mother is a kind of god. *Isn't she?*

We turn down a corridor that stretches for a few yards in front of us. The hallway is dark, except for a tiny sliver of white light spilling out from a half-shut doorway at the end of the dim passage. Once again, the walls are bare and undecorated—without soul, absent of spirit. I notice how some of the hairs on the nape of my neck have prickled a little the same way they do when I walk alone at night in a neighborhood I do not know very well. Just then, I notice something stirring on the carpet stretching out in front of us. I squint, eyes straining to comprehend what I'm seeing in the dark. It's then that I notice that the carpet appears to be moving, muted silver flecks of light circling the rug and flickering there like dots of bioluminescence on still ocean water at night. I look closer and notice that the tiny shapes that are moving are swollen, fat insects. Beetles, to be precise. The creatures are reflective almost, their silver shells glinting softly like pieces of tinfoil reflecting the glare of a flashlight.

"What are these?" I ask, my voice trailing off with such unsureness. I feel foolish even asking since I know I'm supposed to accept whatever I encounter when I come here. That detail was laid out very carefully in one of the many emails we exchanged before my arrival tonight.

"You were told that you were not to question anything," he reminds me. Gentler than I had expected. I'm somewhat grateful for that. "Pay no mind to those little creatures . . ."

I nod slightly, and my attention then drifts back to the slightly open doorway at the opposite end of the corridor. It feels cold and dark where I'm standing, and I sense myself being drawn slowly toward the light, the same way an insect might be drawn to the warmth of an open flame.

"This is where I leave you," he says. "You're supposed to do the rest of this on your own."

The very thought of venturing any farther feels almost impossible for me. However, very soon, I sense my feet shifting slightly and beginning to force me down the length of the narrow and dimly lit passageway. I glance down, careful to avoid stepping on any of the small beetles scattered across the carpet. I'd retch if I heard a crunch while taking another step. Thankfully, I don't. The little insects are safe for now. Until I return, that is. *If* I return . . .

I curse myself for thinking something so grim, so unabashedly grotesque. Why should I presume I'm going to perish when I meet with the person I'm supposed to greet? After all, I sought him out. I made every conceivable effort to come here tonight, to bask in his presence. It seems foolish to invent horrific scenarios of what might occur if things go wrong. *But things* can *go wrong,* I think. There's no way to deny the unpleasantness of the fact. Anything can happen. Anything can occur.

I reach the little door at the end of the narrow passageway.

I glance back and notice that the man has disappeared from where I left him. He was eager to abandon me. But surely he must come back for me when the ritual is done. I hope to God he comes back for me. It feels strange to think of God at a time like this, especially since I've neglected him so much lately. I think about how my mother once told me nonbelievers are so eager to claim they believe in times of turmoil, when they desperately need the assurance. All people are like that—users, manipulators, eager to scheme and make certain that they come out on top no matter what. Am I the loathsome kind of person that my mother once spoke about? Am I so despondent, so miserable and frightened, that I'm willing to pray to some nameless deity I don't normally believe in?

I notice how the floor continues to ripple and undulate like the surface of a lake at nighttime under the shifting of thousands of small, silver beetles. I glance back at the doorway, and the sliver of light feels warm against my face. I sense parts of myself that were unmovable and stiff as bedrock now thawing slightly and threatening to undo completely. *Not yet,* I think to myself. *Dear God, not yet.*

I find myself pressing my hands against the door, slowly pushing the thing open until I'm exposed to what's waiting for me on the other side of the entryway. For a moment, I stand there at the threshold. I'm panting as though I had just run a marathon. It feels strange to admit, but the air seems thinner here. I feel like I might faint at any minute.

I peer into the small room, and I'm greeted by a middle-aged man dressed entirely in white. He looks utterly distinctive and yet completely unremarkable at the same time, if it's even remotely possible to say. His hair is dark, and his eyes are dimmed, glassy, reflective, almost like an ornately decorated bowl made of fine china. He's very trim, but not sickly-looking. There's nothing noteworthy about his appearance that I might be able to recall when I finally leave this room. In fact, he resembles almost a bewildering kind of vessel—a container I could place all my sadness inside, a depository, a sort of reliquary to inherit all my most undesirable longings.

He stirs slowly on the edge of the bed where he's seated. He looks at me with a suppleness I didn't expect from him.

"You're Genevieve?" he asks me.

His voice is saccharine. The words seem to unpeel themselves from the bed of his tongue and lilt, practically *singsongy*—like everything he utters to me is a strange kind of lyric.

He looks almost angelic, perfectly wrought, like the kinds of fancy dishes my grandmother would use on special occasions. It's peculiar to watch him stir from where he's sitting on the most ornate and notable piece of furniture in the room, a large king-sized bed, and move like some celestial guard, a fountain of bloodred sheets pouring out from beneath him.

I clear my throat a little and sense myself moving farther into the room like I've been lassoed by my waist, pulled closer by his every syllable.

"Yes," I reply.

In my peripheral vision, I notice how the room is windowless. There are no other exits except the place where I entered. The walls in this room are bare like the rest of the house.

He steps closer toward me. I sense myself heating red with embarrassment. I don't know exactly why I'm so suddenly unmoored, so lost and unsure in his presence, but he seems to delight in my apprehension.

"Shall we begin . . . ?"

He smiles a little and then holds out his hand.

"How?" I ask, immediately feeling thoughtless for asking another idiotic question. *I should be more trusting,* I think to myself.

But it's too late for that. Whether or not the man trusts me, I cannot be certain. It doesn't matter. The invocation has already been issued. The dance has already begun. Perhaps once I could have retreated, could have sailed across the carpet littered with silver beetles and sprinted out the front door and into the night, never to return again. But certain things cannot be stopped once they're started. We've passed a point when pleasantries can no longer be exchanged, and instead, he can peruse my thoughts, and where we must speak of violence, of unending brutality, of the ghost that haunts me. Or rather, the ghost that I've tormented for years since he first passed. *I am a haunting.* I know that full well. I am a desecrated, revolting thing that's able to exhaust and agonize the dead. It's not that I'm haunted, but rather the simple truth—*I wish to haunt others.* I yearn to possess that which has no meaning, no proper definition. Perhaps he senses this from me, staring blankly at him and wondering what's to become of me now that I've arrived, now that things have actually started.

"There are many ways for this to commence," he tells me, approaching me once more until I'm pinned in a corner of the room. "But I'm afraid you won't like any of them."

"Why is that?" I ask, shivering and sensing my throat sealing tight like he had commanded it to do so. He's capable of magic. This I know too well now. Perhaps I realized it too late.

"Because you're going to have to suffer."

Missing Woman Reported

Posted by **user/laurel_bot** in The Grim Laurels
on November 18, 2021, at 7:57 p.m.

[3 user comments]

The Massachusetts State Police are requesting the public's assistance in locating a missing person. Genevieve Doyle, 47, was last seen on Thursday, October 7, 2021, in the Greater Boston Area. For the last few weeks, local authorities have interviewed family members, friends, and acquaintances of Doyle and have recovered little information into the woman's whereabouts. Doyle is described as a white woman, 5'4", approximately 130 pounds. She has dark brown hair and light blue eyes. Her abandoned car was located in the Suffolk County area on November 10. The car has been processed, but at this time no information is being released as to the results or findings of the investigations. Anyone with information concerning the whereabouts of Genevieve Doyle should immediately contact the Massachusetts State Police at [redacted]. A reward is being offered by the Boston Crime Stoppers for any information that leads to the discovery of Genevieve Doyle.

[Comment posted by **user/shepherdspie23** at 6:34 p.m. today]

Very sad. They mentioned this on the local news again tonight.

[Comment posted by **user/cherryflav3907** at 7:39 p.m. today]

Heartbreaking. I hope they find her.

[Comment posted by **user/cheapy4u38** at 8:17 p.m. today]

They'll never find her. She's with Porcelain now.

Part One

Simeon

It's all a mess. The one out there . . . The one in here . . . the one that's coming. Why is everyone so ready to think the worst is over?

—*Suspiria* (2018)

Chapter One

Dear God, I think to myself, carefully sliding my index finger along the sharp edge of the razor while I squat on the lid of the toilet seat. *This is no way to live. No fucking way to live, indeed . . .*

Day after day, this prickly notion comes to me with hooks and fangs to spear my every waking thought, to wrestle me until my mind is sore and aching. It was innocuous at first. Of course, things are always so deceptively gentle when they first appear to you, especially when they want something from you. I suppose all things in this world want something from you, even something as innocent and as guileless as a thought. However, certain thoughts are carnivorous. I've learned this after years of noticing my mind become more and more polluted, the more upsetting and baleful thoughts taking root easier and spreading further until I'm infected. Yes, infected. Perhaps all human thought is a strange kind of infection, a sort of unseen disease that rots you from the inside out if you're not careful enough. I thought I had been careful. I imagined I was clever when entertaining certain ideas, always attempting to push the more malignant, vindictive thoughts to the outermost corners of my mind where light cannot follow. But lately, more and more, these beliefs come to me when my guard is lowered, when the gates to the shallower lowlands of my mind are open and welcoming to any kind of malevolent trespasser or vagrant. Yes, these thoughts are trespassers. I find myself becoming more vexed by the day as I allow these ideas to plant themselves like perennials in the bed of my mind, destined to be cut down and then regrown every year like a new pernicious bloom.

Still, it's more than obvious to me that this is no way to live—crouching on a rust-eaten toilet in the men's room at work, my fingers skating up and down the length of a razor blade I brought from home. *Just one mere slit,* I think to myself, daydreaming about the self-carnage I could invite with such ease. *Just one flick of the blade and I could open up a river current that's livid and aching to be freed from the most vexing dam of all—my flesh.* Yes, there are days when I wonder if my flesh will slough off similar to the skin of some tropical fruit, shrugging away like some expensive coat until the secret wellspring of blood I've been hiding deep within me unplugs and then rushes out like an uncontrollable geyser. *Dear God, I ache for that!* I think to myself, admiring the way the narrow blade glistens a little in the bathroom's overhead fluorescent lighting. I've thought about killing myself for quite some time. However, ending things is so decidedly permanent. It's the punctuation at the end of a sentence you must complete. There are no other words to be revealed, no other truths to be uncovered. The punctuation at the end of a misused life like mine is final, unable to be rectified or salvaged if you happen to change your mind.

I wouldn't be able to change my mind, after all. I'd be without thought, without pain, without any semblance of reason. Of course, some of these thoughts are attractive to me and possess a certain sense of desirability. But as I gently slide my index finger along the edge of the razor blade with a silent threat to myself, I can't help but wonder if this is how things are supposed to end for me. Naturally,

I never envisioned myself living past the age of thirty-five. I always thought life for a gay man ends when you turn thirty. But as I grow older, I can't help but wonder if I'd be interfering in the way things are supposed to be. *Am I forcing punctuation in a sentence that must remain ongoing?* I remain uncertain even now, sensing my blood coursing in all of my body's main pressure points—a dim throbbing sensation aching me all over. If there were a time to slice myself open, now would be it. I can already envision how it might look when they find me—my bloodless corpse slumped against the side of the toilet like a discarded department store mannequin, a dark shadow of all my wants, needs, hungers stretching across the grime-covered tiled floor. There's no poetry to be found here. But then again, I suppose there's not much poetry in the art of killing yourself. There's nothing poetic about slitting your wrists and slumping over across a toilet half-filled with excrement, all your shamefulness dripping down and pattering along the floor. I've entertained the thought countless times, but never here before, at my place of work. In fact, I feel a little unsettled at how easy it was for me to consider ending things so abruptly in a public bathroom. Have I no shame? Have I no common decency? I think about how my superiors might find me sprawled out on the floor, a blood-buttered razor gripped firmly in my hand. I think of how they might chastise me—even after expiration—and how they might curse me before I had an opportunity to finish my latest spreadsheet about our fourth quarter from last year. *Nobody actually loves you,* I think to myself. *You are worthless to them unless you are giving more of yourself than you can offer.* I suppose that's true of most people. Sometimes what you must give is not nearly enough. It certainly wasn't enough for my beloved Jonathan.

Just as I'm about to press the edge of the blade against the curve of my wrist, I hear a fist pummeling against the bathroom door. A man's voice calls out to me:

"Simeon? Are you in there?"

I immediately know it is Henry, one of the middle-aged men from the accounting office, whose voice is watery and rotted-sounding, probably because he still smokes those god-awful cheap cigarettes, and a dim vapor of smoke seems to constantly shroud him.

The razor slips from my grasp and clatters on the floor. I hold my breath, wondering if he's heard my fumble.

"Yeah, I'm here," I answer, and then silently curse myself for responding.

Why did I feel obligated to answer him? I wonder to myself. *Why am I so accommodating of everyone else's needs but my own?*

So I zipped myself up and excused myself from the washroom. Henry greeted me at the threshold with a look of suspicion. But there was no way he would have been able to guess what I had been doing. It's not like I was browsing on my phone for child pornography like one of our previous associates, who eventually was caught and subsequently fired. Still, there's a part of me that remains cautious. I've already been written up once for what was termed "excessive bathroom time." I certainly don't want to bring more attention to myself now.

"Hurry up," Henry calls out to me from beyond the locked bathroom door. "Mr. Whittaker's asking to see you in his office."

That can't be good, I think to myself. I've only ever met with Mr. Whittaker when I've fucked up in some way—whether it was due to the incorrect numbers included on my spreadsheet or my iciness when interacting with fellow coworkers. Of course, it's never a good sign when your superior wishes to have a word with you. I swipe the razor blade from the floor and pocket it at once. *Why didn't I have the balls to go through with it?* Surely there must be some way I can muster up the courage, the strength, to permanently end things. *Why am I saddled with these meaningless human interactions day after day?*

"I'll be right there," I call through the door, pressing my index finger against the toilet's handle and flushing. "Just a moment."

But I'll need more than a single moment. After all, I've already wasted a lifetime of moments wishing my life were different, wishing I could somehow bring back my beloved Jonathan, promising to the void I'd do anything, would bear any burden to be with him one final time. I hear Henry's footsteps, the squeak of his patent leather loafers on the linoleum floor while he retreats. When I'm certain he's gone, I pull out my wallet and peel the small photograph of Jonathan from where I keep it safe, tucked behind one of my maxed-out credit cards. I gaze at the picture—the way Jonathan's been permanently captured there. It's a beautiful photograph. Jonathan, shirtless and wearing black sunglasses, is lazing on a checkered beach towel on a sandy dune in the hot Provincetown sun. His arm is lifted in the air to prevent me from taking the picture. A smile is slowly creeping across his face, half-formed, nearly there. Sometimes I glance at the picture and wonder if he wanted me to take the photograph. But I can't be saddled with that introspection right now. I pocket the picture and ease myself off the toilet seat. I'm at the door in a matter of seconds, tugging on the handle and stepping out into the corridor. Henry's not waiting for me there. Instead, the hallway is empty.

I make my way toward the main area where most of the cubicles are arranged. I hasten past Henry's workstation and flash him a smile like a simple thanks for alerting me. There's no gratitude in my warmness, however. I know I should be expecting the worst from my superior. In fact, he looks at me somewhat perplexed, like I disrupted him in the middle of something, like I misremembered our previous interaction at the restroom. But surely I couldn't have misremembered something that happened only a few moments ago. Still, I shiver slightly and wonder why he looks at me so queerly, so suspiciously.

Finally, after what feels like eons when it should only have taken me a minute at most to walk from one corner of the floor to the other, I arrive at the threshold of Mr. Whittaker's office—a small, cramped room that resembles almost a broom closet. It's not the spacious, ornate office that one might expect for the vice president of a company. I knock against the door frame and peer through the sliver of open doorway. Mr. Whittaker reclines in his chair with the phone pressed against his ear. He glances at me and signals me to enter the room. I obey with little fussing, sliding inside the office and sitting in the chair across from his desk when he gestures for me to sit. Eventually, he hangs up from his phone call, and his attention snaps to me.

"I've been meaning to meet with you for quite some time," he says, flicking his fingers across the computer keyboard and typing something I cannot see on his screen. "It's such a busy time of year. You know, I'm sure."

He glances down at my hands and notices the large emerald ring on the index finger on my right hand. He sighs and then draws in a deep breath, seeming to admire it.

"That's a curious ring," he says.

I shiver, a little unmoored by his fascination with the ring. Of course, I could tell him the story. I could tell him how Jonathan purchased the ring for me on a work trip to Ireland. Jonathan told me that he had bought it from a curio shop, and the shop owner had told him that the ring had belonged to a man who had been hanged in the village square in the early 1700s. Several people had told the story that the ring held mystical, healing properties. Apparently, it's good fortune to touch the ring of a hanged man. I could have told him all that, but Mr. Whittaker would probably look at me as if my head had just spun around in circles. Instead, I accept the compliment with the little grace I can muster. Mr. Whittaker simpers and then returns his attention to the computer screen.

"I suppose you're curious as to why I've asked to see you," he says.

I swallow hard, not sure how to answer at first. "I know the quarter four numbers I presented at the board meeting were not correct, and I'm working hard to fix them with Accounting."

"That's a small part of why I wanted to see you," Mr. Whittaker says, shrugging. "But it's not the sole reason I sent for you."

I shift uncomfortably in my seat. Naturally, I had expected the worst, and I was right for doing so.

"The board members have noticed your productivity slowing over the past few weeks," Mr. Whittaker tells me. "Of course, we realize that you're under a considerable amount of strain; however, we need to make deadline for certain deliverables, and we keep pushing things back to accommodate your workflow. It's unacceptable and cannot be tolerated."

My eyes lower until I'm staring at the floor. I can't bear to look Mr. Whittaker in the face right now.

"Yes," I say, exhaling sharply. "I know I haven't been as productive as I would like to be."

"Not to mention, the frequent bathroom breaks," Mr. Whittaker says. "Plus, all the days you've been late to work . . . I'm afraid it's sending a clear message to our board that you're not invested; you're not interested in assisting us as we work to meet these benchmarks we've set."

"That's not true," I tell him.

Or is it? Of course I've been distracted for the past several months. What else could Mr. Whittaker have expected from someone who had just lost the love of his life? Naturally, I was afforded a few weeks of paid leave to grieve for my beloved Jonathan, but grief has no expiration date. It's not some switch you can turn on and off as you please. Instead, grief feels like a constant pressure heating inside your gut—a painful reminder when you shift slightly and think it's perhaps abandoned you for the moment. It never does.

"The board and I have been discussing how to handle this," Mr. Whittaker tells me. "We've decided that we're going to recommend you take an extended leave of absence. You've been warned before that this was a possibility. I'm afraid I have no other choice. . . . This leave will be without pay, unfortunately. After a few months, the board will hold a meeting and will make a decision about what's to be done from there."

I sense my heart beating faster and faster, almost like it was a drum of the inevitable doom closing in on me. It feels like the world is swallowing me whole for the sake of its own pleasure. Never mine. My own wants and needs do not matter. I suppose they've never mattered before. *Why should they matter now?*

"It sounds like I don't have any say in this," I say to Mr. Whittaker, and then recoil, surprised by my brashness.

"It's the most sensible thing to do for now, I think," he tells me. "I know it might be painful to hear, but we think it's for the best."

The best for who? I can't help but wonder. For me? Or for the soulless company I've worked at as an administrative specialist for nearly five years? Everything in this world is a vampire. I know that for certain. Everything in this world wants to use you up until you have nothing left to give, until you're a murmur, a pathetic stain etched into the pavement of a roadway heading to nowhere.

"You can take the rest of today off," Mr. Whittaker tells me, easing back into his chair and trying to force a look of relaxation. "Collect your things and clear your desk when you're ready."

I swallow again, my throat burning with a question begging to be asked.

"Am I allowed to come back after a few months?" I ask him, dreading the finality of his answer.

"We'll see what happens," he tells me with a smile that looks so forced, so strained. "We'll see where we are in a few months."

But I already know what will happen at the end of a few months. I won't receive a call from them. My phone calls will be ignored when I finally make a feeble attempt to reach out because my savings account has dwindled to nothingness.

I feel stupid for devoting so much of my time to this place when it abandoned me so callously.

"You need to find new meaning in your life, dear boy," Mr. Whittaker says, reclining in his chair and scratching his marked wrist. "Connect with others. Go out and meet people. Be sociable. It will change your life. . . ."

I swallow nervously. Yes, perhaps he's right. But I've never been much for charming others. I'm only skilled at finding companionship and meaning online. He probably doesn't know this about me. Why should he?

As I turn slightly, my attention is caught by a small gilded-framed photograph arranged on the bureau beside his office desk. The picture is a distorted view of a grove of small hemlocks in some random grove, the image blurred almost like it had been filtered through a warped lens.

"That's an interesting picture," I say to him, stupidly thinking I might worm my way back into his good graces with such a senseless and idiotically kind remark. "A place you've visited?"

Mr. Whittaker glances at the picture and then back at me, his eyebrows furrowed and his mouth frowning.

"That's a picture of my wife," he says so matter-of-factly, and then resumes poring through the pages of notes filed in a small folder on his desk. "I took it last year. . . ."

I shiver slightly when he tells me this because I know for certain that his wife perished three years ago.

I excuse myself from Mr. Whittaker's office and slowly make my way back toward my cubicle to gather my belongings. Yes, even Jonathan. I can't help but think of him, his dimmed, vacant expression glaring at me from behind a portrait inside the empty gallery of my mind. He left me when I needed him the most as well. Perhaps I'm something that can only be used. Perhaps I'll never know the joy of receiving from others.

While I march toward my desk, flitting by cubicle after cubicle, I rub the emerald ring on my index finger and pray for a miracle—a sign that I'll be okay, that everything will pass in time. I'm met with nothing. There's no cosmic signal, no matter how infinitesimal or minuscule. I can't help but think of the poor man who once wore this ring, how the blood must have pooled around the edges when his fingers bloated blackish purple after he was hanged in the town square.

I fantasize about his flaccid body swaying from some wooden post, eventually being cut down by the young, local ruffians who have been assigned to dispose of his corpse. The world can't take anything more from you when you're dead. He was free. *Finally.* The poor bastard was completely and utterly free.

Chapter Two

After I collect my belongings—a few exquisitely framed photographs of Jonathan, a stress toy in the shape of a small mushroom—I pass my work computer to IT Support, a middle-aged man named Walter who constantly carries a sour musk with him wherever he goes. He accepts the gift with little gratitude, almost incensed I caused more work for him due to my own stupidity. He doesn't wish me well on my way. Instead, he forces a half-hearted grunt and then returns his attention to his computer screen, typing a lengthy email to someone.

The whole ordeal feels so anticlimactic. When things come to an end, you expect fanfare. You might expect finality or, at the very least, a semblance of hope that things might soon get better. But instead, everything around me seems to soften with a sort of hazel-colored blur, almost like I was perpetually existing in some well-worn antique photograph. I devoted so much of myself to this company over the five years I worked here. Even Jonathan knew that when he was alive. He'd argue with me sometimes and say that I cared too deeply about what others thought of me, especially work colleagues. But it was all in jest. I know he wasn't truly upset with me. He'd pretend to be sometimes, of course. He'd cross his arms and feign disgust, excusing himself to the other room. But eventually I'd follow, and I'd urge him to make up with a kiss on the cheek.

I feel a hollow ache in the pit of my stomach. It feels so surreal to leave the office for what I know will be the final time. I don't trust Mr. Whittaker's promise to check in. I don't trust anyone anymore, to be totally truthful. It feels as though a screen has lowered across my eyelids, and I'm unable to see people for what they really are. They can present themselves as anything to me, and I'm supposed to believe them. Sometimes I feel like a sleepwalker—a pitiable, pathetic thing that doesn't realize he's dreaming while he's being ferried from person to person, place to place. I'm supposed to accept everything as it is. But what if I don't want to? What if I want more?

I think to wave, to say goodbye and offer a little bit of closure. But I don't. I suppose those kinds of things aren't expected in life sometimes. Very often, things just come to an end without reason, without purpose. There's no rhyme or pretense of explanation. Things simply are the way they are and not meant to be understood.

I make my way toward the elevator. I wonder if someone will rush out and say goodbye as a final effort to end things. But they don't. Nobody seems to care. And why should they? I only worked here for five years. Why should they care about me? I'm nothing. I know that I'm nothing.

After I take the elevator to the ground floor, I step out and cross the lobby until I'm on the sidewalk. It all feels surreal. A blast of cool air hits me in the face with a chilly greeting. Then the sulfur stench of the nearby subway wafts over me. I plug my nose with my free hand and begin to make my way back home. I think about calling for a cab, but what's the point? It's not that far. Plus, it's a beautiful day with clear skies overhead. In fact, the cheerful weather outside seems like an insult—a kind of abuse or a hateful comment about the fact that I've just been let go. I know I shouldn't take it personally. After all, does the universe actually care about me? The universe cares for nothing and no one. We are lost, unfettered in a cruel, uncaring world. Even if the universe possessed the ability to care, I know it wouldn't pay attention to me.

I shuffle along down the street, people weaving around me as my pace seems to slow more and more with every step. I feel groggy, lethargic almost. Like I just had the wind knocked out of me. Perhaps I had. After all, I don't quite know what I'm expected to do now that I'm unemployed. Sure, I have some money saved in a separate account in case things become especially dire. But I certainly can't live off that for the rest of my life. My stomach aches again at the horrible reminder. Things would be so much easier if Jonathan were still alive. I'd return home to him, and he'd welcome me with a warm embrace. He'd talk me off the proverbial ledge after making me a cup of green tea, and he'd tell me all the ways in which we'd survive this. Jonathan was perpetually optimistic like that. He wasn't the kind of sour grape that I've slowly become as I've grown older.

As I round a corner and pass by a small convenience store at the end of the lane, I squint, noticing something stirring in the gutter a few yards away from where I'm dawdling. It's a small, dark shape—half of its body drooping out of sight and into the nearby drain. I find myself drawing closer and closer as more people move around me. It feels strange to notice this thing and to be the only one who seems to care. Just then, I realize what I'm looking at—it's a large rat with its stomach torn open, soft and squishy innards torn from its gut and dangling there like a low-hanging necklace. But the dead rat is not left there to exist in peace. Another rat—this one larger and more aggressive-looking—mounts the poor, lifeless creature and begins to feast on its entrails. I cover my mouth at the disgusting sight while the giant rodent feeds, devouring loops of intestines and burying its blood-soaked snout deep inside the poor, defenseless creature.

For some inexplicable reason, I cannot pull my attention away from the vile sight—the horrible vision of that larger rat feeding relentlessly on the smaller dead one. I close my eyes, and I still see its shiny, blood-buttered viscera dangling like slender, greasy ropes in the sewer, the larger rat feeding without logic, without reason. *This world simply wants to eat other things,* I think to myself, and the thought saddens me. A lowly, helpless rat can't even die in peace, in serenity. There's always some larger creature there to exploit the remains, to gleefully gorge upon its torment, its destruction.

Cannibals, I think to myself, and finally peel away from the grotesque sight. But it will never be a distant memory. It will linger close to the front door of my mind, occasionally knocking there and begging to be remembered. *Yes,* I think. *The world is filled with cannibals.*

I return home later that evening and arrive to a dark, silent apartment. No matter how many days, months, years pass since Jonathan's death, it feels so unusual to return home without being greeted by a friend, a lover, anyone. I wonder if I'll ever grow accustomed to it. It's even more unsettling to live in an apartment building with other people while you live alone, because you're often surrounded by the noise of other residents in different rooms. You hear muffled conversations, dulled music—life being savored by others while I sit here alone, completely unoccupied and ignored.

I shrug out of my jacket, dump my office supplies in a pile near the door, and then head into the kitchen to heat up some leftover macaroni and cheese from dinner two nights ago. After I've finished microwaving my meal, I sit at the kitchen table and open my laptop. Even though Jonathan used to discourage me from the habit, I can't help but browse the message forums on certain websites while I eat—forums dedicated to bored housewives contemplating affairs with their electrician, businessmen sourcing opinions from anonymous users on the craftsmanship of their new necktie. But I think my favorite forums are dedicated to those struggling to comprehend their dreams. I click on a saved link in my browser history, and the page fills in front of me.

The sad fact of the matter is that I desperately need someone to talk to. Naturally, Jonathan was that person for so long. But now that he's gone, what am I supposed to do? Sometimes, late at night, I log onto virtual chat rooms and chat with random strangers. We talk about anything and everything. Sometimes the conversations become sexual, but what else are you to expect? Lonely people have needs, too. I certainly wouldn't be opposed to jerking off with some faceless torso on the video-roulette websites. But, for now, it's merely talking. I try to not be so maudlin, but very often the emotions overwhelm me, and I find myself pouring my heart out across the keyboard. Sometimes the stranger has a kind word for me. Other times, they disconnect and leave me there in the chat room all by myself.

I feel like I'm always the person who's being left behind. I'm never the person who leaves first. I always seem to stay too long for my own good.

But it is early yet, and while shoveling some macaroni into my open mouth, I start perusing the various "Dream Warrior" discussions happening right now—the anonymous users, like me, conversing with one another in real time, moment by moment. It makes me feel included, connected with others, even though I know for certain I will never meet these people. They will never know the real version of me.

Just then, I come upon a forum titled "The Ordeal of Porcelain Khaw." The name attracts me for some reason. I cannot immediately recognize why, but I feel compelled to click the link. After a few moments of buffering, the page loads, and I'm met with a lengthy wall of text written by a user named cheapy4u38. Part of me wonders if I should even bother reading what's been written there. I think of clicking out of the link and returning to the main home page of messages. But something inexplicable forces me to start reading, compels me to go on sentence by sentence. . . .

The Ordeal of Porcelain Khaw

Posted by **user/cheapy4u38** today at 7:34 p.m.

[29 comments]

In my dreams, I think of a book I once read–a collection of Middle Eastern folktales called *1001 Nights*. I don't know why I think about this book especially while I sleep. I read it once during college and was supposed to write a thesis paper about it. Sometimes the most insignificant things in life can inform you in the most surprising ways. However, it causes me to wonder if there's something happening to me that I do not realize–a plot against me and my family. Have you ever seen the film *Rosemary's Baby*? At one point in the film, Mia Farrow's character says, "There are plots against people, aren't there?" She says this during a moment of weakness, her voice quivering a little. I often think of that moment in the film, and sometimes it makes me wonder if there's some horrible plan unfolding against me that I will not realize until it's too late.

I suppose I should tell you about my dream. . . .

In the undisturbed cavern of my thoughts, the place where I've been kept is not merely one room, but rather a maze of interconnected passageways feeding into other private, windowless smaller chambers. I'm only able to approach those rooms while I sleep, when dreams peel back the corners of my mind and fill the loam of my thoughts with different kinds of charms and enchantments.

Sometimes the dreams are so pleasant that I can't bear to rouse myself from sleep. Other times, the dreams are difficult to imagine and hard to endure because they're unpredictable, unpleasant. I suppose I must realize on some level that I've already encountered this strange man—this gaunt-faced, sour-looking gentleman. I've seen him before in a very specific dream that I seem to be able to recall as soon as I see him.

When I think of the dream—when I strain to think of all I remember from the entrails of my imagination—I'm pulled into a dark corridor, and I'm forced down a narrow passage until I arrive at a brightly lit chamber. The walls are bare and concrete like the small room I'm used to, but the lighting is more agreeable, sunnier, and more cheerful. More to the point, the light doesn't feel artificial, thoughtlessly composed. It feels as though we are standing beneath some skylight, the sun bearing down on us with a gentle pulse. A young man waits for me in the room. I don't wish to know his name. I call him Father, and he refers to me only as Mother.

In the way that all dreamers are clairvoyant and able to perceive things that aren't explicitly told to them, I know for certain that Father and I have already coupled together to create a child. Perhaps our child is elsewhere, because I do not see him when I enter the brightly lit space. However, the room's host is present as soon as I arrive. But I do not feel sheepish or out of sorts in his presence. Rather, I yearn for him to accept me, to greet me with the same tenderness I might expect from a devoted friend or a lover. "I hope he likes me; I hope he likes me," I repeat quietly to myself over and over again while I idle there, waiting for an invitation to enter, a visible sign to join them.

Father—I'm unable to see his face, even when I look at him, because his features appear watery, muddled beyond a blurry screen almost—helps me across the room's threshold and tells me how they've been waiting for me to arrive. The host, named Porcelain, waves me over to a small table they've arranged in a corner of the room. The table is covered with various kinds of foods and beverages I do not recognize. But in the dream, I don't seem terribly bothered by the fact, I'm so bewildered by the sight. I sense my feet moving across the floor while I'm guided toward the table, and when I look down, I notice that I've been dressed in new clothing I cannot recognize or recall.

It seems as though we are acting out some sort of theatrical production, an invisible audience grading our every movement. I feel out of place only for a moment, but I'm soon ordered to sit in one of the wicker chairs, and most of my apprehension dissipates as soon as I'm offered something to eat.

"I certainly hope you don't consider it in poor taste that the biscuit is filled with a sweet strawberry jam," our host says. "Especially since so much of what we must discuss today revolves around . . . jams and jellies."

Father shakes his head, stifling some laughter. "If I knew any better, I would say that you arranged it like that."

I watch as our host shifts in his chair, obviously uncomfortable. "Oh, you give me too much credit," he says.

"Well, since the subject has been brought up, perhaps we should discuss it?" Father says.

But I immediately tug on his sleeve.

"Darling, please," I whisper to him gently.

"What is it, dear?" he asks me.

I strain to compose myself in front of our host, offering a polite smile. "Our very thoughtful host certainly doesn't want to discuss the complexities of business right now. Especially not during tea."

Porcelain leans forward in his chair. "Don't you find tea to be a suitable lubricant for conversation?"

"He wants to discuss it, dear," Father tells me, leaning so close that his breath heats the rim of my ear. "That's why he invited us here, after all."

Porcelain smiles. "And the pleasure of your company as well. I assure you."

"You're too kind," I tell him. "But please don't let him bully you into discussing business while we eat. . . ."

Father stirs, obviously becoming annoyed with me. "Darling, there's nothing unsuitable about discussing what we came here to discuss."

"I think our host might be insulted that we took such an improper opportunity to turn the conversation toward business when he was simply telling us about pastries," I remind him.

Porcelain leans in close toward both of us. "I assure you, dear woman, I was thinking no such thing. I'm happy to discuss the matter now if you wish."

"Yes. Of course," Father replies. "That's why we're here."

But I'm too stubborn for my own good. Even in a dream. "Not until we're finished with our food," I tell them. "It's unacceptable to discuss something so—grim—over food that looks so . . . cheerful. . . ."

Father glances at me. The word hanging in the air. "Grim?"

"Excuse me," I say. "I didn't mean 'grim.'"

"Dear, I'm afraid we're wasting our host's precious time," he says. "I imagine he has other engagements to attend to."

I think to make a comment about how he couldn't possibly have other engagements, considering the fact that I've dreamed him here. But my throat seems to seal shut. I'm unable to make use of my voice even in my own imagination. It hurts to realize that I've silenced myself in so many ways.

"I must tell you—I'm in no hurry at all today," our host says. "More than anything, I want to make certain this conversation goes as smoothly as possible. I promise you—I intend to have a healthy, thoughtful dialogue about the situation. It's nothing to fret over."

Father glares at me with such condemnation. "You see?"

I start to fan myself. "Perhaps I'm just a little overstimulated. . . . I should excuse myself. . . ."

"Nonsense," our host says. "Let me fetch a cool washcloth. I'll be just a moment. . . ."

"Very kind of you, sir," Father tells him just before Porcelain heads out of the room and leaves the two of us in peace.

"What on earth are you doing?" Father asks me as soon as we're completely alone.

"What do you mean?" I ask him.

"You're stalling our conversation."

"I'm doing no such thing."

"You're hesitating," he says, rising from his chair and pacing around the perimeter of the table. "You're deliberately trying to prevent us from discussing the matter at hand."

"It's not sensible to discuss right now," I tell him. "Surely you can agree with that."

"Our host is going to be compassionate for only a short period of time. Then he's going to become agitated if we don't move forward. . . . Who knows if he'll kill us?"

I squint at him, wondering if I've perhaps misheard what he's said.

"What did you say?"

"Why are you stalling?" he asks me.

I shake my head, lowering my eyes from Father. "We should never have come here. This is wrong."

"Please tell me you're not reconsidering."

"I already told you how I felt about the ordeal," I tell him. "It's strange. Ghoulish, in fact."

"If he's going to pay, then what do we care?" Father asks me.

"Because it involves our child," I tell him. "Don't you care at all? Or have you already traded him over for the money you've been promised?"

"That's not fair," he says, crossing his arms. "You know it's money for both of us."

"The both of us?"

"Our son, too," Father says.

I shake my head. "You'd sell his soul to the highest bidder."

"I don't suppose you've thought of an alternative?" he asks me.

Of course, in my dream, I've thought of other options for us. I've painstakingly considered and weighed the various outcomes that could become possibilities. Everything feels so utterly hopeless when I dream. It feels like a poisoned well I continually return to sip water from. I don't seem to know why I carry on in such a way, but I do, regardless.

"I don't like the idea of some—gentleman—owning our child . . . to do with him whatever he pleases."

Father rolls his eyes at me. "Certainly not whatever he pleases. The man has character, for God's sake."

"Does he?"

"We've been over this already," Father reminds me, tapping his feet.

But I'm not convinced. "I think we should leave."

"Not until we discuss what we came here to talk about," he replies.

Even in my dreams, a child is a sacred object—a creation to be revered, to be protected at all costs.

"You truly believe that our lives will be better if we make this awful deal?" I ask him.

"What's so awful about it?" Father asks me. "Our son is taken care of. We'll have steady income for the first time in months. I can't help but wonder why you're so against this transaction."

"He's our son," I remind him. "You're giving him away."

"I'm trying to save him," Father tells me.

It's then I notice that when he speaks, his voice thins and becomes brittle, shaky.

He carries on: "I'm trying to spare him the pains of hunger, the agony of existing as something less than human. How many more weeks do you think he'll survive if we go on rationing food the way we have?"

"And you think auctioning him off to some stranger will improve his quality of life?" I ask him. "The boy needs care and affection."

Father nods. "Yes. I agree. He needs someone like this fine gentleman to take care of him. . . ."

But I'll never be convinced. "He won't take care of him. He'll abandon him as soon as the season comes to an end. You're too ravenous for the money to see things clearly now."

Father sits down across from me at the table. "The gentleman will tend to the boy for as long as he's here. And who knows? If your son is competent enough—if they get along well enough—the good gentleman might ferry him out of the country. Is that such an unpleasant thought?"

I sense something raking itself through the meat of my viscera.

"You could bear that?" I ask him. "You could send your child away without even the slightest hesitation?"

"Of course I hesitate. It hurts to know that he'd have a better life elsewhere than here with his parents. But I love him too much to be selfish and keep him."

I shake my head, crossing my arms with disgust. "All you care about is money."

"And you don't?" he asks me. "You don't imagine our lives would be easier if we had an allowance every week from a generous benefactor?"

"It's not worth the price of my child," I tell him.

"If you're going to be stubborn, there's no point in discussing this matter with him and wasting his time," Father says.

"It's already an absurd waste of time."

"Yes," Father says. "Thanks to you and how much you've already stalled us."

"It's not as if we're giving away some animal," I remind him. "Or selling off one of my mother's expensive jewels. Once we hand our son over to him, things will be different. He won't belong to us anymore."

"He shouldn't belong to us in the first place," he says to me.

I'm too shocked to say anything. His words linger in the air and, for a moment, I wonder if I can actually see them—hanging there, like tiny hooks.

"You truly believe that?" I ask him.

"We aren't fit to take care of him the way he deserves."

I sense tears beading in the corners of my eyes. "After all I've done for him . . . all the sacrifices I've made . . ."

"We've both made sacrifices, darling," Father replies.

"Some more than others," I tell him.

There's another long, pain-filled pause. The room is so quiet and still that I can hear the dim pulse of our hearts beating out of tempo with each other.

"I suppose I should tell you something," Father says. "Something I've kept from you. Deliberately. Because I wanted you to come to terms with this decision on your own. I didn't want to convince you of it. . . ."

I strain myself to look at him, prepared to be hurt. "Yes?"

"I visited your father last week," he tells me.

I sense my eyebrows furrow, my eyes narrowing at him. "My father?"

"When I told you that I was going out of town for a few days."

"Yes . . . ?"

"I went to see your father. To tell him everything," he says. "I told him how we've been rationing food. I told him how much our family has been suffering."

Part of me becomes paralyzed. I loathe the idea of my father knowing that I've been complaining, that I've been suffering in silence under the generosity of his care.

"You told him that?" I ask him.

"I first wanted to see if he would offer help," he says. "I thought perhaps he might be willing to do something, anything. . . ."

I swallow nervously, afraid to ask. "And did he?"

"No," he says. "Why should he? So I told him that we had been contacted by a gentleman who was looking for a kind of—assistant. I told him how we had planned to offer our boy. Your father agreed. He told me to go through with it. He said that you might object, but that you'd understand eventually."

"My father said that?" I ask, my speech slurring in disbelief. "But he loves our son. . . ."

"You can love something dearly without holding on to it too tight," Father tells me. "Don't you believe that?"

I shake my head. "I don't know what I believe anymore. . . ."

Father approaches me, looping his arm around my shoulder and pulling me close underneath his arm.

"Surely, you want our boy to be happy and healthy," he says to me.

Yes, of course I want that. Even in the absurdity of my dreams, I want my child to be joyful and intact.

"We owe it to our only son to discuss the matter with this gentleman," Father tells me. "At the very least. We don't have to agree to anything. We don't have to sign anything. In fact, your father insisted that we be totally certain before we make the final decision. Isn't that fair?"

I think for a moment. It feels as though I've been backed into a corner, an invisible weapon aimed at me and prepared to fire at any given chance.

"Yes," I tell him. "I suppose it is."

Our host, Porcelain, eventually returns to the small chamber. He carries a damp washcloth.

"Apologies for the delay," he says, offering me the rag. "Here you are, dear lady. Something cool for you."

I press the cloth against my forehead. It feels heavenly to surrender to the sensation for a moment—to pretend I'm elsewhere, to imagine I'm no longer dreaming.

"Very good of you," Father tells him. "She was feeling a bit feverish, I'm afraid."

"I certainly hope it's nothing too serious," our host tells us, glancing at me with a visible concern.

I continue to dab myself with the wet cloth, and I wave his apprehension away. "No. Nothing at all. I'm already feeling much better. . . ."

"Perhaps something else to drink?" Porcelain asks me.

But I'm not thirsty right now. "Maybe later . . ."

Porcelain sits down across from me at the table. He straightens his tie a little. "I wish I could offer something else. But, as you know, the accommodations here are primordial. You're sure you don't need anything?"

I smile as politely as I can. It vexes me to realize that even in my dreams I'm incapable of being truthful. The imitation of politeness has been engraved so deep into me that I wonder if I've been completely hollowed out, if I'm able to perform anything other than niceties for the sake of friendliness.

"I feel fine," I tell him, even though it's a lie. "I promise. . . ."

Porcelain doesn't appear convinced, though. "I suppose as long as you're sure.

"Sir, we needn't waste any more of your precious time," Father says. "I gather you have other far more important matters to address than our silly arrangement."

Porcelain shakes his head. "I'm afraid you're incorrect, my good man. Our negotiation today is my sole priority. We'd be foolish to be so cavalier about the whole ordeal, considering the fact that the matter involves your precious boy."

It feels so gruesome to hear our host refer to our son as "precious." He seems to luxuriate in the pronunciation of each syllable, almost as if he were attempting to taste the very word.

"Yes," I add. "We simply want to be respectful. . . ."

"Certainly, dear woman," our host responds. "Are you comfortable enough here?"

I merely nod.

Porcelain begins to laugh, amused. "I imagine it must be considerably pleasant to be so comfortable after enduring such hardship for quite some time. It makes the comfort even more rewarding, more fulfilling."

I think about what he's said. I suppose in some ways he's correct. After all, it feels liberating to have finally stepped outside the confine of my little cell, to venture down a passageway and find myself in the company of others in an identical room.

"Yes. I suppose so," I tell him.

"I'm afraid I couldn't relate," Porcelain tells me. "You see, so much of my life is based on comfort. I don't bother going out in the heat. If I do, I can afford to find shade. A scarcity here in your country. I certainly don't expect you to understand how devoted I've become to finding comfort. It's a luxury that not many can claim as their own. I suppose the most insufferable thing about being comfortable all the time is that you never truly know what it's like to be uncomfortable. Therefore, little grievances that might annoy the average man become completely unbearable for me. It's like drinking champagne at every meal. Why on earth would you settle for water? After all, that's what peasants drink. . . . Then, of course, champagne loses its taste, its flavor after time when you grow so accustomed to it. There's a burden to being comfortable all the time. You misplace your appreciation for it. Until you find yourself completely and utterly without it . . ."

"Is that where you find yourself now?" Father asks him.

"Yes. I'm afraid it is," he replies. "I've only been in your fine country for less than a month, and I still feel so uncomfortable. More to the point, so out of place. I often wonder if it's sensible for me to stay."

"Yes?" I ask.

"Well, it's a thought I can't help but entertain," Porcelain says. "Leaving everything here and returning to my home. I would certainly be more comfortable there. . . ."

I'm not pleased with where this is heading.

"If I may . . . perhaps those decisions should be made before we discuss everything," I say to him.

Porcelain grins at me. "You're worried I'll up and leave after we've made our little bargain. . . ."

"Well, naturally . . ."

"I can assure you that if we are able to come to some sort of resolution today, I'll be more than delighted to stay here . . . At least until the end of winter."

"That's still not much time," I remind him.

Father beside me swats at my arm. "Darling."

I realize I continue to talk out of turn. I sense my cheeks heat, and my lips start to quiver.

"I'm sorry," I say. "I'm just—hesitant."

"Naturally," our host says. "And why shouldn't you be? Your only son holds considerable value."

"It's not just that," I confess.

Porcelain tilts his head, perhaps a little unsure of himself. "Oh . . . ?"

"I want to see to it that this deal is made with his best interest in mind," I say.

"Naturally, my dear woman," he says. "Naturally. Shall we discuss the matter now?"

He unfolds a pair of spectacles from his shirt pocket and slides them on. Then he picks up a small pen and leather-bound notebook arranged at the far end of the table. I didn't notice them before, and it seems as though they just materialized in the space the same way that all dreamers can conjure certain items as soon as they're needed.

"I suppose we should start with very basic details," he says. "You needn't be concerned about being totally precise with your answers. We'll, of course, have the boy examined by a doctor here before our arrangement begins. But I'd ask you to answer everything to the best of your knowledge. . . ."

"Yes, of course," Father says.

"Very good . . . Now. First point of business. The age of the boy. How old is he?"

Father looks at me suddenly with an unsureness that all fathers seem to possess when questioned about their child.

"He turned twelve two months ago," I reply.

Porcelain jots a note down on the paper. "Excellent . . . His height?"

I stammer, uncertain. "Oh, I'm afraid we don't know—"

"You couldn't make a reasonable estimation?" he asks me.

Father shakes his head. "I'm afraid we haven't taken him to a doctor in quite some time."

Our host makes a note on the paper again, his eyes lowering with a look of obvious disappointment. "I thought as much."

"He's about as tall as his father," I say. "If that helps at all . . ."

"Let's see," Porcelain says, eyeing Father. "Stand up, will you . . . ?"

Father rises from his chair and stands awkwardly at the end of the table. Our host studies him for a moment. Then he makes a note in his notebook.

"We can have my private doctor record the boy's measurements," Porcelain says. "I take it you don't know the boy's exact weight, either?"

"I'm afraid not," I tell him. "He's very slender, though. He had a belly for quite some time, but, thankfully, he's grown out of it."

"So, you'd argue that the boy is healthy?" Porcelain asks.

"Oh, yes," Father replies. "Most certainly. Very healthy indeed."

"Not opposed to physical labor?"

"Certainly not," Father says.

Porcelain makes another note in his little leather-bound book.

"Of course, we wouldn't want to overwhelm him with too much work, though," I add.

"Darling, be sensible," Father tells me. "Our gracious host needs to know if the boy is capable of work or not."

"Hair and eye color?" Porcelain asks me.

"His hair is black," I say. "Just like mine. Eyes are brown, of course."

"A handsome young man, I take it?" Porcelain asks.

Of course I'm partial because he's my boy. But I know for certain others might think so as well.

"Very handsome," I reply.

Porcelain makes a note. Then he leans forward in his seat, whispering as if he were about to reveal something truly delicate.

"The next question is somewhat sensitive, but I'm afraid I must ask it for reasons you'll come to understand in time," he says. "Has the boy developed hair in the pubic area?"

"Yes," Father replies immediately.

Porcelain makes another note.

It feels unnatural to share something so private, so intimate, with a stranger. But the logic makes sense in the world of my dream.

"I'm afraid he's rather hairy actually," I tell him. "Despite his age. I think he's a little embarrassed about it, to be truthful."

"It's perfectly natural," Father says. "I was the same way when I was his age. Boys are supposed to develop like that. I'm sure our host would agree."

"Naturally," Porcelain says, his tone souring slightly. "But you wouldn't be opposed to having the boy shaved? So that he can perform his duty more efficiently?"

"Not at all," Father answers.

"Yes, I suppose that would be fine," I say. "If it's for the sake of his employment."

Our host makes another note. "Excellent," he says. "Now, I have one more question, and then we can move on to your concerns. . . . Is the boy excitable?"

Father's face scrunches, obviously a little unsure. "Excitable?"

"Yes," our host replies. "Would you describe him as unpredictable and fidgety? Or would you describe him more as even-tempered and patient."

I swallow, my throat burning a little. "He's still a child, of course."

"Naturally," Porcelain says.

"So it stands to reason that he might need a few more years before he becomes gentler and soft," I tell him.

But our host doesn't appear satisfied with my answer.

"You're saying that he's prone to outbursts?" he asks. "That he's expected to be difficult while he's employed here?"

"No. That's not what she's saying. Right, darling?" Father asks me before returning his attention to our host. "Our son is very undemanding. He's a very permissive and courteous young man."

"I'm delighted to hear it," Porcelain says, making another note on the paper.

"But that's not to say that he's utterly perfect," I remind him.

Father grits his teeth at me. "Darling . . ."

"We certainly don't want to lead our host astray," I tell him. "Do we, dear?"

Porcelain slants his glasses to the tip of his nose and then squints at me. "Then he is difficult?"

"He's a twelve-year-old boy," I say. "His enthusiasm, his impulsiveness—it's all to be expected. Isn't it?"

Porcelain lowers his head slightly, closing the notebook and removing his spectacles. "I'm afraid I beg to differ, madam. I was always taught that children should be seen and never heard. The carelessness and the recklessness that you describe lead me to believe that he might not be a good fit for this position, I'm afraid."

"No. She simply misspoke," Father tells Porcelain, almost pleading with him. "It's—a misunderstanding. I assure you that our son would be very dedicated. An ideal employee. Very kind and gentle, too. I would never want such an opportunity to be lost merely because she was a little careless with her words. . . ."

Our host sighs. "I suppose I won't know for certain until I actually meet with the boy."

Father exhales deeply like a small knife had been removed from his gut. "Yes. We'd be delighted to arrange that. Any time you see fit."

"I'm afraid we're getting ahead of ourselves," Porcelain reminds him. "Certainly, you both must have questions for me."

Father seems to glance nervously at me. His eyes widen, almost begging me to keep quiet and refrain from asking anything. Of course, I'm going to disappoint him.

"What will our son's responsibilities be?" I ask our host.

"An excellent question, my dear. I hoped you might ask," Porcelain tells me. "Well, you both already know that I'm someone who can't bear to be uncomfortable. In the simplest definition possible, your son would be tending to my comfort. Day and night."

"Sounds simple enough," Father says, glancing at me with another look of hope that I'll be satisfied with his response.

"I'm afraid I'm a rather discerning person," our host says. "So his success depends entirely on whether or not he'll be devoted to the post."

"Naturally," Father replies. "He will be. I assure you."

Porcelain throws a scowl at Father. "I don't need your assurance. I need the boy's."

"What kind of comfort will he be providing for you?" I ask.

"Whatever I request from him," he says. "I'm afraid there's no proper list of expectations. He's merely expected to perform his duties reasonably and with considerable enthusiasm. I don't believe those demands are out of the question."

"Certainly not," Father adds.

Porcelain sighs again. "I'm afraid I've kept something from the both of you. . . . Something I probably should have specified in the letter I wrote. A small caveat. It's an expectation that I have."

I lean forward in my chair. "Yes . . . ?"

"Perhaps the most unbearable aspect of being a guest in your country is the insects—the bugs, the flies, the mosquitoes," he tells us. "They're impossible to avoid. . . . Needless to say, it's excruciating for me to step outside each and every day in the heat and be hounded by thousands of insects for hours. I'd prefer to be flayed alive. Don't you agree?"

Father looks to me for a sign of approval, but I have none to give.

"I guess we're simply used to it," he says to him.

"Yes," Porcelain says. "Such a pity. You're accustomed to being uncomfortable, living in agony. . . . Well, I'm afraid I cannot bear the discomfort any longer. After all, I've spent so much of my life being comfortable. It's impossible to exist without that same level of care and tenderness. I suppose you could ask why I came to your country in the first place. Surely I'm not expected to get by and merely endure while I'm here. I deserve the comfort I've been accustomed to. Just as you deserve the discomfort you've endured and continue to endure . . ."

I'm afraid I cannot bear the cat-and-mouse game any longer.

"What exactly do you want our son to do for you?" I ask him.

Porcelain flashes me a hideous grin of teeth stained the dark color of amber. "There's a clever trick that some of my associates have practiced. They've shared it with me and urged me to consider adopting a similar practice."

"Yes?" I say.

"My associates have taken to hiring young peasant boys to follow them around while covered in jelly," he says. "The idea is that the insects will be attracted to the boy while the gentlemen are expected to conduct business in the god-awful heat."

"And your acquaintances claim that this–unusual–practice works?" Father asks him.

"Of course," our host says. "I wouldn't go out of my way to suggest something so absurd if I wasn't totally sure it would work. In fact, I was golfing last weekend, and one of my dear friends was kind enough to loan me one of his . . . jelly-covered assistants. It was one of the most–comfortable–experiences I've had in your country the last few weeks. So, naturally, I thought I would seek out my own."

I can hardly believe what he's saying. I sense my breath quickening, my heartbeat hammering away.

"You want our son to follow you around outside and be devoured by insects?" I ask.

Our host laughs a little. "You make it sound so obscene."

"Isn't it?" I ask him.

"Dear. Please," Father says to me, patting my thigh.

"I take it you wouldn't approve of something like that?" our host asks me.

"Absolutely not," I tell him, pushing Father's hand away from me.

"Darling," he says, trying to soothe me. Then he glances at our host. "She doesn't mean that. I assure you. . . . She–she's just a little upset."

"Forgive me," Porcelain says. "I didn't think the idea would displease her so much."

I shake my head, and when I speak, I can hear how I no longer seem to carry the words calmly but instead begin to shriek. "Our son would be nothing more than a meal for mosquitoes. To lather him in jelly? And expect him to endure being devoured every day bit by bit?

"You might be interested to know that similar practices existed in Ancient Egypt," Porcelain tells me. "Peasant children were often coated in honey and ordered to walk behind the pharaoh in order to attract pesky insects."

"I'm very sorry," Father says. "If you wouldn't mind, perhaps we could have a moment to discuss together in private?"

Porcelain nods. "Yes. Of course. Take all the time you need. I'll be waiting outside."

Then he withdraws, slinking out of the small, windowless room and finally disappearing from our view. Whether or not he remains close by to eavesdrop, I don't seem to care much.

When we're quite alone, Father reaches across the table to put a hand on me. But I pull away from him at once.

"Don't you dare try to say anything to me," I tell him.

"You're going to spoil everything," he says.

"Everything's already been spoiled thanks to your greed," I remind him, leaping out of the chair and circling the small room like a captured beast.

He looks at me, shocked. "My greed?"

"Yes," I tell him. "Your gluttony. Your need for more than you deserve."

"I'm trying to provide a better life for us," he says.

"Are we truly suffering so terribly?" I ask him.

"You think we aren't? This gentleman has been kind enough to receive us today—to discuss the possibility of taking on some of our debts and giving us a weekly allowance. A very generous allowance indeed."

I glance at him and wonder if I've heard him correctly. "And you think it's worth the safety of our son? You heard what he plans to do to him."

"I imagine he won't want to work with us now," Father says. "Not after how you've insulted him."

"I've insulted him? He wants to make a meal of our son. Wants to cover our boy in jelly so that he can be eaten by insects bit by bit, day after day. It doesn't sound like employment. Sounds more like a punishment. Practically medieval."

"You're thinking about it too literally," Father tells me, seeming to be becoming more and more annoyed with my questioning.

"And you're not thinking about it at all," I say to him. "You could truly live with yourself? You could endure the guilt of knowing that you had sent your son to suffer?"

"At least I won't have to bear witness to his agony any longer," he says. "So much of the world is utter cruelty. To be alive is to be aware that you will be hurt, damaged, beaten down. I can't bear the thought of knowing I've allowed our son to suffer under my care. I'm a poor imitation for a father."

I look at him, afraid to ask the question, afraid of what he might say to me to hurt me. After all, he's told me time and time again how good it feels to hurt another living thing. "All living things want to feel more important, more powerful than the other," he's told me. I wonder if this is his moment to finally undo me, to unravel me until I'm threadbare—a gibbering miscreation that will thoughtlessly agree with every single deception he uses to trick me.

"Am I such a poor imitation of a mother?" I finally ask him.

"He will look after the boy," Father says gently. "You know he will."

But I still shake my head. "A middle-aged man—no relation to the family—tending to a young, innocent boy. It's reprehensible."

"What exactly do you think will happen?" he asks me.

"Besides the obvious?"

He follows me until I'm cornered against the concrete wall. "You're clearly thinking about something. . . . What is it?"

I take a deep breath. I've prepared myself for this. "Our son will become that man's property. To do with him whatever he pleases. He told us that. What happens when our son is no longer useful to him?"

"You're so certain that will happen?" he asks.

"You don't think so? He could hurt our boy. Break him apart beyond repair . . . You know full well that people like him have already taken so much from us."

Father rolls his eyes and folds his arms. "Please. Not this again."

"Why do you detest the reminder?" I ask him.

"I detest how much it upsets you. You assume the worst of everyone," Father tells me.

"You don't suspect there's another reason why that man wants to take our son from us?" I ask him.

"Another reason?"

"Perhaps something you're not considering," I say.

Father recoils. I think perhaps he finally understands what I'm trying to convey but cannot bring himself to actually consider it.

"I'm not interested in your grim fortune-telling," he tells me. "The man intends to pay handsomely for our son."

"Yes. Of course, there's a reason why," I say.

"You're too distrustful."

"You'd accept a cup of tea from the devil himself."

"Just come out with it and tell me," he begs. "What on earth could that man possibly do to our boy?"

Once more, my cheeks heat. It's too horrible to say. I can't bear to ladle the words from where I've hidden them deep inside my throat.

"He's going to come back in here and expect an answer from us," Father reminds me.

"You don't think it's peculiar that he asked about our son's . . . pubic hair?" I ask him.

Father stammers a little, shrugging. "Well, of course it was–somewhat strange. But I later assumed that it had to do with the jam that our son would be covered in during his employment. The boy would obviously have to be smooth and hairless to accommodate the man's instructions."

"It seemed almost like it was some kind of–bizarre sexual preference," I tell him.

"A preference?"

"You don't think that?" I ask.

"Well, certainly he had to ask an uncomfortable question," Father tells me. "It's a sensitive topic, after all."

"And then there's the fact that he and his associates pass the boys around like little trophies," I say. "He told us that one of his friends had loaned him a jelly-covered boy to use. . . . Our son would be–passed around–" I cover my mouth, hardly able to let the obscene words pass through my fingers. "An object for their pleasure."

I collapse at the table, burying my face in my hands and sobbing quietly. Father draws close to me, kneeling and trying to comfort me as best he can.

"You truly believe that will happen?" he asks me.

My breathing is shallow, and I force each word out with such coaxing. "How could it not? Our son will become some meaningless article. Some soulless body capable of only following orders."

"That's not true," he says.

"Why are you so determined to go through with this?" I ask him, wiping some of the dampness from my eyes. "You could walk away at any time. You choose to keep us here. You won't change my mind."

"Yes. I know," he says.

"Call him back in here," I order him.

Father looks at me, astonished. "Already?"

"Yes."

"You've decided?"

"Tell him that we're not interested," I say. "We've considered his proposal, and we're politely declining."

Father trembles slightly, resting a hand on my shoulder. "Darling," he whispers.

"Please," I say, cutting him off. "Don't make me beg."

Father makes his way toward the room's only entryway. He's about to call out, but he doesn't. He turns to face me one more time.

"I can't," he says.

I'm about to elbow past him. "I'll call him in myself."

"No. Wait," he says, gripping my sleeve. "I can't tell him that we intend to decline. . . ."

"Why?" I ask.

Father will not look at me. He speaks slowly, unsurely. "Because I've already accepted his offer."

There's another long, painful pause.

I can scarcely believe what I've heard. I sense my mouth hanging open, my hands unsure what to do and fumbling together nervously.

"You–accepted already?"

"Yes," he says. "He provided a contract, and I signed a few days ago. . . ."

"You signed a contract?" I ask, thinking that perhaps if I repeat him enough it might undo some of the harm he's already caused.

"I–didn't want to alarm you," he says. "I had hoped that if we met with him today, you might change your mind. I hoped that you might be open to the idea of sending our son to work with him."

I shake my head in utter disbelief. "How could you do this?"

"He's already paid us our first week's allowance," Father tells me.

"He paid you already?"

Father's eyes lower. "I was hoping to surprise you."

"And what about our son?" I ask.

"What about him?"

"When is he expected to begin work?"

"Tomorrow," he tells me. "That's why the gentleman was so adamant about meeting today. . . . I'm afraid things are already in motion. . . ."

I sit in the chair and close my eyes, listening to the ragged sound of my breath.

"There was a part of you that always knew I would say no to this plan," I say. "Wasn't there?"

"Yes."

"You signed our boy's life away," I tell him.

"Shall I send for the gentleman?" he asks me.

I continue to stare at the wall, imagining how I might pull each brick away bit by bit until the room is nothing but rubble, until I'm forced to dwell in the wreckage.

"Yes," I finally answer. "Ask him to come in."

"Things will get better for us. I promise," Father says.

He places a hand on my shoulder, but I shift away from his touch. Then he moves toward the doorway and calls out. There's a long pause. Eventually, our host reappears and glides into the small, windowless room.

"Well. I trust everything's in order?" he asks, glancing at me. "My good woman . . . ?"

"My wife isn't feeling well, I'm afraid," Father tells me.

"Shall I send for a doctor?" he asks.

"No," I say. "I'm fine. Please don't bother on my account."

Porcelain resumes his place in his chair at the head of the table, glancing at the both of us. "Well, I trust you've had enough time to discuss the delicate matter?"

"Yes," Father replies. "I've told my wife that the contract has already been signed."

Porcelain chuckles a little. "So there's no point in the charade anymore. An ideal situation."

"Sir . . . Will you assure her that our son will be looked after?" Father asks.

"Well, of course I can assure–"

"No," I say, cutting him off. "I don't need any assurances."

"Dear?" Father says, looking at me and about to reach out to touch me when he seems to suddenly remember not to.

"Darling, will you please leave?" I ask him. "I'd like to speak to the gentleman alone. . . ."

Father glances at Porcelain and then back at me with a look of worry. "Are you certain that's a good idea?"

"Please," I beg him. "Offer me this kindness."

There's another long pause. Father finally settles and agrees to the arrangement. He tells me how he'll be waiting outside the room if he's needed. I thank him before he moves out of the chamber and leaves us unsupervised. Porcelain and I sit in silence for a while. Perhaps both of us are a little unsure how to act around the other, unsure where exactly to begin.

"Maybe something else to drink?" he asks me.

"No," I say. "Thank you."

He clears his throat and leans forward. "There was–something specific you wanted to discuss with me?"

"Yes," I tell him, squeezing my hands together so tight that I wonder if I've broken my fingers in half. "Something I'm–too frightened to ask . . ."

"I can assure you, dear lady, that you needn't be frightened," he tells me.

"Well, now that he's gone . . . I was hoping we might be able to speak frankly," I say to him, lowering my voice a little.

"Naturally."

I shake my head at him, steeling some of my resolve. "I don't want any false promises. I don't expect any words of support. I merely want you to be honest with me. . . ."

"Dear lady?"

I peer into his eyes, hoping I might see a flicker of truth there. When I find nothing, I finally ask him, "What do you intend to do to our child?"

"I'm afraid I don't understand," he says, grinning at me.

"What are you going to do to him?" I ask. "Are your plans to actually care for him? Or are your desires more self-serving?"

It's then that Porcelain does something that makes my stomach quiver. He glares at me with a hideous grin and chuckles deep from his belly.

"I think you already know the answer, dear woman," he says to me.

"Yes, I think I do," I tell him. "However, I want to hear you say it. . . ."

Porcelain exhales deeply. Perhaps he wasn't prepared to reveal such confessions today, but I'm only too eager to pry everything out of him.

"I'm going to dismantle your precious boy," he whispers. "Bit by bit. I'm going to crack him apart like an eggshell. Expose his soft, pink innards and gorge on all that remains until he's completely empty and useless to anyone else. . . . Is that what you wanted to hear me say?"

I sit without movement. Yes, I had expected all of this.

"I presume his father and I will not be permitted to visit him while he's working for you," I say.

"My dear woman. I'm not some cruel, godless primitive," Porcelain tells me. "I recognize that the boy needs love and affection from his parents—the people who raised him. You'll be allowed to meet with him occasionally."

I already know there's a caveat to accompany his promise.

"But not unsupervised," I say.

"That's correct," he replies.

I close my eyes, wondering if the air circulating in the small room has become thinner and thinner over time since we first arrived here.

"He belongs to you now," I whisper.

"I'm afraid he does," Porcelain says.

I swallow hard. Then I rise from where I'm sitting, and I inch toward the nearby doorway.

"Will you promise me one thing?"

"My dear?" he says.

"When you're torturing him slowly, will you remember to remind him that his mother will always love him?" I ask. "No matter how much he's broken or shattered . . . Please tell him that. . . ."

Porcelain does not reply. He sits there without comment, observing me as I'm about to cross the threshold and leave.

I turn back one more time.

"What happens to him when you've finished your cruelty?" I ask. "When you've exhausted all possibilities from him? What then?"

He regards me with a devastating look, a horrible glare that seems to tell me I will be destroyed by his answer.

That's when the dream comes to an end. . . .

I finish reading the wall of text pasted on the primitive-looking web page, and I sense myself slow for a moment—every movement an excruciating ordeal, something difficult that must be done no matter what. I click on the comment section and begin to scour some of the postings that have been made already. *Have you dreamed this person before?* But it's then that I arrive on a comment that perplexes me and confounds me all at once. In fact, the comment is so alarming, so perturbing that I read it aloud to myself: "Porcelain Khaw is a real person. . . . Or rather, a real thing . . . An ageless entity. A cosmic furnace . . . I think he visits you in your dreams. . . ."

I go over the name again and again—*Porcelain Khaw.*

His name feels familiar and yet so unnatural at the same time, like something I've secretly rehearsed without actually knowing, without realizing I would one day encounter him. His name feels so hideously inevitable, and when I whisper it out loud, I sense myself crimp a little, bend in ways like I'm being ordered into submission.

CHAPTER THREE

I can't help but think about how someone once told me—I can't recall exactly who—that when we stand on the shore and the tide curls onto land, the surf isn't actually coming toward us. Instead, we are being slowly pulled into the water, if we stood calmly in one place without moving. I'm afraid I can't quite tell whether that notion softens me a little or disturbs me to the point of never idling on the beach ever again. I haven't visited the beach in years. Partly because it's such a far drive from where I live, and also partly because I'm terrified of how my thirty-eight-year-old, well-worn body will look in a swimsuit. I don't work out much, and my body is no longer taut and firm as it was when I was a specimen of manhood in my teens or early- to mid-twenties.

Regardless, there's something uniquely distressing about the idea of being slowly dragged into the oncoming surf—wrenched from our place of safety and then pulled farther and farther out. I suppose I've always felt as though I were dawdling on an empty beach, my poor, broken body being slowly pulled inch by inch into the rising tide. I sense my stomach drop, realizing that I've wasted so much of my adult life idling in one place. Meanwhile, seawater seems to pour in all around me, and I know it won't be very long until I'm fully submerged, until I'm claimed by the climbing drift.

Instant Messaging Conversation Between <simeonlink_86> and <babyfacexoxo>

[**simeonlink_86** has entered the chat group The Grim Laurels]

[**babyfacexoxo** has entered the chat]

1:34:25 <babyfacexoxo> Hey, wanna chat?

1:34:49 <simeonlink_86> You a guy or a girl?

1:35:05 <babyfacexoxo> Gender's more complex and nuanced than that . . . For fuck's sake . . .

1:35:17 <simeonlink_86> Just wanted to know . . .

1:35:24 <babyfacexoxo> Why?

1:35:37 <simeonlink_86> Seemed like an easy thing to answer

1:35:49 <babyfacexoxo> Gender's never an easy thing. Even if you're comfortable with what's in between your legs.

1:36:01 <simeonlink_86> Why's that?

1:36:09 <babyfacexoxo> Because gender is never static. It's never just one thing. It's many things . . . and nothing, all at once . . .

1:36:20 <simeonlink_86> Forget I asked . . .

1:36:34 <babyfacexoxo> You're the first person who's asked me what's between my legs on this site . . . I wonder why you care so much . . .

1:36:44 <simeonlink_86> Because it's easier for me to jack off with other guys . . . Girls usually want nothing to do with me . . . And that's fine.

1:36:57 <babyfacexoxo> Well, sure. If you're going to reduce them to nothing more than a gender role . . .

1:37:09 <simeonlink_86> If you have such a problem, you can skip me and connect to the next fuckwit.

1:37:22 <babyfacexoxo> Maybe I don't want to.

1:37:30 <simeonlink_86> You want to jack off?

1:37:41 <babyfacexoxo> That's the only thing you do on here?

1:37:56 <simeonlink_86> Gets me off quick so I can go to bed . . .

1:38:06 <babyfacexoxo> I don't like the idea of comfort.

1:38:18 <simeonlink_86> In general?

1:38:27 <babyfacexoxo> No. Specifically, your comfort. I don't think it's a good thing. I think it's good for us to ache from time to time . . .

1:38:35 <simeonlink_86> I've already done enough of that

1:38:49 <babyfacexoxo> Have you?

1:38:59 <simeonlink_86> You don't believe me?

1:39:08 <babyfacexoxo> I don't know you. I suppose I can't say one way or the other.

1:39:13 <simeonlink_86> You act like you know me . . .

1:39:23 <babyfacexoxo> If I knew you, I'd make sure you were never comfortable a day in your life

1:39:34 <simeonlink_86> Why's that? You hate me?

1:39:45 <babyfacexoxo> Because discomfort tests a person. Truly. I kind of want to know what you're made of . . .

1:39:56 <simeonlink_86> You sound like you want to jerk off . . .

1:40:11 <babyfacexoxo> Not everything is built around sex.

1:40:25 <simeonlink_86> You're right. Everything in this world is built around suffering, though . . .

1:40:37 <babyfacexoxo> You think that?

1:40:56 <simeonlink_86> You don't?

1:41:05 <babyfacexoxo> I think you've been comfortable since you were a child. I think you've never known agony a day in your life . . .

1:41:17 <simeonlink_86> You seem sure of yourself on this

1:41:29 <babyfacexoxo> How couldn't I be? You come to a grief chat room to jack off with randoms, for fuck's sake

1:41:38 <simeonlink_86> We're allowed to process misery differently

1:41:50 <babyfacexoxo> Is it truly working for you?

1:42:05 <simeonlink_86> I never said it worked . . . It's a distraction, I suppose

1:42:19 <babyfacexoxo> You're so eager to be distracted for the sake of comfort

1:42:30 <simeonlink_86> Wouldn't you want a little bit of comfort if you were constantly existing in agony?

1:42:42 <babyfacexoxo> Jacking off with local strangers isn't the kind of distraction that lasts, though. Surely, you know that.

1:42:53 <simeonlink_86> Unless you know of an alternative?

1:43:07 <babyfacexoxo> You probably wouldn't even believe me if I told you

1:43:19 <simeonlink_86> There's something in particular you're thinking of?

1:43:27 <babyfacexoxo> Have you ever heard of a group known as "the Wretches"?

1:43:39 <simeonlink_86> Can't say that I have

1:43:49 <babyfacexoxo> They're a small, exclusive group that meets in the church recreation hall on Spruce Street. You know the one?

1:43:58 <simeonlink_86> Yeah. I know it . . .

1:44:09 <babyfacexoxo> They meet there every Thursday evening at eight o'clock

1:44:17 <simeonlink_86> What's so special about them?

1:44:26 <babyfacexoxo> They've been around for a few years. I only just started going to the meetings a year or so ago . . .

1:44:39 <simeonlink_86> They're a support group?

1:44:48 <babyfacexoxo> In a way, yes

1:45:03 <simeonlink_86> I'm not much for talking in person to strangers. Online is one thing. But not in person . . .

1:45:16 <babyfacexoxo> Most of their communication is visual

1:45:29 <simeonlink_86> Visual? How's that?

1:45:57 <babyfacexoxo> They're a group of camera enthusiasts, I suppose you could say. All the members of the group have recently lost a loved one. They take photographs of inanimate objects and look for their departed in the pictures . . .

1:46:14 <simeonlink_86> They take photographs and then look for evidence of their loved ones?

1:46:29 <babyfacexoxo> You'd be surprised what some group members have seen . . . Just last week, one of our newest members noticed her husband's smile in the back of a leather armchair . . .

1:46:30 <simeonlink_86> You can't be serious about this

1:46:44 <babyfacexoxo> I thought you wouldn't be interested

1:46:59 <simeonlink_86> It's not that I'm not interested . . .

1:47:09 <babyfacexoxo> So, you are?

1:47:23 <simeonlink_86> I guess I don't know what to make of it . . .

1:47:39 <babyfacexoxo> Some of the photographs that have been taken are very convincing . . .

1:47:50 <simeonlink_86> You believe them?

1:48:09 <babyfacexoxo> How could I not?

1:48:22 <simeonlink_86> You've seen the things they've seen?

1:48:35 <babyfacexoxo> Does it matter if I have or not? The picture therapy seems to work regardless of my opinions about it . . .

1:48:52 <simeonlink_86> They meet Thursdays at eight?

1:49:09 <babyfacexoxo> You need an invitation to go

1:49:18 <simeonlink_86> How does that happen?

1:49:34 <babyfacexoxo> I invite you . . .

1:49:47 <simeonlink_86> What's your name?

1:50:33 <babyfacexoxo> The rest will happen when you arrive

1:50:46 <simeonlink_86> I don't know if it's really my scene

1:50:59 <babyfacexoxo> I can tell you with the utmost certainty that this is not the place for doubters

1:51:12 <simeonlink_86> You're still not going to tell me your name?

1:51:24 <babyfacexoxo> You know enough

1:51:38 <simeonlink_86> Will you be there at the meeting?

1:51:46 <babyfacexoxo> Maybe . . .

1:51:58 <simeonlink_86> Is there anything else I should know before I go there?

1:52:09 <babyfacexoxo> "Don't look forward to the day you stop suffering, because when it comes you'll know you're dead."

1:52:18 <simeonlink_86> Who said that?

1:52:32 <babyfacexoxo> A playwright I admire. He died choking on a bottle cap . . .

1:52:44 <simeonlink_86> I'm sure he would have preferred not to suffer so . . .

1:52:53 <babyfacexoxo> But what a waste if he hadn't . . .

[**babyfacexoxo** has left the chat]

[**simeonlink_86** has left the chat]

Don't look forward to the day you stop suffering, because when it comes you'll know you're dead. The quote fills my mind while I take a hot shower that morning, scrubbing myself with a half-melted bar of soap. I wonder if our suffering is the only thing keeping us alive. Perhaps we idle on that imaginary beach for most of our lives, the current slowly pulling us from our safety until we're dragged into oblivion. Maybe that's what it feels like to die.

I eye the razor blade I abandoned on the bathroom counter and wonder if I should make good use of it. Perhaps it would be kinder to my rescuers to get the fucking ordeal over with while in the shower. All the blood would be so easy to clean. They'd find me slumped, crouched over the drain where the current collects. Of course, I could easily swipe the razor blade from where I had left it and go to town on my poor, trembling wrists. I could slide the edge over my skin and open a sacred wellspring that cannot be tempered once the valve is undone. But then there's a queer part of me that doesn't wish to think about such cruel, obscene things. There's a part of my mind—ever so small and unimportant—that yearns to know what might become of me if I pull myself away from the approaching sea.

It's simple to stand in one place and allow yourself to be claimed by the poisonous, the fatal. But it's a fine art to remove yourself, to pull yourself away from the attractive invitation of the abyss.

Thankfully, I have enough willpower today to eye the razor blade as nothing more than an empty threat—a vacant kind of invitation to the end. There are no true answers for me to be found at the other end of that blade. Once I make the decision to use it, everything's over. *And do I actually want that? Do I yearn for that?* I'm not entirely sure. Part of me is so captured by the idea of the small group of photograph enthusiasts that I learned about the other evening. What were they called again? The Wretches? It's a curious name, but I'm sure it has some meaning. It's then I recognize that human curiosity is a wonderful thing. Sometimes it's the very thing that keeps us tethered to this place—the all-consuming ache to simply know more, to find out, to search for meaning. I realize that I'm curious about them. Curious enough to prevent myself from slicing my wrists open in the shower on a Tuesday morning before four a.m.

When I'm finished, I climb out of the shower stall and dry myself with a nearby towel. I look in the mirror, and I deflate as soon as I greet my reflection in the glass. I look tired. There are lines wrinkling underneath my eyes. My hair is wiry, unkempt, almost like a sparrow's nest. I haven't been to the barber in weeks, and I curse myself for letting my routine maintenance slip away so noticeably. But to be truthful, nothing seems like it matters without my beloved, sweet Jonathan. There are no more special parties for us to attend as a couple—no excuses to go to the salon to be pampered for an hour or two. There are no more lunches with dear friends. There are no more invitations to Provincetown in the summer. In many ways, it feels like the approaching tide has curled away from me and, in fact, doesn't want to take me with it. Our life together was once filled with so much happiness, so much joy. Now it's nothing but lonely mornings without conversation, without the tenderness and care I've come to know for so long. Instead, a discarded razor blade on the bathroom counter seems like a more worthwhile companion.

But only for a moment.

I get dressed and head out of my apartment, riding the elevator down to the ground floor, where I exit and make my way out of the building. It's chillier this morning than I anticipated, and I pull my jacket a little tighter around my throat, quietly wishing I had added a scarf to my ensemble before I left home. I walk a few blocks, and it's not long before I arrive at the small skate park at the end of the avenue. I can hear the various teenagers shouting and yelling before I see them performing tricks with their skateboards to impress some of the young girls watching from the sidelines. As I make my way toward the gated entrance, I notice my ex-wife, Evelyn, waiting for me there. She's dressed in a smart-looking brown leather jacket with a matching belt lassoed around her waist, and her eyes are obscured by black sunglasses. I wonder if she'll do me the courtesy of removing her glasses when speaking to me so that I'm not just staring at my reflection the whole time I'm talking to her. She doesn't, unfortunately. I greet her with a half-hearted hello, and she offers a polite smile.

"How's he doing?" I ask.

She inhales sharply and then exhales, resting her hand on the nearby fence that separates the sidewalk from the skate park. "He's been asking about you all morning. Always excited to see Dad."

My eyes follow where Evelyn looks, and it's then I see my sixteen-year-old son, Carter, securing his helmet and chatting with another boy around his age near the edge of an elevated platform. The only real thing I notice about my son is how happy he looks—how delighted and how joyful he looks while climbing around the skate area. It's admirable—that level of cheerfulness, that sense of pleasure and satisfaction. I sense myself quiver slightly, realizing I haven't felt that way in quite some time. I suppose you're only meant to feel those things when you're a child, when you're young and foolish. But then the world takes those feelings away from you bit by bit, the same way seawater eats away at the shore. I'd give anything to be young and foolish once more.

"Want me to take him for the morning?" I ask Evelyn.

"What about your work?" she asks.

I shift uncomfortably. If I could peel myself out of my own skin, I would.

"I'm taking a leave of absence for now," I explain to her. "We thought it would be best."

Evelyn removes her sunglasses, her eyes searching me for the truth.

"Something happened?" she asks.

"Not everything has a secret meaning," I tell her, even though I know I'm lying. There's a secret meaning for each and every thing we say—plans hidden from obvious sight, intentions permanently disguised. "Sometimes things work out the way they work out. . . ."

Evelyn bites her lip, and then her attention eventually returns to our boy. "You're content with it for now?"

"I'm making the best of it," I tell her, shoving my hands into my coat pockets when a gust of wind braces me.

Evelyn rests a hand on my shoulder and squeezes tight. "If you ever need anything, you know you can call me."

Yes, of course I realize that. But part of me is afraid of reaching out to Evelyn. While she's been a devoted and caring mother to our boy, there's something about Evelyn that makes me think she dwells too comfortably in the past. *Our* past, to be precise. Naturally, things became heated when I came out of the closet a few years into our marriage and explained to her how I had never felt any sexual attraction toward women. I know I wounded her. Still, there's always a sense of sorrow when we come together, almost like she was perpetually mourning the life we lost together—the imitation of love we shared for many years before I acknowledged the fact that I had been deceiving her.

Surely I never expected her to forgive me after deceiving her for so long and for the sin of coupling with Jonathan a few months after our divorce was finalized. But Evelyn seems patient and composed any time I meet with her. It's inspiring and also infuriating how one person can be so resilient. Still, there's a part of me that can't help but wonder if she's waiting for me, if she's biding her time until I tell her that this was all a joke and that I'm prepared to love her unconditionally once more. I know that day will never come. Of course I care for her, and I love the perfect boy we created together. But I will never be in love with her. I hope she knows this. But there are times when she squeezes my shoulder or clasps my hands that make me feel unsettled, like she's waiting and wanting, yearning and hoping.

"I appreciate that," I tell her, trying to simulate a polite smile. But it probably looks distorted and warped. "I'm doing okay for right now. . . ."

Evelyn slides on her sunglasses once more. "If you're free for the day, maybe the three of us could go to breakfast before Carter has to go to school. Eileen's is right around the corner. You used to love their blueberry pancakes."

Indeed, I did love their pancakes. But part of me is unsettled at the thought of sitting down to a breakfast with Evelyn and our son. All three of us together. Like a perfect little family. The family I know for a fact that Evelyn dreams about. I can't continue to lead her on, to make her feel confident in the idea of me remaining in the picture. Of course I'll love Carter no matter what. But I know I'm a poor excuse for a father. I can't bear the idea of dragging both Evelyn and Carter into the rising tide with me. I'd much rather leave them onshore while I'm pulled away.

"I would love to," I tell her. "I miss Carter. . . . I miss you, too. . . ."

I notice how Evelyn's face softens when I make my confession—how her lips curl a little and her nose twitches a bit.

"We miss you," she says softly.

I wonder if she's going to take hold of my hands and caress them. It wouldn't surprise me. It might cause me to tremble. It's been so long since I've been touched by another person. I've forgotten what the sensation might feel like. . . .

"But I have some things to take care of today, I'm afraid," I tell her.

"Like what?" she asks me, squinting.

Of course she wants to make me say it. Evelyn was always like that—eager to confront, too delighted to provoke me no matter what.

"I . . . have some errands to take care of," I tell her. "I don't want to interrupt Carter while he's playing. . . . Will you please tell him how much I love him?"

Evelyn swallows a little. I can tell she's hurt. I keep on hurting this poor woman. I wonder when she'll want to be rid of me.

"I'll tell him you love him," she says gently. "It would mean more to him if it came directly from you. . . ."

I know she's right. A boy deserves to be told how much he is loved by his father. That's what will make him a man. That's what will keep him sane when the world tries to demolish his spirit, when it attempts to disturb his soul.

I glance at Carter while he scales the platform toward the ramp. I think of going over to him and kissing him on the forehead. Something my father never practiced with me. I'm about to step toward him, but something prevents me from doing so. I think for a moment I'm going to push past the indecision, to shock myself out of my reluctance to reclaim all the love my father never shared with me.

But I don't.

Instead, I swivel slightly and make my way out of the skate park until the sounds of my son chatting with his friend dim to a distant thrum. I want to show him how much I love him, how much I care. But something always prevents me from actually doing it. *What will it take? What will it take to finally be the kind of doting, loving father that my son actually deserves?*

As I stroll toward my favorite café at the end of the block, my thoughts turn to Carter over and over again. It feels decidedly unusual to slip away before offering the boy a hug, a kiss, anything. I love him with my entire being; however, I must realize that I've done nothing to raise him, to care for him the way a proper father should and is expected to.

There are times when I wonder if my own child detests me—if he wastes hours away imagining a world where I'm not present, where I'm not able to pretend to care for him. *What would be the difference anyhow?* I've done nothing to coddle him, to nurture him the way a loving parent should. Carter has every right to hate me, to despise me the same way I dislike myself. He's always been such a precocious boy, after all. It wouldn't surprise me in the least if he harbored some secret grudge against me all while dutifully playing the role of the sullen, attention-starved teenager.

I suppose I never quite fit the qualifications of a proper father. *What am I, after all?* A disgruntled cocksucker with a hang-up on the man I loved, who, in turn, abandoned me right before his terminal cancer diagnosis. Carter deserves so much better than that. Naturally, I've done all I can to love him and be there for him when his mother told me he needed me. But a boy needs a father's love constantly. It's not just a switch you can turn off and on when it suits you. Fatherhood never suited me, I suppose. It's queer to admit that, however, since I desperately wanted to have a child with Jonathan.

While I drift along the sidewalk crowded with other people, I notice a few children traipsing after their parents and holding on to their hands while they move along the pathway toward the school located near the end of the road. I think of how delightful it might have been to have had a child with Jonathan. He was always so tender and soft around children. We visited his aunt in Minneapolis over the Christmas holiday, and his niece had just had a new baby boy. I recall watching Jonathan hold the child near the fireplace, cradling its head and whispering something to him while the little miracle dozed in his arms. Even if I was never confident in my role as a parent, I knew Jonathan would make up for the both of us. Of course, Jonathan met Carter a few times at the local park when I was asked by his mother to visit because my attendance had been so scarce, to say the least.

I recall watching Jonathan observe Carter while the boy played. He was so gentle, so affectionate with Carter, of course. But there was something rigid about his composure whenever he interacted with the boy. I seem to remember that now. It's something I didn't quite notice while it was happening, but it stands out in my memory now that he's gone. Jonathan seemed so uncomfortable, so out of place whenever Carter would ask him to play or would ask him a question. Jonathan stammered, unsure of himself. In the moment, I assumed it was merely because my son had caught him off guard. But as I'm further away from the events now, I can't help but wonder if it's because Jonathan was uncomfortable, especially around Evelyn. Naturally, he accepted the fact that I'd been married to a woman previously. But I wonder if he ever really appreciated the fact that such a relationship came with certain baggage, certain taxes on the soul.

I continue to make my way along the sidewalk, and I sense my mind unfurling more memories of Jonathan. I'm pushed from one corridor of thought to another. Finally, I arrive at a moment I hadn't remembered for quite some time. It occurred a few weeks before Jonathan's cancer diagnosis. I recall how we were enjoying an evening at home. He had built a small fire in the fireplace and was tending to it while I was reading one of the many books I start and then never finish. I remember how I watched him from the corner of my eye—how he stood there framed by the hearth and lingering like some virile specter. To me, Jonathan was godlike. He was more powerful than I could possibly comprehend. I set my book down on the table beside me and watched him for a moment until his eyes snapped to me, recognizing I was staring at him.

"What's the matter?" he asked me, his brow furrowing.

"Nothing," I said gently, releasing a little smile. "I'm not allowed to look at you?"

He simpered, amused. But before he went back to tending the fire, I called to him again.

"Do you ever think about us having a child together?" I asked him.

I recall how he shifted slightly, his head tilting a little to one side with an inquisition he was obviously too scared to issue at first.

"A child?" he asked.

"I hear they're quite fashionable," I said, laughing.

But he didn't seem so amused. Instead, he looked concerned. Yes, I remember that now. In the moment, I thought he looked surprised, perhaps a little startled. But as I look back on those events now, I remember how he looked somewhat frightened at the idea of having a child with me. I still wonder why he reacted like that.

"I've seen you with Carter," I told him. "You're always so soft and gentle. The way a father should be. For God's sake, you're better with him than I am. . . ."

"That's not true," he told me, shaking his head.

I waited for him to say something else, but he didn't. Instead, he idled there with his attention drifting back toward the crackling fire.

"Well . . . ?" I said, trying to prompt him. "What do you think?"

Jonathan shoved his hands into his pockets, and his eyes seemed as though they were avoiding me at all costs.

"I guess it's something we can talk about sometime," he told me.

"So, let's talk about it now," I said to him, trying my best to pry him open more and more—a stubborn chestnut about to split apart. "I think it's something we should consider. . . ."

"What about Evelyn?" he asked me.

I recall how the question astonished me a little. *Why did he ask about her? Why did he care so much what she might think?* I stirred in my seat, sensing my stomach heat with a dull ache.

"I don't see what she has to do with any of this," I told him. "She knows full well that my life's different now. . . . My life is with you. . . ."

But Jonathan shook his head slightly, glancing away from me. "Simeon, she still expects you to be a father to your boy. . . ."

I remember how I sensed a sharp pang of guilt in the center of my chest when he told me that. After all, I knew—and still know—that I hadn't been a worthy father to my sweet, beloved Carter. The boy would undoubtedly have to grow up and come to terms with the fact that his father would rather fuck men than be a respectable parent.

"And I will be," I told him. "But don't you want to have a child with me?"

I think of how Jonathan grew silent for a moment.

"Things don't always stay the same," he told me. "Things change over time. . . ."

"Are you saying that you don't want to have a child with me?" I asked him, rising from my chair.

I recall how my voice quivered with pain.

"No, I'm not saying that," he assured me. "I'm only saying it's something we should really and truly think about."

In the moment, it felt like a little sliver of hope that I could grasp onto.

"So, we can talk about this later?" I asked him. "Further down the road?"

"Yes," he promised me. "*Later.* When we're ready . . ."

But *later* never came for us, sadly. Jonathan was diagnosed with brain cancer a few weeks after our conversation, and very soon I would be forced to make the necessary funeral arrangements for him.

Chapter Four

Email Addressed to Simeon Link from the Wretches

from: The Wretches <wretch@[redacted].com>

to: Simeon Link <simeonlink_86@[redacted].com>

date: March 5, 2025, 11:34 p.m.

subject: An Invitation for Simeon Link

Dear Mr. Link,

It has come to our attention (thanks to a thoughtful group member who recently interacted with you via another online forum) that you may be in need of our aid. Although we typically engage in a rigorous screening process before admitting any person into our club, we've decided to lift certain restrictions in order to properly assist you. We're very interested in welcoming you to our group tomorrow evening (March 6, 2025) at 8:00 p.m. Of course, you'll be observing the small gathering as an outsider; however, we will make every effort to see to it that you'll be as comfortable as possible.

You might be unfamiliar with our association, so it's my honor to explain some of the details of the group to you before you make your first appearance in our circle. The Wretches initially took life in October of

2008 when the group's founder, Melvin Cartwright, lost his beloved wife, Louise, of thirty-seven years. Melvin was devastated by the loss and found little comfort in the several grief-counseling groups he attended over the few months following Louise's untimely demise. Melvin, an amateur photographer, found himself drawn to taking pictures of everyday life in order to cope with his loss. It wasn't until one day when he noticed something unusual staring back at him from a photograph he had taken of a small fountain in the local park. Melvin recognized a familiar face hidden among the nearby shrubbery--the face of his beloved Louise. In that moment, Melvin became convinced that his wife was attempting to communicate with him from the other side, from the place where all spirits are sentenced to dwell.

Enraptured with the idea that his wife was making an effort to appear to him in his photography, Melvin conferred with various friends and showed them what he had seen. Although some were skeptical, many encouraged him to continue taking pictures and seeking out his dear wife in unusual places. It wasn't until he began sharing his photographs online that he developed a unique local following among those afflicted with a similar sorrow. Realizing that many like-minded people could benefit from this kind of therapy, Melvin organized the very first meeting of the Wretches and held the gathering at his home in December of 2008, a few weeks before Christmas. Naturally, the first meeting was an enormous success, and Melvin was truly touched by the outpouring of love and support from those who were also grieving in the community.

Of course, over the years, the group has shifted slightly in design. However, the integrity and the purpose of the organization have never faltered. The group's sole purpose? To provide a safe space for those who are grieving to witness the wonder of the world around them, to recognize the sheer fact that the dead, indeed, do live on and surround us at all times. Although Melvin Cartwright passed away in 2015, this mission statement has never wavered in the years of the organization's existence and has been upheld by the many thoughtful and kindhearted members of the group who keep Melvin's cheerful memory alive to this day.

I expect you will have many questions, and it will be my honor to answer more of them in person tomorrow evening at 8:00 p.m. We expect to see you at the church recreation hall located on Spruce Street. You are not obligated to bring anything to the meeting. If you desire to continue visiting with us, that will be determined by your presence at the initial meeting you attend. Naturally, if you have any logistical questions before our gathering, please do not hesitate to reach out.

We sincerely look forward to meeting with you and restructuring the way you process grief with the enchantment of photography.

Best wishes,
Daniel Westmacott

I look at the small, framed photograph I keep beside my bed on the nightstand. Of course the picture is of Jonathan. *But is it actually of Jonathan?* No. I suppose not. It's of his ghost. I don't necessarily mean the appearance of his spirit or phantom, but rather him in the past tense. A memory. A faraway recollection. He exists only in that small frame now. Captured there, never to be set free. Permanently a young man at the age of thirty-four, three years before the cancer eventually took him from me, three years before our love soured and became rotted because of his disease. If a photograph is a kind of ghost, then I suppose cancer is a kind of cannibal. *But does any of it actually matter?* Both things will destroy us in the end. . . .

But do we actually discard photographs? Not always. We hold on to them. We pin them to the refrigerator. We frame them and keep them in a place of honor on the mantel. Is it because we wish to be haunted? Perhaps we take photographs because we yearn to be tormented, disturbed by the past, reminded of what once was and what will never be ever again. A photograph can be a dismal, sad thing—a memory you'd prefer to neglect, but instead it follows you, pursues you until you finally relent and place it beside your bed in a small, wooden frame with gold etchings.

Feeling restless, I find myself seated at my desk and hunched over my laptop screen. Even though it's late at night, I don't feel too fatigued. Sleep isn't an option right now. I haven't been sleeping well the past few nights anyway, so I'm surprised I'm so alert, so awake right now. I make the decision—however unwise, however imprudent—to do an internet search for the Wretches. More specifically, anything I can find about testimonials from those who have joined and found peace existing among their ranks. I type in the search bar: *the Wretches photography grief group*. The small icon beside my cursor flutters slightly until a bunch of search results floods the screen.

I peer down the list of options sprawling before me and find myself unsettled at how documented the group has been since its inception. I wonder why that surprises me so. After all, it seems like such an exclusive club. Why would they want to advertise themselves so much? It seems perfectly reasonable to me that so much of their presence in the world is practically untraceable online. Not all things in this world exist online. Vice versa as well. Not all things online are apparent in the actual world.

I hover my mouse over some of the results that pop up along the page, but nothing seems to pique my interest. I scroll down farther, slowly nearing the end of the results and sensing myself shrink at the realization that I probably won't find exactly what I'm searching for. It's then I come across the link to a blog post titled "Der Mensch lebt von Illusionen: My Short Time with the Wretches." I think to myself how that sounds somewhat promising. I click the link, and I'm spirited to a primitive-looking blog post from the early 2010s on a page with a hideous tangerine-colored background. The text is written entirely in jade green, so it's somewhat difficult to read everything at first. I highlight the entirety of the blog post, copy it, and then paste it into a separate Word document so that I can read it better.

After pasting it there in the document, I begin to read:

Der Mensch lebt von Illusionen: My Short Time with the Wretches

Posted by **meryl_in_blue** on October 9, 2011, at 3:47 p.m.

*[Click **here** to share with your followers]*

[7 comments]

If you're reading this, I imagine you know the very basics of a group referred to as the Wretches. Then again, perhaps you don't. I probably shouldn't assume such things. Regardless, they were touted to me as a highly selective coterie of grieving individuals who are fascinated with the idea of the dead dwelling inside photographs. More specifically, they are interested in the phenomenon of deceased loved ones making appearances to the grieving in all kinds of imagery, especially photographs taken by the living with the intent to view messages from the departed. Naturally, like anyone else, I found myself especially drawn to this group of individuals for a myriad of reasons. I had recently lost my mother and was finding it difficult to navigate the complexities of being a woman in an indifferent and uncaring world—especially as a single mother to a newborn baby boy.

My mother and I were not terribly close while she was alive. In fact, I hardly saw her during the last year she was living in a rehabilitation facility on the outskirts of Haverhill, Massachusetts. Still, once she passed, I was filled with such an overwhelming sense of sorrow, a sadness that I had missed out on so much of the joys of being a daughter and possessing a doting, caring mother. When I first arrived at a meeting for the Wretches, I felt very out of place. I had assumed that many of the people there might welcome me and assure me that things would get better, that I would feel welcome over the course of time—however, no such kindness occurred. Instead, I continued to feel very much out of place, wondering if I had made the correct decision, worrying that I had initiated some sort of ritual that could never be undone.

It was after the first meeting that I began to look for signs of my mother in everyday objects, to search for meaning in the mundane, to hunt for a reason in the ordinary, the routine. Like I was instructed, I purchased a special camera and made good use of my time to try to capture hints of my mother's essence in various things. Eventually, so much of my existence became wrapped up in the question of whether or not I could locate her, whether or not I could be successful in finding her by the time we were supposed to meet next. It felt like some impossible challenge that I was already predetermined to fail. That said, it wasn't long before I took a particular photograph and did a double take, wondering if I had perhaps noticed something unusual in the corner of the picture. There, hidden amongst pots and pans in my kitchen cupboard, was the vague silhouette of a woman's face. I was convinced. The face belonged to my mother.

However, the more I looked at it, the more the definition of what I presumed was her face began to dissipate, began to curl away from me. Is it because things lose meaning if you struggle to define them properly? Why had I strained in earnest to find evidence of my mother's presence after her death? All of my existence began to feel hollow, even almost artificial.

It's my belief that so much of the Wretches' popularity continues with those who are feeble and grieving fresh departures is because so many people rely on illusion to survive. What was the name of that play about the faded Southern belle who goes to live with her sister and her sister's womanizer of a husband? At one point, she cries out, "I don't want realism. I want magic!" So many of those who find success, who find joy and comfort existing as a Wretch want to deny realism and instead embrace the power of magic. So much of life is being confronted with the harsh truth of the reflection. These people simply want to exist in a place where there are no mirrors, there are no truths. Instead, there is only magic.

It was when I discovered this that I realized I would not be able to continue on as a Wretch. I have concluded all of my dealings with them and have made no attempt to get in contact with them. Still, I worry that someone from their organization will come to me again, will seek me out and question why I refused to carry on with them. Perhaps if they come to me one day, all I'll be able to say is this: "I do not wish to dwell in the state of illusion. I'm much more comfortable with the truth. . . ."

After I finish reading the final sentence of the woman's blog post, I sense my eyes going over her last sentences again and again. *"I do not wish to dwell in the state of illusion. I'm much more comfortable with the truth. . . ."* I wonder if I feel the same way. So much of life is about suffering, about being uncomfortable. I wonder if I'm more inclined to accept the realism or if I prefer the magic. I open the blog post on the computer screen once more, and I look for other entries written by this person. It's then that I recognize that's the final blog post she wrote. I sense myself shrivel a little at the realization, at the horrible possibility that something happened to her. *Why did she stop posting? What became of this poor woman who was so adamant against the Wretches and their magic?*

I think of every excuse not to attend the Wretches' private ceremony tomorrow night. I invent every plausible defense, every reasonable kind of ailment I could suffer at a moment's notice that might call me away, that might disrupt my sense of self and possibly explain my noticeable absence. But very soon I come to the awful realization that no disruption could keep my curiosity away from their small gathering. I'm far too invested, far too curious in what might happen if I make the decision to go. After all, there are only two outcomes in every given situation: what might happen if you do go and what might happen if you don't. Do I necessarily want to live in a timeline where I didn't attend, and I'm left to grieve all alone?

Instead of debating whether or not to go, I lie down in my empty bed and think of Jonathan. My mind rolls over the recollection of his image again and again until my eyes eventually close, and other gentle thoughts arrive like well-dressed patrons milling about inside the theater of my mind. There's a part of me that wonders if I'm actually remembering him as he was, or rather if I'm inventing him the way I'd like to see him. There's every possibility that I've added a certain level of charm and wit to his character in my dreams. Of course, that's not to say that he was ever completely lacking in those subjects, but I can't help but recall how reserved he often became around my friends. Or our friends, in general. He always preferred quiet nights spent in our apartment as opposed to going out and seeing others. I never objected to this because I truly loved being around him, but still, I wonder if I've misremembered aspects of his character now that he's been gone for so long.

Sometimes, when I dream, I invent new, strange scenarios for the two of us to endure as though they had actually happened. I don't question the subject of the dreams when they finally arrive to me. I seem to accept everything the way all dreamers lovingly accept whatever their mind tells them to recognize. I find myself stirring in bed, tossing in between the sheets, and wishing this damn bed weren't so empty. Very often I'll build a small pile of pillows on the side of the bed where Jonathan used to sleep, and I'll cling onto them while I doze. I like the way the cushions feel between my legs when I grip them tight. Sometimes it feels like Jonathan never left, never abandoned me so carelessly. Yes, I suppose there's a part of me that feels somewhat abandoned, like I had been some neglected child forced to endure a birthday on their own and without presents or frosted cake. In my heart, I know Jonathan would never have left me if he'd had the chance. But still, I wonder why he was so hesitant about adopting a child with me. Surely we would have been exceptional parents. We would have raised a beautiful, healthy boy and taught him the ways to become a happy and successful man. There are times when I dream about what might have happened if Jonathan and I had actually raised a child. Curious enough, in every dream, there's some formless specter lingering there, eager to spirit our baby boy away from us. Sometimes the treachery is obvious, and we are not deceived. But other times, the disloyalty is more complicated, and we cannot help but be fooled. Perhaps we would have been poor imitations of parents if ever afforded the opportunity. Maybe we would have auctioned our child off to the highest bidder, to allow some perfect stranger to do with our boy whatever he might will.

I turn over onto my side, bedsheets snarled around my legs, and I force my eyes shut. I try to sleep. *Sleep, sleep. Please come to me,* I think to myself. *Let me dream. Let me float away until I'm rested on some invisible lily pad, gently floating through the tide of my thoughts.* I try to empty my mind so that I'm not upset or disturbed before sleep claims me, but I'm still hounded by the awful possibility that perhaps Jonathan did not want to raise a child with me because he knew we would have wounded that boy. Every parent is capable of harming their child. In fact, perhaps it's better for the parent to do so, because the world is going to be too eager to harm what you've created. I suppose that wouldn't matter much to me and Jonathan, considering two men cannot conceive naturally. Perhaps that's another reason why he didn't want to accept having a child with me. Perhaps it was too much to accept for such a pittance of a reward. I'm still not sure of the answer, and that uncertainty shatters me. I crumple a little, sleeping on my side, and eventually I feel myself soften until I'm unspooled and floating there. Sleep comes to me, and I dream of sweet Jonathan, of the child we never had, and a soulless figure—his skin shiny and reflective like a freshly polished mirror—begging to claim our boy as his. He holds out a contract for me to sign, to will away the life of my precious boy. I shove the pen aside and refuse to print my name on the line. I would never let my son be devoured.

Part Two

Predator and Prey

Tell me, at what precise moment does an individual stop being who he thinks he is?

—*The Tenant* (1976)

Chapter Five

There's a term I keep thinking of while I make the drive out to the church recreation hall at the edge of town. It's a French term I learned once in college history class: coup de grâce. It refers to the final blow to kill a wounded person or animal—a mercy killing. Naturally, this kind of butchery was more prominent during certain historical periods and included all sorts of dire situations, like when a mortally wounded soldier could not be aided by doctors and was, therefore, put out of his torment. Those who received injuries during failed execution attempts might have received similar treatment as a more humane way of making them more comfortable in their final moments.

I can't quite figure out why I continue to think about this strange term while I grip my gloved hands on the steering wheel, aiming the car ahead at the empty highway stretching in front of me. Of course, there's a part of me that wonders if there's some sort of cosmic execution for those who have suffered enough—a more compassionate way of ending your existence after enduring so much for so long. I suppose I've come to the realization that I'm too frightened, too apprehensive, to end things for myself—to finally pull the trigger, to tighten the noose, to slide the razor across my wrist at long last. I shift in my seat, uncomfortable, when I come to the realization that

I'd much prefer that someone else put me out of my misery. Perhaps that's what I've been looking for when I go searching in those online chat rooms with random strangers. Perhaps I'm searching for the perfect candidate to trust with the end of my existence.

If there's anyone on this planet who deserves something similar to a coup de grâce, I would argue that such a person would be me. I've endured such heartache, such despair, for so long. How can I carry on when I know full well that nothing good will be coming my way for the foreseeable future? After all, I don't possess any high hopes for the Wretches. Even if they are able to momentarily distract me from my grief, my despondency, there's every possibility that the sadness will return even more poisonous than before. Grief is like that. Grief is a living thing that binds you, constricts you like a large serpent, and then grows the more that you feed it. I suppose I've been feeding my grief, my sorrow, for quite some time. It would be impossible to stop at this point. Of course, this is no way to live, and I know that full well. It's a reminder I see every time I glance in the bathroom mirror.

It's frustrating to continue fantasizing about your own demise but lack the shrewdness to actually go through with the damn thing. *What will it take? What will it take to persuade me to finally do it?* I can't be certain. That's why a coup de grâce is so necessary, so vital to my happiness. I'd give anything to be executed humanely, to have my shaved head positioned beneath a freshly sharpened blade and then to feel the rush of cool air while it comes down upon me, prepared to strike and hit its perfect mark. I yearn for someone to recognize my suffering, my sense of hopelessness, and to take matters in their own hands—to put me out of my misery so that I'm not burdened with the responsibility or the discomfort. Naturally, I know that's a lot to ask of another human being—to charge them with the responsibility for your demise. But perhaps I'll locate this kind, benevolent soul at the small gathering tonight. Perhaps they'll make themselves known to me the moment I enter that recreation hall.

I sense my foot easing off the accelerator as I take the exit on the side of the highway and drift into a new lane flanked by small rows of brightly lit houses. I peer into the nearby windows, and I wonder about the lives hidden away in each of those homes. I wonder what secrets they might be keeping from the rest of the world—their joy, their aching, their cheerfulness, their despair. Such things are impossible to live without. Of course I know this. Still, I yearn for humaneness—the gift of being given permission to walk away, to end things and to still maintain a semblance of my dignity.

Eventually, I pull into the parking lot, and I park at the end of a row of vehicles. I observe several people milling about the entrance of the building, a few others shouting greetings at those who are approaching. There's something churning in the air like electricity outside my window that tells me things could change tonight. *Indeed,* I think to myself. *Everything could change in a matter of seconds.* After all, a coup de grâce takes a mere moment to enact. I wonder if I'll discover the person brave enough to help me here tonight—to issue that final blow, to help a poor, defenseless fawn with a leaking wound.

I drift through the double doors of the church recreation hall, after informing the gentleman guarding the door that I'm expected, that I've been sent by someone online named babyfacexoxo. It feels ridiculous to utter the faceless person's screen name aloud, but it's the very thing that gets me past the threshold, so I cannot be too self-conscious about it. Once I enter the room, I immediately take note of the large wooden figure of Jesus Christ presiding over the empty space like some unsolicited referee, some everlasting celestial observer to our shared suffering. He's life-sized and carved from what appears to be rustic-looking driftwood. The most unusual aspect of his presentation is his face. As his mouth is twisted open in the usual expression of agony while nailed to the wooden crucifix, it's unsettling to note how the figure's eyes have been hollowed out completely. In their place are large silver-looking orbs that are mirrorlike.

I find myself being pulled closer and closer toward the wooden figure. I pale a little, noticing how weathered I look, how downtrodden, how upset to be here. *Why have I come?* I wonder to myself. Surely I could have made every excuse to keep myself away. I could have declined their very polite invitation. But still, something drew me here. I can't quite tell what it is, but it disturbs me all the same.

Framed next to the large wooden figure of Christ is an oil portrait of a young man. Or at least I presume it's a young man. To be truthful, I cannot adequately tell. I squint, struggling to examine the person's face, and it's at that moment that I realize the paint has been smudged where the figure's face is supposed to be—a handprint and a shapely swirl defiling the image and covering the area where the young man's face once was. He's dressed in angelic white, and he's sitting at the edge of a sprawling bed with both arms outstretched to the viewer, welcoming them to his sparsely lit chamber. I glance at the gilded plate at the bottom of the frame in hopes of learning the piece's title, but the damn thing has been filed away, scratched by something.

After I'm finished examining the statue of a tortured Christ and the damaged portrait of the faceless young man, I make my way over to the arrangement of collapsible chairs organized in the center of the room. I notice a middle-aged woman with black hair pulled back in a bun sitting on the far side of the makeshift circle. She looks soft and gentle, so I approach her, and I ask if I can sit next to her. She doesn't say much to me aside from removing her handbag from the chair beside her and motioning for me to take a seat. I pass her a polite smile and thank her for allowing me to sit next to her. She's receptive to my thanks but doesn't say anything else to me. Perhaps she wants to, but she's been instructed to be careful around those who are not yet officially welcomed to their group. I suppose, in many ways, I'm still an outsider to these people. These strange and beguiling people. I watch them as more file into the room and take their seats, filling the rest of the large circle of chairs. Part of me wonders if I'll meet babyfacexoxo here tonight. *Will they reveal themselves to me? How will I know it's actually them?*

Occasionally my eyes drift toward the large statue of Christ glaring down at us from his perch, from his venerated place of sacrifice and martyrdom. *If only there had been a kind enough soul present during his demise to issue a coup de grâce,* I think to myself. But then again, if that had happened, his suffering would have been meaningless and empty. I stare at the effigy of Christ pinned to the nearby wall, squinting at him and wondering why the damn figurine is here in the first place. Everything about his presence seems so objectionable—his gruesome expression of permanent anguish, the etchings of blood leaking from his bound hands, the obscenity of his nakedness. I wince a little, recognizing so much of *his* misery in my own. I find myself shivering when I glance into the silver orbs fixed in his eye sockets, and I see my pitiful reflection echoing there like an antique film I cannot shut off.

Eventually, after what feels like hours of endless waiting, a middle-aged man rises from a chair near the exit and approaches those of us waiting in the circle. He's wearing a knitted sweater and khakis. I can't help but notice how painfully artificial he appears. He resembles something not quite human, something almost uncannily human but not familiar with any of the characteristics that make a fully formed person. It's then that I decide to refer to him as Void.

"Good evening, friends," Void says, greeting the small crowd of twenty or so faces. "We have a full agenda tonight, so I propose we get right into it. . . . I'd like to call upon one of our kindest and most thoughtful patrons. Mr. Philip Jeffrey."

I watch in silence as Void withdraws to the back of the large room and makes way for an older gentleman assisted with an ornate-looking cane. I notice how his wrinkled hands grip the silver handle fashioned in the shape of some large insect. I can't quite tell if it's a spider or a beetle since the old man's fingers are long and cover most of the decorative ornament. Does it actually matter? I suppose it does only to sate my curiosity.

I observe while Mr. Jeffrey takes his place at the center of the circle like some kind of sacrificial lamb. Just then, the lights in the room begin to dim, and a large projection screen descends from the rafters above us. A projector stationed in the rear of the room and operated by a middle-aged woman with dark hair and glasses whirs alive and sputters, coughing like the engine of an old luxury car. My attention snaps to the screen when I notice a large image coming into frame, the projector struggling to focus on the picture. It's an image of storm clouds threatening with rain. In some strange way, the picture looks almost menacing—something unsaid in the muted whisper of a rumble of distant thunder you can't quite hear.

"You'll recall we had some nasty weather around this time last week," Mr. Jeffrey says to us. "I went outside with my camera because I felt something . . . that strange kind of feeling you must feel when you're certain something's about to happen. You're not sure what, but you know something's coming. . . ."

I glance around at the others in the circle observing Mr. Jeffrey while he speaks, struggling to discern whether or not they seem to agree with him. I suppose that feeling of inevitability is present in every living thing—especially animals during bad weather—but it's a matter of listening to that voice. It's at that precise moment that I come to the awful realization that I haven't engaged with that inner voice in quite some time. I convinced myself I didn't need to, for whatever reason. I guess I thought that if I couldn't shield Jonathan, couldn't protect him from whatever eventually destroyed him, what's the point of listening to such a voice?

"I looked up at the clouds, and I saw something," Mr. Jeffrey tells us, his voice trembling a little from the excitement. "I saw my wife's face in the clouds. Her sweet, loving face. Framed there, peering down on me . . . Do you see it?"

I watch as the image is enhanced on the screen, the projector zooming in on a dimly lit corner of the photograph. I squint, my eyes narrowing at the picture, and I find myself filled with such an urgency to locate the face he's talking about. For some inexplicable reason, there's a desperation moored somewhere deep inside me that aches to believe this old gentleman. I want to see what he sees. I want to believe it's really and truly there.

Just when I'm about to give up, the projector enhances the image once more, and a woman's face arrives into focus. It's a gentle, warm expression, her face nestled in the pocket between two dark clouds.

As the photograph comes more into alignment, there's a collective sigh among those of us who are sitting in the circle. Then there are, of course, the oohs and aahs filtering among us. Finally, the excitement settles, and there's a stillness lingering over the room.

"Naturally, I've seen her face in many things before," he tells us. "Antique teapots. Sand on the beach. But this sighting felt more intentional. Felt more like a clear message from her . . . I wish I could tell what she was trying to say. . . . It feels so—deliberate. . . ."

"Notice how the lips are thin but obviously smiling," one of the younger ladies in the group exclaims, her eyes fixed on the projected image.

"She's not smiling," another older gentleman contests. "It's an obvious look of ache and despair. See how the mouth pulls downward?"

"You're both wrong," a third voice chimes in before Void takes charge of the room, hastening toward the center of the circle and motioning for all to be still, to be silent.

"As much as I appreciate a lively discussion, this is Mr. Jeffrey's photograph," he says. "His interpretation is the most important."

Mr. Jeffrey seems to soften, wilting a little but thankful for the group leader's guidance.

"Mr. Jeffrey, what do you think of the photograph exactly?" Void asks the old gentleman. "What are your thoughts?"

Mr. Jeffrey clasps his hands together almost like he's praying. His eyes lift to meet the image thrown on the screen. He's silent, and there comes a time when the room is so still, so quiet, that I can hear my heart thumping inside my chest—tirelessly beating again and again, yearning to be heard by anyone who will listen.

"I suppose this kind of picture makes me realize that I won't ever understand everything about my wife," Mr. Jeffrey says. "It helps me come to peace with not knowing. . . . If you understand something, you can possess it. You can claim ownership over it. . . . I don't wish to do that to her. I want her to be free. . . ."

Void's lips crease with a polite smile. "That's lovely, my friend," he says, and then turns to the rest of us, encouraging us to clap. "Let's hear it for Mr. Philip Jeffrey."

The room erupts in applause and cheering while Mr. Jeffrey accepts the attention with an awkward wave and a forced grin. Eventually, when the room quiets down again, Mr. Jeffrey moves out of the center of the circle and resumes his normal seat on the far end, directly across from where I'm seated. Part of me feels foolish for thinking I saw the face in Mr. Jeffrey's photograph. *Did I actually see that?* I wonder to myself. *Could it be true?* Of course, I suppose anything's possible. However, it feels so decidedly unlike me to hold on to a belief so desperately, to ache for something to be true. I shift in my seat, uncomfortable, and I notice how Void seems to be eyeing me from across the room. *God, please don't call on me,* I think to myself. I couldn't bear it. My attention is caught again by the effigy of Christ presiding over this paltry court of our anguish, and part of me wonders if I see the damn thing's lips quiver, about to speak and order me to obey. Just as I'm about to curl inward completely, Void locks eyes with me and points me out to the other group members.

"Ladies and gentlemen, we have the distinct honor of welcoming a newcomer to the Wretches this evening," he announces, glaring at me with almost a look of challenge, as if he were attempting to discern whether or not I actually had the guts to be here. "Sir, would you like to stand up and introduce yourself?"

I hesitate a little. Perhaps I don't have the guts to be here, to show my face and pretend to be invested in their gathering. I wince, disturbed by the recollection of the old gentleman's photograph. I can scarcely believe what I saw. Was it actually true? Naturally, the human mind is capable of processing many curiosities. But could it be that I actually saw that poor old man's dead wife in the storm clouds of that picture? I feel strange, unsure of myself and desperately wanting these things to be true—to be a believer in this rare sacred art form of an unusual kind of photography. But the more I stay here, the more I linger among these people, I sense myself wanting to be liked, to be accepted. I find myself silently begging them to show me more pictures—to test my curiosity, to sate my interest.

I allow a moment to compose myself, finding that I've become short of breath. When I finally steady my breathing, I slowly rise from where I'm seated, and I glance around at the crowd of dim, somber-looking faces. There are no smiles, no warm expressions to greet me. Rather, they all seem to glower at me like I'm interrupting their evening, as if my presence is a horrible intrusion upon their mourning. *Perhaps it is,* I think to myself. *Perhaps I'm not meant to be here.*

"Hi, everyone," I say, my voice trembling a little. "I'm Simeon. . . . I was invited here this evening by . . ."

But my voice trails off, unsure. I don't know exactly who invited me here, after all. It feels queer to admit it was a random stranger in a chat room. They'd never believe that. So, instead, I let the unsaid words dangle in the air for a moment before continuing.

"I lost my husband a few months ago," I tell them. "His name was Jonathan. . . . He was . . . Well, he was perfect in every way. . . . Incidentally, he loved taking pictures as well. Loved going to the park and taking photographs of other people, wildlife, anything that captured his attention . . ."

I glance around the room of faces, desperate for a look of kindness, of acceptance. There's none to be found, unfortunately. In fact, part of me wonders if some of them might unhinge their jaws and charge at me with fangs exposed.

"Why did you come here tonight?" Void asks me from the other side of the room, circling the periphery of the circle of patrons. "What do you hope to get out of these meetings?"

I hesitate once again, wondering if this might be a trick question—the final opportunity for them to either accept or reject me.

"I suppose I came here to see if I could . . . see Jonathan again," I say, clearing the catch in my throat. "I want to know if he's still around me, still watching me. . . . I just—want to feel his presence again. . . . That sounds silly to say. . . ."

"If it's the truth, it should be said," Void says to me, and then addresses the small crowd. "Let's give Simeon a round of applause."

They all clap their hands, cheering for me, but so much of their praise feels forced. I notice how several group members lean over to the person they're sitting beside and whisper something in their ear. I want to know what they've said. I know that they're talking about me.

An hour or so passes, several group members moving into the center of the circle and narrating their process for taking a picture that's projected onto the large screen. Over the course of the evening, there are some pictures presented that I can clearly see strange, tortured-looking faces in inanimate objects. However, there are just as many photographs presented when I struggle to decipher human faces. I feel broken, like I'm not properly calibrated to see what they see, and it makes me quiver slightly, my stomach coiling into a tight knot. I feel especially guilty when a young woman—probably the youngest person here—takes command of the room and explains how she saw her dead mother's face in the tiling of her kitchen counter. But when she presented the picture to us, there was nothing to be seen there. Quiet murmurs filtered throughout the crowd, silent questions of her integrity. I soften, feeling sorry for the poor girl. I watch her as she takes her seat after a lackluster presentation and her head remains lowered, as if out of humiliation. More than anything, I want to believe her. *But at what cost?*

Finally, the meeting comes to an end, Void taking charge of the room.

"Folks, tonight was an excellent meeting," he says. "We'll see you again next Thursday at eight. . . . Perhaps our new group member will have something to share with us then?"

He throws a look at me—an obvious challenge—and then drifts out of the center of the circle of chairs.

I sense my heartbeat quicken, a drum pounding away inside my chest. Naturally, I had expected they might want me to play the game. *But so soon? Does this mean I've been welcomed to their group?* I can't be certain. I grab my jacket from where I've draped it on the back of the foldable chair and throw it on. I pass a polite smile to the woman seated beside me, who's already on her phone and taking a picture of the floorboards. Perhaps she sees something I cannot. I begin to make my way toward the exit when I suddenly notice a young man weaving through the crowd and heading directly toward me with such intent, such purpose.

He's probably one of the youngest men here. He's obviously very fashionable, as he wears a white knitted sweater, dark jeans, and a handsome pair of crocodile loafers. He's trim and boyishly handsome. In many ways, he resembles the kind of innocent young-looking men I used to seek out for the sake of pleasure at the bars before I finally met Jonathan. For a moment, I think back to those nights—sweaty, uncoordinated groping with a random stranger in the bathroom stall of some club while electronic music drifted in from the nearby dance floor. Naturally, I had felt free. I had felt liberated to do whatever I pleased, to stick my cock into anyone I saw fit enough to receive. But that novelty eventually wore off when I came to know my sweet, beloved Jonathan, when I realized that you could be monogamous and gay at the same time.

I curl inward a little, observing the young man make a dash toward me across the crowded room. I prepare myself, forcing a smile.

"Hey," he says, offering his hand to shake. "My name's Kent. . . . I really like what you said about your late husband. . . . I'm sorry for your loss. . . ."

I shudder, still a little uncomfortable accepting condolences. Every expression of sympathy seems to serve as a reminder that he's actually gone, that he's never coming back to me.

"Thank you," I say, shivering as our hands touch and we shake. "I'm Simeon. . . ."

"What do you think of our little group, Simeon?" Kent asks me, shoving his hands into his pockets and smiling.

"I guess I didn't know exactly what to expect," I tell him. "But I'm glad I came. . . ."

"You think you'll be a regular?" he asks me. "We've had a few come to the group and then never show up again. . . . Maybe it's not for them. I get it."

I shake my head, unsure. "I'm still trying to decide if it's for me, I suppose. . . ."

"Do you have a camera?"

I flash him my cell phone, laughing. Embarrassed almost.

He laughs, too. "I meant a real camera," he says. "Something of quality."

My eyes lower. I can't lie to him. He seems to recognize this immediately, his voice softening a little when he speaks to me.

"I can help you find one, if you'd like?" he offers. "I know the best kind to look for. Especially if you're not familiar with good quality cameras . . ."

I glance about the room, watching group members weave around us while we speak. Some of them seem to eye me with a look of sincere questioning: *Should you be here? Do you belong here?* I can't be bothered with answering those inquiries now.

"I wouldn't even know where to begin looking," I tell Kent. "Or how."

"I know we just met," he says, passing a small business card to me. "But if you ever want my help, please just reach out. I'm always around. . . ."

I glance at the card and read what's printed there: *KENT SIMMONS. Landscape and Still Life Photographer.* His cell phone number and email address are printed below.

"Thanks," I say to him. "I'll definitely keep this in mind."

"It's never any trouble," he tells me before slipping away and walking out the door leading toward the parking lot.

I push his business card inside my coat pocket and then wrap a scarf around my neck, pulling it tight. One final time, I glance back at the giant effigy of Christ presiding over the church's recreation hall. He's still there, of course—forever caught in the exquisite passion of his final persecution, the incredible sensation of bondage, of human torture and brutality. But now that the lights in the room have lowered considerably and the space is nearly dark, I notice how the silver orbs fixed in those hollow sockets where his eyes should be glow like twin flames, like small fires that will be kept burning until I return next time. *If* I return next time, that is.

I shove my hands into my coat pockets and make my way out of the recreation hall, moving into the parking lot. I glance up at the dark night sky flecked with tinfoil-looking bits of broken starlight. I wonder if I should swipe my phone and take a picture, but what's the use? I don't see any faces there. Will I ever see Jonathan's face staring back at me? I don't know. But it's a lovely thought to consider while I make the drive home, my mind turning over and over again the possibility of seeing his face in every single object I pass on the roadway—every stop sign, every highway marker, every passing billboard. I can't help but wonder when Jonathan will finally make himself known to me. Occasionally, I glance in the rearview mirror and wonder if I'll see Jonathan staring at me from the back seat. But the reflection is empty. He's not there. So I just keep driving and driving until I feel as though the road might peel away from underneath my vehicle, until I finally reach the edge of the shore and I'm pulled into the tide rising with blood.

Chapter Six

Nothing seems to calm my nerves as I make my way into my apartment building, press the small circular button beside the lift, and then climb on board when the elevator finally arrives. I feel so out of sorts, and it perplexes me. I wince a little, sensing my stomach broiling with a strange feeling of unease while I idle in the elevator and wait to arrive at my floor. Ever since I was little, I've found it a strain to compose myself around other people. I always felt as though I had to perform, had to be something I wasn't so that they might like me. Usually at the end of crowded events, I feel drained, utterly emptied, as if I had given small but meaningful pieces of myself to each person there and let them mindlessly gorge upon me until they were sated. Of course, it was kind of that young man to approach me, to show an interest in me, but will I actually go through with seeking him out for his help? At this point, I'm not so sure.

Instead, I find myself curling inward, aching to be alone. Thankfully, the small elevator is empty, and I thank God I won't be forced to make unnecessary small talk with any neighbors. Eventually, I arrive at my designated floor, and I hasten down the lengthy corridor until I'm at the doorway to my apartment. I fish inside my pocket for the keys, pull them out, and then twist them into the lock, heaving the door open until I'm finally inside my safe space—the place where I don't need to perform in order for others to like me or care about me, the place where I don't need to edit my grieving to make others more comfortable. Their comfort doesn't matter to me. What matters is how I feel, how I react and grieve. I try to remind myself of that again and again. It's been said to me countless times on the many self-help tapes I've purchased since Jonathan passed, but no good, decent thought seems to linger for too long in my mind.

In fact, while I idle there in the apartment entryway and shuck off my jacket, I wonder if I should play one of those tapes I purchased. After all, it's been so long since I've listened to them, and I know I could certainly use the emotional boost. But something in my mind argues against it. Something whispers to me that I'd much prefer to remain miserable, that I'm more interesting or somehow more valuable to the world if I suffer, if I simply carry on and endure in pain. I don't know if I believe that voice inside my head, but the pernicious little creature speaks with such conviction and clarity that anything it says could sound true if delivered earnestly and intelligently enough.

I think to heat up some of the leftovers in the Chinese takeout cartons inside the fridge, but I'm not hungry, even though my stomach grumbles and aches slightly. Instead, I'm too fixated on the idea of Jonathan—the very thought of seeing him again, the notion of witnessing his face in random objects. I wonder if he's been present with me all this time, and I've been too stupid, too foolhardy to notice. Yes, perhaps I wasn't paying close enough attention to the world around me. Grief does that to you, after all. It poisons everything in its path and alters how you view the world. I can't help but recall how, when Jonathan passed away, I once received an unexpected phone call from Evelyn. The voice I heard on my voicemail was rough, impossibly grating—nothing like the sweet, lilting voice I knew of her before. Instead, everything she said in her voicemail seemed to bear a threatening, almost menacing kind of tone. It's now I realize that so much of my view of Evelyn changed after Jonathan died—almost as though she's been replaced by someone else pretending to be her. There's a part of me that wonders if that's possible—if Evelyn has been replaced by someone, *something.*

I make my way into the bedroom and flop down onto the mattress, undoing my belt and shucking off my pants. I lie there for a moment, gazing upward at the ceiling fan spinning above me. It hums gently, the blur of some celestial eye peering down on me while I stir on Jonathan's side of the bed. I grab hold of the pillows, squeezing them tight and pushing one of them between my legs until I roll over on my side like a sleeping toddler. It's then that I feel myself start to quiver a little. It isn't long before I sense some wetness beneath both of my eyes. I blink, more beads of tears webbing there. *Fuck,* I think to myself. *I don't want to do this again. I don't want to cry. I've already wasted so much time crying.*

Instead, part of me wants to scream. I want to holler until I'm hoarse, until the neighbors call the police because they think someone's being butchered in my apartment. But I can't. For the sake of *their* comfort, I cannot do that. So I do the next best thing and bury my face into one of the pillows, screaming into the cushion until the sound breaks apart and I'm left to do nothing else but sob.

I dread the idea of going to bed. Sleep means temporary relief from the sorrow that's not supposed to follow me into my dreams. However, it also means that I'll be forced to wake up and remember the horrible truth—that Jonathan's not here, that I'll possibly never see him again, that he's been taken away from me because I never deserved a love like his.

My mind eventually sours and turns to thoughts of my old place of employment—the office I dreaded visiting for the past several years, the small talk I tolerated for the sake of a paycheck, the abuse I endured because we're told it must be normal, and because we must suffer a little bit if we wish to inherit pleasure in the next life. Of course, I don't believe in any of that nonsense. Still, I can't help but think of Mr. Whittaker and that strange picture of the grove of trees on his desk—how he had said it was a photograph of his deceased wife taken not very long ago. It seems too ridiculous to believe at face value. Perhaps he haunts her in ways that I think of when I consider haunting my sweet Jonathan and how I'd give anything to subject him to my thoughts, my musings, my most misguided fantasies.

I lie on my back and observe the ceiling fan spinning above me again. I pretend that I can see Jonathan's handsome face buried somewhere in the fan's seemingly permanent blur. But I know it's just a trick, a kind of deception that my mind likes to play on me when I'm feeling especially maudlin. I close my eyes and pray that I won't dream of him. Instead, I'll dream about random photographs of antique furniture, and I'll dream about large statues of Jesus Christ made from old driftwood. Those things are safe and cannot harm me. At least, for now . . .

There's a part of me that wonders if I'm a simple mark because of my heartache, because of my despair. Does my misery allow me to become malleable, moldable, by those wishing to do harm to me, to control me? I don't know the exact answer, but it's a thought that unsettles me while I strip naked and climb into the shower for my morning rinse. As the warm water sprays me and I grab a nearby bar of soap to lather my skin, I think about calling that young man I met at the recreation hall last night. I feel a little foolish, thinking of calling him so soon after first encountering him. Perhaps this is why I've struggled to date after losing Jonathan. I don't understand certain signs, certain routines practiced between men who are interested in other men. Everyone else seems so capable of speaking a secret, dead language that I'm not allowed to learn no matter how much I beg or plead to be taught.

Yes, this is why I'm unable to capture the attention of other men on the few nights I go out to the bars and clubs in the neighborhood. The other men in the room look at me with such condemnation, as if they know I'm grieving, as if I'm visibly tainted and they think that some of my misery will pollute them, too. Perhaps it will. Perhaps that's why so few of my friends continue to check in on me any longer. It's obvious to note that their presence has diminished in my life ever since Jonathan died. After all, Jonathan was so charismatic and charming. Maybe he was the only reason these people came around me in the first place. Then, after he died, they decided I wasn't worth salvaging. I was a lost cause, irredeemable goods. I'm ashamed to say that I feel like that most of the time.

After I finish washing myself in the shower, I climb out of the stall and wrap a towel around my waist. I gaze at myself in the bathroom mirror for what feels like hours, and I feel so disgusting, so pitiable and wretched. I notice how specific parts of my body have begun to droop and sag. My skin is no longer firm and taut in certain areas, but rather fleshy and pouchy there. I can't help but notice the stretch marks sprawling from one end of my stomach to the other. I loathe the way I look. I can't imagine being naked with another person in bed. I might die of humiliation. Jonathan always accepted me, always adored the subtle imperfections, the slight blemishes. But I can't help but wonder if he would still love me, still care for me after I've neglected the gym for so long. My body is no longer the firm and carefully constructed effigy of masculinity I so desperately tried to maintain day after day, year after year.

As I stand there, my reflection glaring back at me from the glass, I recall the last time Jonathan and I made love before his terminal diagnosis. I recall how I unbuttoned my shirt, his nimble fingers teasing the hair on my chest. Then his hands wandered below my waist, and he undid my belt, unfastened my jeans until my pants and underwear were around my ankles. I think about how he took all of my cock in his mouth, his tongue carefully working around the shaft while he groped my balls. I think about how he begged me to finish inside his mouth, to let him know when I was close to orgasm. I did. I sensed myself release deep inside his throat, and I recall pressing against the back of his head while he choked, gagging a little. I remember how he stepped away from me, hastening into the kitchen and then swiping a bottle of water from the counter. He downed some of the bottle, gargling for a moment and then spitting out in the sink. I recall thinking how that was queer. After all, he had always swallowed me so enthusiastically before. *What changed? Or was I merely making an issue out of nothing?* I thought nothing else about it at the time, but the more I consider it, the more I wonder if I somehow disgusted him, if the taste of my cock was vile for him to endure. He had always enjoyed going down on me previously, savoring the way I tasted, cherishing the way I smelled. But something seemed to change right before his diagnosis. He seemed more reserved, more discriminating. I can't possibly think that he was falling out of love with me, but perhaps he was simply tired of being so submissive. Perhaps he was coming to terms with his own masculinity and wanted to shift roles in the bedroom. I would have done that for him. God knows I would have done anything for him.

I drift into the bedroom and dry myself. It's then I notice the small business card that Kent gave me last night. It's lying on the nightstand beside my bed. I grab the card and run my fingers over the raised letters and numbers printed there on the soft eggshell-colored background. I think about picking up my cell phone and dialing his number. But what could I possibly say? After all, is it too soon to contact him? Then again, what else am I waiting for? I'm curious about how he might respond, how he might possibly help me. Besides, there's every possibility that I'll be able to see Jonathan again because of his assistance.

Without giving it a second thought, I swipe my cell from the bed and dial Kent's number. I wait a few moments, and just before I'm about to hang up, the call connects and Kent answers:

"Hello?"

I clear my throat a little, unsure. "Hi. Is this Kent Simmons?"

"Yes . . ."

"Hi, this is Simeon," I tell him. "We met last night at the recreation hall."

Kent's tone seems to change immediately to more cheerful, more sincere. "Oh, yes. Of course. I'm—happy to hear from you. . . ."

I'm surprised to hear that he's so pleased that I've called. I imagine it might feel so unusual to say that to someone you just met. In fact, his cheerfulness catches me off guard for a moment, and I don't quite know how to recover.

"Listen, I know you said you might be able to help me find the right equipment to participate in the group," I say to him. "Any chance you might be free tomorrow . . . ?"

Kent hesitates on the other end of the line a little, probably conferring with his calendar. "I . . . think I could make that work. . . . How does two o'clock sound?"

"That's perfect," I tell him.

"Meet me at Tremblay's," he says. "The electronics store on Bennington Street . . . You know it?"

"Yes," I tell him. "I'll be there."

"See you then," he says, then hangs up.

When the line disconnects, I lower the phone from my ear. It feels strange to have made plans with a perfect stranger; however, it also feels exciting, somewhat exhilarating. I sense my stomach clench a little, a reminder of my worry. I try to ignore it, throwing on a shirt, then hoisting up a pair of pants around my waist.

Just then, my phone rings, and I can't help but wonder if it's Kent calling to cancel, to reject my invitation. But it's not. I read the caller ID tag: Evelyn. *What on earth can she possibly want?* I wonder to myself. I think to press Accept Call. But I don't. Instead, I send her to voicemail and bury my phone inside my pocket.

The next day, I drift through the double doors and make my way into the lobby of the large electronics store on Bennington Street. The place was once a children's toy store and has since been remodeled over the past several years to suit the needs of the new business. However, the faintest signs of the toy store endure to this day—the shadow of a large sign in the shape of a rainbow imprinted on the far wall, some of the paneling still faded pink and blue to differentiate the boys' section from the girls'. I find it amusing how even the spirit of a failed business can haunt a new one. Everything in this world is so desperate to be remembered, to be recalled by those who remain, who still endure.

As I meander into the lobby of the store, I'm greeted by a young salesman wearing a pair of thick glasses, his dark hair parted to one side. He asks me if I'm looking for anything in particular today, and I tell him that I'm just browsing. Of course, it's not true, and I could probably use his help. But I want Kent to have the honor of assisting me today. After all, I forced him to come here with me in the first place.

I find myself drifting down aisles of different gadgets and equipment I recognize slightly but cannot claim to know their intricacies closely. Jonathan was more finely tuned to the latest trends in technology. I've always seemed to resist those changes, those advancements for whatever reason. After all, it took me so long to accept the fact that I needed a new cell phone and took great pains to retire my nearly prehistoric flip phone. I suppose most of my aversion to new things is the fear of change. In fact, it somewhat pains me to be here in this store right now. It reminds me so much of Jonathan and how excited he would be to browse.

Eventually I spot Kent loitering at the end of an aisle, and I wave to him. He recognizes me and immediately makes a dash toward me with a polite greeting.

"You weren't waiting long, were you?" he asks.

"No, not at all," I assure him. "I just got here. . . . Good to see you so soon . . ."

He starts to make his way toward the glass counters situated on the opposite end of the store, where a few other shoppers have gathered to browse.

"This way," he says. "Most of the camera equipment is over here. . . ."

I follow him until I'm standing at the glass case, peering inside and inspecting the various cameras organized on display. Of course, I have no idea what separates a good one from an inferior model. Regardless, Kent appears so sure of himself as he browses the case and points out several models that are the best quality. He asks the salesperson at the counter to open the case and allow us to look at several of the models. Kent explains the differences between some of the various cameras, and even the salesman seems impressed with his knowledge. Kent seems especially smitten with the idea of me purchasing a digital single-lens reflex camera (or DSLR, for short). Even though it's an older type of camera, he says it's a wonderful investment. He also makes a point to state that there's a mirror inside the camera that helps capture the photograph. I'm not quite sure why he considers this to be a selling point, but I'm amused with his passion and excitement for showing me the several camera models.

After reviewing a few options, Kent asks the salesman to let us think for a few moments. The salesman agrees somewhat reluctantly, peeling away from us but still loitering in earshot.

Kent and I drift farther down the glass cases filled with all kinds of cameras and equipment. There's, of course, the expected lull in conversation, that corrosive and awkward pause between subjects. Naturally, I had expected this. But Kent appears unbothered. I'm sure I look so uncomfortable, so out of place. I catch my reflection in one of the glass cases, and I notice my mouth is pulling downward in a permanent frown. It makes me appear so much older than I actually am, and I nearly pale at the horrible sight.

"How long have you been attending meetings there?" I ask him, prying my eyes away from my reflection and moving farther down the aisle while he leads the way.

"A year or so," he explains. "My husband died of an aneurysm two years ago. . . . I thought I was going out of my mind. . . . The whole world around me changed. It felt almost—*polluted*."

I swallow hard. I know exactly what he means.

"I struggled to see the good in carrying on," he says. "I didn't want to. . . . Until I was invited to a meeting at that place . . . And then everything changed for me. . . ."

I sense myself soften a little.

"That's how it felt for me, too," I tell him.

I hesitate slightly, wanting to ask him something I've been wondering since I attended the meeting the other night. I'm afraid of how he'll respond, but I know I'll curse myself if I don't follow through.

"Is it actually true?" I ask Kent. "Is it possible to see our loved ones in these pictures?"

"You saw the evidence the other night," he replies. "You still doubt it?"

I stammer, unsure. "I just—I'm worried it won't happen for me. . . ."

"Maybe because you're not open to it yet," he says. "There are doorways in this world. Once they're opened, they can't be closed. . . . This is one of those thresholds."

My eyes lower, and I sense my shoulders drop slightly. "I just want to see him again. . . . I'd give anything for that. . . ."

"What was his name?" Kent asks me.

"Jonathan," I tell him. "He died of cancer. . . . Truthfully, I've wondered if he's been lingering around me since I first lost him. I turn my head sometimes, and I wonder if I see him out of the corner of my eye. Almost like he was waiting there for me to notice."

"It sounds to me like he wants to be noticed," Kent says, moving back toward the display case and pointing at one of the cameras there.

Of course it's the DSLR. The one with the mirror inside. I'm hesitant at first, but there's something about this camera in particular that seems to call to me in quiet, unassuming ways. It's not one of the newer models near the front of the store. Instead, it's more moderately worn, scuffed—like it's already witnessed a wealth of beauties and brutalities to last an entire lifetime. I wonder what kind of person owned the camera before it was relegated to a display case at a store here in town. Naturally, I think of the spirits, the wraiths existing within this small apparatus—the secrets they could tell me if they had a mind to.

"Some ghosts are tricky like that," Kent says, smiling.

I lean in close toward him, testing how far I can push him. "Do *you* believe in ghosts? Spirits that haunt us?"

Kent looks around the store, making sure there are no nearby eavesdroppers.

"I've seen a ghost before," he tells me.

I recoil slightly, and I can sense myself firming with a distinct feeling of unease.

"You have?" I ask him.

"I've seen hundreds of them actually. . . . They look different than you might imagine," he says. "They're little wisps. Like glittery specks of tinfoil. Reflective almost . . . a kind of mirror . . ."

I wonder if I've misheard him. "You've seen hundreds? Where?"

Kent shoves his hands into his pockets and shrugs. "I shouldn't bore you with those details now. . . . Shall I call for the salesman?"

I laugh, uncomfortable. "You can't expect to tell me something like that and leave it there. . . ."

Once more, Kent looks around like he was being graded by some invisible advisor.

"Look," he says, swallowing hard. "Ghosts are kinds of mirrors, you see? They reflect everything closest to them. Sometimes you don't even have to die to become a ghost. They're made softly, quietly, over a period of time. . . . Do you get what I mean?"

Of course I don't understand a damn word he's saying. But I'm too embarrassed to let him know that, to reveal just how thickheaded I can be. Instead, I nod politely and pretend to have understood. Surely there must be some truth to what he's telling me. If ghosts are kinds of mirrors and reflecting only what they're closest to, then perhaps the memory of my sweet Jonathan is less withered than I imagined. Perhaps he's closer to me than I realized.

After I tell the salesman that I'd like to purchase the camera, he excuses himself to the stockroom and then returns a minute later with a battered-looking box with a picture of the camera printed on the side. He suggests purchasing a small black leather satchel to carry the camera in as well as a few camera-cleaning products. When we're finished, he packs my items in a large tote bag and then sends us off with a polite smile.

Kent and I make our way out of the store until we're on the sidewalk, the sun bearing down on us as if through a magnifying glass.

"Have you thought about where you might like to look first?" Kent asks me.

"Jonathan used to love visiting the park near our apartment," I tell him. "I was thinking of going there. . . ."

"That's a fine place to start."

I hesitate again. "Would you like to join me? You could show me where I might have better luck looking. . . ."

Kent frowns a little. "I'd love to. But you must do this on your own. . . . Your loved one might not want to make his presence known if I'm there. . . . It must be done alone. . . ."

"Oh," I say, feeling like I do at the bar after I've attempted and failed to chat with one of the younger men loitering near the counter and waiting for the bartender's attention. "I guess that makes sense. . . . I can't thank you enough for coming here and showing me which camera would be the best. . . ."

"Any time," Kent says. "You have my number. Call me whenever, okay?"

I nod slightly. I can tell his offer is sincere by the way he looks into my eyes and doesn't glance away.

"Yeah," I say. "I'll call you sometime. . . ."

Before I can say anything else, Kent has already turned and is making his way down the sidewalk away from me, weaving around mothers toting their children and businessmen saddled with briefcases. I watch him drift farther and farther away until he turns a corner and vanishes completely from my sight.

I realize I'm standing in place and decide to get moving. I duck into a nearby coffee shop, order an espresso, and then sit down at an empty table in the far dimly lit corner of the café, where I begin to unbox my camera equipment and prepare for an afternoon in the park.

It's chillier than it was yesterday, and I thank myself for thinking ahead and bringing my favorite scarf from home. It's the black scarf that Jonathan bought for me when we spent a quiet weekend in Burlington, Vermont, on Valentine's weekend a few years ago. I loop the scarf around my throat and struggle to recall the day when we visited that small boutique near our hotel. It pains me to realize that so many memories with my sweet Jonathan have rusted, discarded in the dimmest crooks of my mind. Of course, that's not to say that I don't often think of him. But very often I'll recall another memory I have neglected and will feel such pity for all the other recollections I've chosen to abandon. I curse myself for not remembering everything as swiftly as I once did. It seems to me that every day Jonathan's silhouette in my mind grows softer and softer. I wonder if he'll be smeared away after too long. I dread that horrendous thought.

I soon find myself wandering the colonnade that separates the sidewalk from the public gardens near our apartment. Others are traipsing about the portico. Lovers are bound hand in hand with attention fixed on each other. Children play with one another on the apron of grass nearby while their parents supervise, probably passing silent criticisms among each other. It's then I notice that music is being played over the park's loudspeaker system. They sometimes play music throughout the day when the weather is clear. Today's choice is Cole Porter's "Begin the Beguine," performed by Ella Fitzgerald. I hum along, not quite sure of the lyrics. Of course, I know the tune because Jonathan was so intrigued by classic songs from the American songbook. I think about his record collection in our apartment—the stack of vinyl sitting in the far corner of the room and gathering dust because I cannot bring myself to touch any of his possessions since he passed.

I mill about the walkway, observing people while they move past me. I think to take their picture, wondering if I might capture the flicker of Jonathan's essence in their bewildered expressions as they pass me. But that's probably not likely. I won't find Jonathan in the bemused appearance of others. But where on earth could I possibly find him instead? I drift down the steps and circle the large fountain arranged at the center of the garden. Several people are idling in the area, and I wonder if they observe me while I take a photograph of the fountain. I peer at the camera screen and ponder if I might find Jonathan's face hidden somewhere. But I don't, sadly. I groan loud enough for onlookers to glance at me and then pass soundless comments to one another, probably exasperated with my presence here. I creep away from the fountain and decide I need to venture farther into the park. To a place where I won't be followed, where I can be alone with my camera, where Jonathan might be willing to make himself known to me.

Eventually I find myself at a small vine-threaded trellis leading to an open area organized with several wooden benches. I wonder to myself if I've been thinking too literally about the possibility of seeing Jonathan's face. I wonder if I'm not open to the idea of seeing him in some random object. Perhaps I don't actually believe it's possible. It's not likely for me to suddenly believe in something I've decided against. But I've already made such an effort to try this. I can't help but wonder why I've decided to be so stubborn.

I take a photograph of one of the nearby benches and squint slightly, peering into the camera screen. I hold my breath, praying I'll somehow find Jonathan hiding somewhere in the photograph. But he's not there. It's foolish to think that he would make himself known to me after all this waiting, after all this time.

I'm about to leave when a gust of wind blows past me, and I observe how some of the vines on the trellis lift like the hem of a lady's skirt. I do a double take, wondering if I've somehow noticed something hidden among the network of vines climbing there. *It's not possible.* I sense my mouth hanging open slightly as I approach the trellis step by step, careful not to upset anything, to scare anything away. I hold the camera up to my face and press the button. *Click.* The photo's captured. I stare at the screen, and I can feel my eyes widening in total disbelief. *It can't be,* I think to myself, shaking my head. I squint, pulling the camera closer toward my face so I can see the screen properly. Something in the photo stares back at me—a young man's face hidden among the shadows of the vines creeping up the side of the freshly painted trellis. *Can it be . . . ?* Yes, it's Jonathan's face. He's buried in the curve of one of the vines curling there like a black electrical wire.

My hands tremble and begin to feel sweaty. I worry that I'll drop the camera. I stare at the screen for what feels like hours, studying the way the shadows and plants have collected there to resemble the vague outline of his sweet, gentle face. It seems totally incredible. *But what more proof can I possibly need to believe that it's him? Why can't it be him?*

Fearful of damaging the only proof I have of my sweet Jonathan appearing to me after his demise, I tuck the camera inside my black leather satchel and begin to make my way out of the park. Cole Porter's "Begin the Beguine" follows me while I drift out of the public garden and onto the crowded sidewalk. I hum the tune off-key, and I think of Jonathan. For the first time in many months, I feel as though he's here with me. *Stay this time,* I tell him quietly, while I amble toward my apartment building.

Please, God. Stay with me. Stay. . . .

Chapter Seven

As soon as I return to my apartment, I rush to my laptop and drag several cords out of my computer bag beside my desk. I plug one of the wires into the camera and then insert the other end of the cord into the receiving end on my laptop. The screen flickers alive, and I notice a small icon pinned in the top right corner of the display that reads *Import.* I click and then observe as my camera begins to hum, the screen glowing with a dim pulse. It isn't long before the photos have been imported, and I save them inside a newly created folder on my desktop. I hover the mouse over the photograph I'm most interested in, and I click twice, the photo expanding until it fills the entirety of the screen. I sense my heart flutter a little, my breath becoming shallow, as I gaze at the photograph—the unexplainable picture that defies all sorts of logic and yet exists all the same. I wonder if this is what it must be like to see a ghost. Of course, I've never witnessed one before, but I've often thought of how I might react to some kind of wraith making its presence known to me, its muted blue shape, its form drooping slightly like wilted petals from a discarded flower. I've wondered if I'd be afraid, if I'd recoil in shock or cover my mouth and struggle to comprehend. But Jonathan's picture does not frighten me. I'm not fearful of gazing at the screen for too long. I would consider myself foolish if I thought I could be afraid to observe something so gentle, so discernibly tender and kind.

I click on File and then select Print. I hear my printer buzzing awake in the next room while it prints the photograph. I hasten into the den, and I collect the picture, studying it once more and trying to savor its complexity, its subtle intricacies. I'm sure I could gaze at this picture all day and notice new and wonderful things about what I've captured in that split second. Just then, I notice how my stomach seems to heave, sour-tasting bile rising into the pit of my throat and seething there. It's a feeling of worry that I cannot seem to push away—the barbed and dangerous thought of timing and how I might not have seen Jonathan if I had waited another moment to take the photograph. Yes, perhaps he was only able to make himself known to me in that brief instant. I sense my shoulders drop with a feeling of defeat, worried that I might not bear witness to Jonathan ever again. Perhaps it's all about timing. Yes, it's obvious that I captured him at the perfect time; however, there's every possibility that I won't be as lucky in the future.

It's then I wonder if I'm able to capture Jonathan's essence twice in the same day. Of course, I know full well it's greedy to consider this. But my enthusiasm can't be tempered. Just as I'm about to unplug my camera from the computer and hunt around my apartment for signs of his presence, there's a knock at the door. I shiver at the sound, unsettled at the very thought of a visitor so late at night. I close my laptop and set the printed photograph on the kitchen table before making my way toward the foyer. I peer through the peephole at eye level, and I'm greeted by Evelyn's face, her expression misshapen and watery-looking, like I was gazing at her from the other side of a small fishbowl. I open the door, and she greets me with a half-hearted smile.

"I was hoping you'd be home," she says, pocketing her car keys and removing her sunglasses. "Can I come in?"

I nod, stepping aside and motioning for her to enter. She does, glancing around the room while she drifts from corner to corner. It feels as though she's inspecting the area, surreptitiously looking for something.

"Where's Carter?" I ask her. "He's not with you?"

"He's old enough to stay home by himself," Evelyn explains. "I was hoping you and I could speak alone."

"Something bad?" I ask, swallowing hard.

But Evelyn merely smiles, trying to calm me.

"You have anything to drink?" she asks, hurrying into the kitchen and beginning to rummage through each of the cabinets until she locates a half-empty bottle of red wine.

I observe her in silence as she pops the bottle open and then pours herself a glass. She takes a sip and seems to soften slightly, her protection lowering bit by bit. Then she tilts the bottle at me with an offer, but I wave her away. Wine usually gives me headaches if I drink too late at night.

"There's something you wanted to tell me?" I ask her, pulling out a chair at the kitchen table and sitting down.

Evelyn approaches me slowly, the wine circling in her glass while she rocks it back and forth.

"I wanted to check in on you," she says. "You seemed so distraught the other day. I wanted to make sure that everything's okay. . . ."

I swallow nervously, not wanting to reveal too much. Evelyn always has a way of undoing my resolve until I'm clay to be molded, to be shaped by her. Of course, she's talented at knowing what people need and when they need it the most, but there's a part of me that's fearful of her, fearful of what I might do if given the opportunity.

"Everything's fine," I tell her, my voice quivering a little. "I'm sorry I had to step away the other day. . . . I just had a lot on my mind. . . ."

Evelyn sits across from me at the table. "You're allowed to have a lot on your mind. I just want to make sure you're not torturing yourself because of the job thing. . . ."

I shrug a little, not really wanting to talk about it. "I'll get by for now. . . . Maybe it's best to take some time off and focus on myself."

Evelyn reaches across the table and touches my arm, tugging on my sleeve. "If you ever need anything, I hope you'll let me know. . . ."

Just then, she notices the photograph I printed out. I think about swiping it from the table and shoving it inside a nearby drawer, but I'm not quick enough for her. She's already grabbed it and begins to examine it.

"What's this?" she asks.

I clear my throat, more bile rising there. "It's a new kind of therapy I'm trying. . . . Jonathan used to love taking pictures, you know? I thought I'd try it, too. . . ."

I watch Evelyn as her eyes go over the picture again and again, carefully studying it with her mouth hanging open slightly. I wonder if she sees it, too. I wonder if she sees Jonathan's face buried there in the trellis. Of course, she must see it.

"Do you notice anything in the photograph?" I ask, leaning forward in my chair.

"Like what?" she asks, eyes flashing to me and then back at the picture.

"Anything," I tell her. "Like shapes or colors . . . Anything that catches your eye?"

I stir in my chair, hoping and praying that she says something, anything. If she notices Jonathan's face, then I know for certain that

I've captured something truly remarkable here. But, of course, I can't tell her about what the picture actually is, because then it might inform her opinion, might sway her in one direction or the other. I need her to witness the miracle all on her own. Swallowing some of the bile that's climbed into my throat, I watch her for another moment while she gazes at the printed photograph. *Does she see it? God, I hope she sees it. . . . Please let her see it. . . .*

"It's a lovely picture," she says, setting it down on the table again and offering me a polite smile. "Very pretty . . ."

My eyes widen a little, waiting for her to say something else, anticipating some kind of miraculous revelation to be finally exposed.

"You don't notice anything else?" I ask her.

She squints at me, tilting her head to one side. "What am I supposed to see? There's something else in the picture . . . ?"

She's about to snatch the photograph from the table for a second look, but I'm too quick for her this time. I grab the picture and fold it until it's small enough to fit inside my pocket.

"Nothing," I tell her. "It's nothing. . . ."

I bite my lower lip until I can taste blood. I feel so foolish, so astonishingly stupid for believing I captured Jonathan's essence in a mere photograph. Of course, such things are nonsense. There's no possible chance that Jonathan will ever make himself known to me. I've kept a shrine for him in my mind, delivering thoughts to feed him each and every day. But such offerings are useless. I know this now. *Perhaps I'm the one who's haunting him.*

"Are you all right?" Evelyn asks me. "You don't look well. . . ."

But I wave her away, struggling to keep my composure in front of her. When she finally leaves, I can dissolve, I can crumple until I'm sobbing, broken.

"I think I'm just a little tired," I tell her.

"I don't mean to pry," she says. "Are you okay financially? I know how quickly the city can use up your savings. . . . I just want to make sure you're okay. . . ."

I hesitate a little, and I suppose Evelyn can observe my reluctance to answer, my bashfulness when it comes to money.

"I've been better, I guess," I tell her. "But I'm not suffering yet. . . ."

Evelyn shakes her head, tips her handbag open, and pulls out her purse. "I don't want to see you suffer, Simeon. . . ."

She pries open her wallet and produces a small wad of cash. Counting the bills, she passes me a couple hundred dollars. But I recoil from her immediately. I can't possibly take her money. I would feel so disgusted, so unable to fend for my own being and provide for myself in Jonathan's absence. What would it mean to take Evelyn's hard-earned money? Would it mean that she's more capable of caring for me than I am?

"There's no shame in grabbing hold of a rope when someone throws it your way," she tells me, forcing the cash into my palm until I finally accept it.

I uncrumple my fist and gaze at the bills she's placed there. Of course, it's kind of her to still care about me, to still hope I might need her help every now and then; however, there's a part of me that remains unsettled at the idea of accepting Evelyn's offer. I sense myself shiver, wondering if I've accepted some hideous bargain I'll never escape. Even worse, I feel as though I owe her things. I owe her my time, my company, my friendship.

"Would you like to stay and watch some TV?" I ask her. "Maybe have some more wine?"

She smiles, beginning to rummage through the nearby cabinet

until she finds another wineglass. I watch her as she pours more wine into the glass and then passes it to me.

A few hours pass, and we eventually find ourselves curled together on the couch, the television playing some old black-and-white horror movie from the 1950s about mutant insects. I occasionally glance at Evelyn, whose attention is permanently fixed on the screen. There's a part of me that still cares for her, still desperately wants to be cordial and loving with her. After all, she was the first person I ever made love to. We had met in college during my sophomore year, and I was so enraptured with her confidence, her charisma. So much of that wit and sureness has not dissipated over the years like it does with most people; instead, it's blossomed considerably, and I often find myself struggling to keep up with her magic.

I can't help but think about how long it's been since I've touched another person. Friendliness and affection from others seem to dissolve slowly after you lose a loved one. You become marked, tainted—a vile thing that could corrupt others with the same kind of heartache, misery, impurity.

It's strange to understand that Evelyn still cares for me after all the pain I've put her through, all the despair and the deceit I invoked just to sate my own sexual appetite. Of course, she said there was a part of her that always knew I was gay, but I wonder if that's the truth. I wonder if she feels the same way I do sometimes—forever haunted by an irredeemable love, acutely aware of an unrelenting desire for someone, something that will never quite be reciprocated. It's odd to admit it, but I suddenly find myself curious about her again, wondering if there are any secrets remaining on her body that I never solved during our marriage.

I notice her hand resting somewhat close to mine on the edge of the couch where we're relaxing. My fingers creep toward hers, and finally our hands brush together. She winces, perhaps a little startled by my touch. But she doesn't shrink away or recoil like I half expect her to. Instead, she takes hold of my hand and squeezes me tight until I can feel her heartbeat quivering in her every finger. It's an unmistakable sign. I finally have the answer that I was yearning for.

I aim the remote at the TV, and the screen goes dark. Our watery-looking reflections greet us in the dark mirror. Evelyn turns to me, looking for some kind of explanation.

"Can we fuck?" I ask her softly.

I thought of asking if we could "make love," but I can't bring myself to utter those words. That was something reserved exclusively for my beloved Jonathan. Of course, I still care for Evelyn deeply, but I don't want us to make love. I want us to mate like feral beasts. I want our coupling to be primal, animalistic, perhaps even a little hate-filled.

Evelyn accepts my invitation, climbing off the couch and leading me toward the bedroom. Before I realize it, she's kissing me and undoing my belt. For a moment, I think to excuse myself to the bathroom to clean up. Even though I've already washed myself today, I worry that I'll offend her somehow. There's a peculiar kind of stench that attaches to a person after they lose a loved one. It's a powerful, offensive kind of musk that marks you and lets others know that you've been abandoned, that you are uniquely and utterly alone. I think to wrench myself away from Evelyn and tell her I'll be right back. But I worry I'll hesitate even more if given the opportunity. I worry that I'll back out of the whole thing and leave her feeling disgraced, humiliated for trusting me once more.

We slip into the bedroom, peeling bits of clothing off each other and scattering them across the floor in a trail. Evelyn pulls me onto the bed, and I'm on top of her, our mouths devouring each other's. Very soon, she rips my underwear from me and grabs hold of my cock until it's pointing at her, living-looking and throbbing. I'm surprised at myself for being so excited, so eager to fuck. I think about swiping one of the condoms from the bureau beside the bed. I'm not even sure when the damn things are supposed to expire. I bought them a few months ago when I was routinely hitting the bars and nightclubs in the neighborhood, hoping to bring home one of the many men I met throughout the course of the night. In the few times I went out, there was only one guy who ever made it home with me. He had begged me to fuck him while we were riding the elevator, but his tune soon changed when we arrived at the bedroom. He gave me a quick blow job, spat me out of his mouth in the bathroom sink, and then excused himself, claiming he had a migraine. The whole experience had felt so clinical, so unnatural and forced. It feels different with Evelyn now, and I'm grateful for it.

Without hesitation, I push myself into her until I'm completely buried there. She whimpers a little, and I sense the place between her thighs quivering slightly as I force more of my cock into her furrowing cunt. Evelyn grabs hold of me and pulls me tight until our bodies are pressed together. I grunt, wishing I could somehow fill her with my sadness, my sorrow. Of course, I know it's a disgusting notion to consider, but I secretly wish I could pass all the poison of my heartache, my misery to her when we're done.

After, Evelyn climbs into the shower and asks if I'd like to join her. But I wave her away, swiping a washcloth and sponging the gluey, white fluid from the tip of my shriveling cock. She appears a little disappointed to be turned down, but she seems to recover quickly with a polite smile and a half-hearted nod as she disappears into the shower stall. While she's in the bathroom, I find myself gazing at my reflection in the floor-length mirror positioned in the far corner of the bedroom.

What have I done? I wonder to myself, eyes searching for a visible explanation, a sign—anything.

I gaze at the reflection, and I do not recognize the man I see dawdling there. His eyes are vacant, hollow. His shoulders droop with a permanent apprehension, a horrible defeat. I feel such pity for the reflection of the man I see there.

Jonathan would never have loved a miserable wretch like you, I think to myself.

I walk into the kitchen, and I grab the photograph I hid from Evelyn. I gaze at the picture for what feels like hours, trying to convince myself I believe in what I've captured—that I've actually seen Jonathan once more, that he's finally made himself known to me after eons of waiting, hoping, praying. But the more I gaze at the picture, the more his face seems to wither away from me, almost like he was eager to hide in the nearby underbrush, as though he no longer wishes to be seen. I squint, trying to convince myself that his face is still there. But I know full well it's not true. I toss the photograph aside and collapse into one of the kitchen chairs, burying my head on the table and beginning to sob.

I have composed myself by the time Evelyn gathers her things and heads for the door. We offer each other awkward pleasantries, suddenly forgetting how to interact with each other. It feels like we're trying to pretend nothing happened, that we didn't surrender to our more shameful desires, that we're better than what we've become.

"Maybe I could swing by again," she tells me, sliding into her jacket and eyeing me with a hopefulness that I feel obligated to return. "With Carter . . . Or maybe without . . ."

I soften a little, sensing myself unspool at the mention of his name. I miss him terribly. Why am I so unable to offer him the affection, the tenderness, and care that he so rightfully deserves? It's not helpful to him for his father to love him only from a distance. I want him to know how much I care for him, how he's one of the best things that has ever happened to me.

"I'd love to see him," I say to her, shoving my hands into my pockets and leaning against the nearby wall. "You're always welcome here. . . . The both of you . . ."

Evelyn then grabs hold of my hand and kisses each of my fingers, squeezing them tight with a gratitude I didn't realize that she carried.

"Call me, won't you?" she says, then pulls the handle and disappears out through the doorway and down the corridor leading toward the elevator.

I watch her until she climbs onto the lift and the doors close shut, casketing her and taking her away from here. When she's finally gone, I creep back into my apartment and fasten the locks on the door until I'm entombed here for the night.

I still cannot quite explain what came over me, what made me crawl into bed with my ex-wife and seek her out for comfort, for companionship. After all, I thought I held no attraction for Evelyn. I was utterly convinced of it for the past few years while falling in love with Jonathan. I was convinced I had abandoned every thought, every fascination, every bit of attraction for her in the past after I came to care for and love my husband. Still, I thaw at the idea of Evelyn. Naturally, I could never love her the way I once had, the hollow, insincere way I always pretended to care for her while we were an item, while we struggled to make it work and care for Carter together.

I drift back into the kitchen, and I locate the photograph I took in the park earlier today. I think about tearing the picture up, ripping it to shreds, and then tossing the confetti remains into the waste bin. But something prevents me from doing so, a feeling deep inside that whispers to me to hold on to the photograph just in case.

Just in case? I wonder to myself. *In case of what?*

But there's no discernible answer for me to uncover as I stand there in the middle of the kitchen, my heartbeat quickening while I gaze at the small, printed picture. I suppose it's possible to consider the fact that even though Evelyn did not observe the face I saw in the picture, there's a small chance others might see it. I couldn't have been wrong. Could I have? Could I have been so stupid, so desperate and eager to believe in something that I willed the silhouette of Jonathan's face to appear there in the photograph? *It's entirely possible,* I think to myself as I gaze at the picture more and struggle to envision the outline of where his nose was, the dim shape of his hair that I adored. It's peculiar how I once so easily saw his shape, his figure fixed there near the corner of the photograph. Now I find myself unable to comprehend where he's gone, where he's disappeared to. Perhaps he's still somewhere in the photograph, hiding there, hoping to be found, yearning to be discovered by me once more.

I make my way from the kitchen into the bedroom, and I place the photograph on the nightstand beside my bed, propping it up against one of the framed pictures of Jonathan that I keep there. I wonder if I might find his shape, his silhouette again in the morning after I've slept. *Yes, perhaps that's all I need—a decent night's sleep.*

But soon I find myself stirring beneath the weighted blanket, kicking sheets off me until I'm exposed and shivering beneath the spinning overhead fan aimed directly at me. I observe the strange shape that the ceiling fan makes while it rotates in a frantic blur—a giant, ever-vigilant eyeball peering down at me. Or perhaps, even worse, an infinite loop—a circular pathway that leads me back to the place where I began again and again until I'm sick to my stomach, until I'm on my knees and coughing up blood from the aching nausea of infinity.

It's early in the morning when I crawl out of bed and stagger into the kitchen to make myself some breakfast. I wipe the scabbed crust from my eyes, my head pulsing with the possibility of a migraine after another night of strange dreams—imaginings of some grotesque, faceless figure sitting on the edge of a large bed and beckoning me to come closer. I pull the carton of eggs from the refrigerator and crack two into a pan over the stovetop, and find myself thinking of the photographer, Kent. Over and over again. No matter how much I strain to think of other things, I can't help but return to him. Of course, there's a part of me that wonders what he might think of the photograph I took in the park yesterday. I trust his opinion, his kindness. I know for certain he won't only tell me things I yearn to hear. He'll tell me the truth. At least I hope he will. I feel somewhat foolish for thinking so highly of him in the first place. After all, I just met him. How can I possibly place so much trust, so much care in him upon first meeting? I've been taught time and time again how the world is filled with nothing but cannibals—soul-sucking parasites eager to feed off the scrawnier, the second-rate. The way in which they locate and devour their sustenance completely defines them the same way it defines all of us.

I think about how I first encountered these intrusive thoughts years ago, even while Jonathan was alive. I can't help but recall how they burdened me with such weight, as though they were arranging concrete bricks to be piled on my back until I finally succumbed to the enormous pressure, the immeasurable weight. Even though I know it's a terrible idea, I make my way into the living room and pull out the journal I kept years ago. The entries were written during a particularly bleak time in my life when I was doubting myself at work and especially doubting my relationship with Jonathan.

I tip the journal open and thumb to a random page:

August 16

There's no possible way to disguise the unpleasantness of this truth.

I promised myself I would be as candid and as honest as possible with myself, even when it's nearly unbearable and excruciating to do so—to realize things are more pleasant in memory than they actually were.

That said, there's no correct way to say this. So, I'm just going to come out and say it—ever since I began working on these journal entries, I've been thinking of horrible things. I've found my mind swollen with thoughts I've never even considered before. Whether or not they were there to begin with remains inconsequential as they have willfully and quite stubbornly made their presence known now.

I find myself unnerved and wondering if perhaps this level of discomfort will become more prominent as I wade deeper and deeper into these diary entries. I also wonder if perhaps the thoughts will become more intense as I continue to work on my writing. Of course, I cannot for the life of me understand or appreciate how exactly the thoughts will get worse. However, it's an unfortunate fact of reality that things can and will always get much worse.

To give you a glimpse of the thoughts my mind seems to be entertaining as of late, I'll keep it as brief as possible. I've been entertaining thoughts of doing things to hurt my husband, Jonathan. I've been meticulously considering all the ways I could possibly hurt him without him suspecting I'm at fault.

I can't help but wonder if Jonathan were given the opportunity, would he hurt me? Undoubtedly, he would. How could I possibly be so naive to think that he wouldn't? I suppose in our community, it becomes a matter of doing it to the other person before they do it to you.

It also raises a question I've been considering for quite some time: Are queer men capable of engaging in monogamous relationships? I don't believe so. I think, on some level, most men are programmed to couple with any viable source of pleasure. Most of the men I've dated have cheated on me or, worse, abandoned me when I was developing a strong connection with them.

I don't think Jonathan would be as faithful to me if I hadn't shown him how much I suffer, how much I ache. In fact, I can't even pretend that I've been a dutiful and faithful husband for the entirety of our marriage. Even though I've never confessed this to him, I'm perfectly content to admit that I engaged in sexual relations with a younger man during the first years of my partnership with Jonathan. It was a chance encounter at the hotel where I was staying for a work retreat in Providence, Rhode Island. I seized the opportunity and had sex with the young man, who had attended one of my panels and said lovely things to me after the discussion was finished. Of course, I never told Jonathan what happened in Providence. But there's a part of me that wonders if he knows and either doesn't care or merely accepts the fact that gay men are not destined to stay tethered together forever.

Regardless of the outcome, I've still been entertaining these horrible thoughts about Jonathan and all the things I could do to hurt him.

It feels so cruel, so decidedly ghoulish to glance back on what I once wrote. I feel so disconnected from the person who wrote these entries. In fact, it feels like I'm reading a work of fiction, a random journal written by a perfect stranger. *Is it possible for memory to distort and warp perception so ruthlessly to the point where we are deceived?* I wish I knew the answer. I thumb to another page and begin to read again:

August 21

This morning, I thought about taking my precious Carter to the zoo and feeding him to the alligators.

Did I really just write that?

Fuck. I can't believe I wrote that out and put that horrible thought on paper.

I don't know why I thought of something so abominable.

Okay, perhaps that's not entirely true. As I wrote previously, I have been entertaining decidedly gruesome thoughts. However, the thoughts never involved me going out of my way to do something to physically harm my precious Carter. Instead, most of the thoughts centered around something inexplicable and inevitable happening to Jonathan and me while Carter becomes an innocent victim of the catastrophe.

I find myself troubled at the idea of being alone with my thoughts—thinking such horrible things about Carter and what I could possibly do to him to harm him.

Of course, it's one thing to think of drowning your child in the bathtub—holding his head under the foamy water until his little arms stop thrashing against you—but it's another to invent horrible excuses to justify why you need to kill him.

I can't bear to admit it, but there's actually a quiet part of me that thinks I'm correct in my idea of murdering Carter. I wonder if it's because of how I've been feeling lately, especially about my new identity as a gay man. After all, the queer community does tend to eat one another. But often the argument exists solely for queer people. I would go so far as to argue that the entirety of the world is a cannibal.

People eat other people.

More than anything, the human being wants to assert their dominance over another less powerful human being. It's been this way since the earth was forming and new. It will be like this even after the radiation from the atomic bomb wizens our frail, little bodies.

Why would I choose to raise a child in a world filled with such unrestricted hatred and violence? Although it pains me to admit this simple fact: Carter would be far better off dead.

I've thought about how I might go through with it—how I might wipe him from the world until he's nothing more than a stain. I couldn't bear to do anything physical to him. I would never forgive myself.

Then I'm reminded how Jonathan wanted us to take a trip to the local zoo this coming weekend. We'd show Carter the lions and the giraffes and the elephants. But then I recall how there's a large pool where they keep the alligators. The exhibit contains a large apron of greenery that slopes down toward an embankment where the creatures usually take their afternoon sunbath at the water's edge. Below the area where zoo patrons mill about is a large pool where the alligators are permitted to swim. Although the creatures are well outside of arm's length, one could easily lean over the edge of the handrail and drop something into the enclosure.

It's then I imagine myself strolling over to the handrail after most of the visitors have left the area. I've wrapped Carter in a small blanket. His favorite print: periwinkle-blue elephants wearing waistcoats and black top hats like posh, distinguished gentlemen from the 1920s.

When I'm certain nobody's watching, I imagine myself unwrapping Carter from the blanket until I can see his face. I think of admiring him for a moment. But I know if I do that, I'll hesitate even further. So I think of tossing the small infant into the enclosure. I imagine I hear a vulgar splash when his little body hits the water. Although I'm too squeamish to observe for too long, I look over the handrail and watch as the alligators crawl from where they've been sunning themselves on the embankment and as they glide into the pool, where they begin to circle their shrieking prey.

It might seem heartless to consider something so vile, so monstrously evil. But one must understand how the world takes pleasure in obliterating small, gentle things—especially children. I think dropping Carter into the alligator enclosure for him to be eaten by those animals would be a far more preferable way to go than to be systematically tortured by every single human he's to interact with for the remainder of his life.

Let the alligators eat him.

I'd sooner die than offer his little corpse up to you cannibals.

August 25

I took Carter to the zoo today.

Nothing happened. So you needn't worry.

But I thought about it. I certainly entertained the thought. As quickly as it came, it abandoned me when I held him in my arms and drew closer toward the handrail overlooking the alligator exhibit.

It was the perfect opportunity, too. Everybody else was beginning to disperse. The afternoon crowds were thinning because of the heat.

Eventually, there came a point when Carter and I were completely alone near the alligator exhibit, and I was cradling him as I loitered near the walkway looking over the large enclosure of junglelike greenery.

Jonathan had offered to go to the concession stand and buy us two sodas before we began to make our trek back toward the zoo entrance. So I was there. All alone. With Carter. The moment I had been quietly dreading. After all, who was to say I wouldn't follow through with my plan? There was a part of me that remained unsure. I wondered if I was capable of doing something so monstrous.

My fingers begin to untighten as I held my precious boy. I felt myself begin to loosen.

But just then, something miraculous happened.

Something I hadn't expected.

I peered down into the enclosure and saw three alligators sunning themselves on the edge of the lagoon. As I pulled the blanket from Carter—about to send him plummeting down into the murky brown water—I noticed one of the alligators thrash excitedly and hurl itself on top of one of the other creatures. With the snap of its jaws that seemed to decide the matter almost instantly, I watched as the animal tore the foot from another alligator. Then, visibly pleased with the work it had done, the creature slid into the water on its belly and vanished beneath the oily black surface.

How could I possibly justify sending my poor, innocent child to his death at the hands of other cannibals?

Carter deserves better than that, after all.

It then occurred to me that so many animals are eager consumers of one another. Practically every species has been known to resort to some form of cannibalism. Although humans tend to literally cannibalize as a final resort when situations turn especially dire, animals have been known to go out of their way to eat their own kind. They think nothing of it.

It's unnerving to consider—the small mother rabbit that decides to eat her young, the poisonous insect that devours their partner after having engaged in intercourse.

At least animals don't pretend to be charming sophisticates with noble pedigrees thanks to generations' worth of Ivy League educations. They never attempt to be anything more than what they really are—savage creatures with the unrelenting appetite to feed.

Still, it didn't seem fair to me to subject Carter to such a horrible and needlessly cruel end. Especially if animals are just as cannibalistic as their human counterparts.

It dawned on me that it would be difficult to locate someone—something—to kill Carter who couldn't decidedly be classified as a cannibal.

After all, every living thing on this planet wants to eat another living thing in some way, shape, or form.

The horrible thought continues to ferment like rotting fruit inside my brain—how can I possibly kill Carter without subjecting him to "death at the hands of a cannibal"?

Once Jonathan returned with the sodas, I tucked Carter back into his stroller, and we steered him through the rest of the zoo. We noticed the sun dipping lower and lower in the sky, and eventually we decided to make our way toward the exit. Jonathan and I didn't talk much on the ride home. It wasn't because he had seen me dangling Carter too close to the edge of the handrail overlooking the lagoon. It was simply because we haven't talked that much lately. Whether or not our silence between each other will last, I can't be certain. It doesn't necessarily bother me. In fact, I somewhat enjoy it. Now I have all the time I need to think about what's to be done with poor Carter. Something must be done about him, after all.

He can't live in a world full of cannibals.

Not for much longer.

I slam the leather-bound journal shut and shove it inside the end table drawer, hiding it behind a stack of random papers like some artifact that could explode into flames at any moment. I should never have looked. I know that now. I know full well that the person who wrote those entries has perished, the very notion of his existence—a thing of the past. Thank God for that. I don't quite know what compelled me to seek out those diary entries, why I was so infatuated with rereading them again and again. Haven't I suffered enough already?

It's then I wonder if I enjoy the idea of misery, if I secretly delight in the agony of despair for some inexplicable reason. Of course, anybody could argue that misery and despair help us come to terms with hardships, that they're necessary feelings to endure in a world that's already become so muted, so dulled. But there's a part of me that wonders if I find enjoyment in my own heartache, if I've already surrendered to the hardship in my mind and have discovered joy, perhaps even exhilaration in such unrelenting hopelessness. I can't quite tell.

Then another thought comes to me and frightens me so much that I shudder uncontrollably, my skin starting to itch. Am I a self-devouring cannibal?

Trying to occupy my mind with other matters, I swipe my cell phone from the kitchen counter and thumb across the screen until I arrive at Kent's contact icon. I press down and call him. The phone rings a few times, and just as I'm about to hang up and try texting him instead, the line connects.

"Hello . . . ?"

"Hey, Kent, it's Simeon again," I say, my voice trembling a little. "I hope I'm not calling too early."

"No worries," he says. "I've been up for an hour already. What's up?"

I eye the photograph I took yesterday on the kitchen table, studying it, and aching to see Jonathan's silhouette buried somewhere in the shrubbery. Sadly, I'm met with nothing.

"I took a few pictures yesterday," I tell him, trying to imitate a tone of excitement as best I can. "I was hoping I could share them with you before the next meeting. . . ."

Kent's voice firms on the other end of the line. "Did you—see something?"

I swallow hard, my throat burning.

"You *did* see something," he says.

"I'm—not really sure, to be honest," I tell him, hesitating slightly. "I think I need a second opinion. . . . Can we meet sometime today?"

"I'm free after two o'clock," he tells me. "Meet in the park?"

"Sure," I say. "I'll be there at two—"

Before I can say goodbye, the call disconnects.

I slide my phone onto the kitchen counter and then pick up the photograph that's held my attention since I first printed it out. Once more, I search every corner of the picture for a sign of Jonathan—a nose, an ear, a freckle, *anything*. But I'm met with nothing. It's as if his very presence has been vacuumed from the picture entirely, dried away like beads of water underneath a hair dryer. I worry that the same thing will happen to him in the privacy of my mind one day. I'll suddenly notice that he's very much absent. I'll wander the corridors of my thoughts and won't find any trace of him. The way he laughed, the soft whimpers he made while we were making love, the way his cheeks dimpled when he smiled—all those memories completely erased and sponged from the bed of my memory. I hold the photo tight against my chest—hoping that such things are merely thoughtless fantasies, hoping that I'll continue to be haunted by him no matter what. I'll never be fully prepared to let him go as long as I live. . . .

As I make my way toward the neighborhood park to meet with Kent, I can't help but notice how I must resemble some kind of miserable war criminal returning from battle, secret murder threaded into my skin and stinking like the sulfur of gunfire. I've wondered for so long why others won't pay me any attention when I go out to the bars and the clubs on the weekends, my soul aching for companionship, my loins yearning for touch. I think other men can tell when another has been wounded, invisibly damaged, and, therefore, is not useful. It's exhilarating to defile someone, to mark them as your territory, to break them in and claim them as your possession. But it's an entirely different matter to couple with a perfect stranger and know full well that they've already been broken, that they bear the mutilations, the wounds of so many previous lovers. When you make love to those kinds of people, it probably feels like you're making love to a ghost, a lonely spirit aching for a semblance of affection, a modicum of hope that they might one day redeem the love that abandoned them. But where's the joy in that? Where's the pleasure, the excitement in fucking someone who's already been ravaged? The job's already been done. It's an honor to destroy someone, to undo the very last filament of their resolve and feast upon their trust until the pearl-white claw of bone has been picked clean. But what could another person possibly find enjoyable about mating with me? I belong with the broken, the ruined and damaged. I sense my shoulders drooping slightly with an invisible weight as I recognize this, as I comprehend the truth of why I'll continue to be alone.

I finally arrive at the small neighborhood park at the end of the avenue, easing the gate open and drifting through the colonnade that separates the city sidewalk from the private garden area. It's a cloudless, sunny day. I notice parents milling about on the lawn, monitoring their children. I hear the distant noise of music playing over the loudspeakers in the park. Today's song—*Rhapsody in Blue* by George Gershwin. I hum a little while I make my way over toward an empty bench situated at the end of the colonnade, looking out over the gardens.

I sit there for a few moments before I pull the photograph from my coat pocket and stare at the image once more. I beg my mind to cooperate and allow me to see the dim silhouette of Jonathan's face once more. Am I foolish enough to believe I've captured something as rare, as completely unexpected as my dead husband? I wonder what on earth could be wrong with me. Of course, the Wretches made the whole ordeal sound so simple, so straightforward. But perhaps I'm not cut out for this kind of grieving, this strange sort of mourning. Perhaps it's best if I leave this alone. In fact, I wonder if there's any point in wasting Kent's time.

Just as I'm about to crawl off the bench and make my way out of the park, I notice Kent at the end of the nearby pathway and heading toward me with a smile. He's at my side in a matter of seconds, pulling off his leather gloves and shaking my hand.

"You haven't been waiting too long, have you?" he asks me.

"No," I say, shaking my head. "I just got here."

I shift slightly while he sits on the bench beside me.

"You have something to show me . . . ?" Kent asks. "Something important?"

I clear my throat, a little anxious at first. In fact, part of me wonders if I'll excuse myself and leave him sitting here. I could do that. Easily. I could shrink away from him and abandon him on this bench in a matter of seconds, making my way back to my apartment to latch the door shut and close myself off to the rest of the world. But what good would that do? It certainly wouldn't help me come to terms with my beloved Jonathan.

"Before I show you what I came here to show you, I wanted to ask you something," I tell him.

Kent nods, anticipating.

I hesitate again, biting my lower lip.

"Do you—actually believe in seeing these faces?" I ask. "Do you really think these are pictures of our loved ones trying to contact us?"

Kent's lips furrow with a playful smile, almost like he expected such an impertinent, foolish question.

"You've seen the pictures," he tells me. "You still don't believe?"

I shudder, worried I've offended him. "I guess what I mean to say . . . This isn't some kind of collective neurosis? This is true? This is real?"

"Let me be the judge of that," Kent says. "Show me the picture."

Bile climbing in my throat, I feel my stomach lurching at his demand. I've never been comfortable with accepting orders. But, for some inexplicable reason, I find myself softening in Kent's presence. I want him to tell me the truth. Even worse, I want him to like me.

I uncrumple the photograph and pass it to him, observing his eyes as they intensely scan the image over and over again. He stares at the picture for what feels like hours. *God, why won't he say something?*

"Is it—bad?" I ask him.

Finally, Kent peels his attention from the picture and gazes at me, dampness beading in the corners of his eyes.

"It's miraculous," he whispers, whimpering out of shock. "One of the most stunning pictures I've ever seen . . ."

My heartbeat quickens, my cheeks heating. I can't quite believe what he's telling me. Does he actually see this? Or is he telling me what I want to hear?

I hesitate, cautious to ask. Finally, I do: "You can see my Jonathan?" I say to him.

"As plain as day," Kent says, his finger tracing the vague outline of what I presume to be Jonathan's face in the photograph.

I tilt the picture slightly, and I strain to see what Kent sees, but I cannot. For some reason, I'm still unable to see what I once so briefly saw. It feels like a bizarre kind of penance, a sort of awful toll for witnessing something so exquisite, so unabashedly magnificent. You can only see it once, and then it's gone forever.

"You think the Wretches will appreciate this?" I ask Kent.

"They're going to be overjoyed," he assures me. "I can't wait for you to show them. . . ."

I drag the photograph from his hands and stare at it once more, thinking if I blink hard enough, I might catch sight of Jonathan. But it's no use. He's not there.

"I was thinking against it actually," I tell him quietly. "I wasn't sure about it. . . ."

Kent recoils, surprised. "You can't be serious. . . . Simeon, you have a gift here. You must share it with our group. . . . I'm certain they'll make you a member after this. You'll be one of us. Wouldn't you like that?"

But Kent's promises are hollow-sounding, dull, and insincere. I'm instead far too focused on the photograph to pay any heed to what he's telling me. After all, I'm not entirely sure if I want to belong to anyone, anything. Except for Jonathan, that is.

"Want to grab a coffee?" Kent asks me. "There's a cute little French café about a block away from here. . . ."

"I know it," I tell him, folding the picture and sliding it deep into my coat pocket. "It's one of my favorite places."

Kent eases himself off the bench and motions for me to follow as he walks toward the gated entrance at the opposite end of the colonnade. I follow him a few paces behind, but my mind is very much elsewhere. *One of us,* I think to myself, amused at the very notion of pledging allegiance to some group without actually believing in what they say. *What would that make me? A deceiver? A liar . . . ? Or perhaps even something far worse . . .*

Chapter Eight

I arrive at the church recreation hall a little earlier than anticipated, and I find myself with time to spare. I sit in my car while it idles in the parking lot for a few minutes, thumbing through some unread messages on my cell. I soon come across an unread text from Evelyn:

Call me when you can? Carter keeps asking if he'll see you this weekend.

I feel a dull ache coiling like a sliver of glass scraping the pit of my stomach, so I shift in my seat until the horrible feeling melts away. But not completely. It's still there when I shudder slightly, when I feel a little cramp of discomfort. Of course, I love Carter with my whole heart, my entire being. But I know full well that I've been so absent, so decidedly lackluster as a father. It makes me wonder why the boy is so adamant about seeing me on the weekends. After all, the poor thing doesn't even really know me. He probably wouldn't care to ask his mother to send for me if he knew the truth about what I am, the loathsome person I've become in such a short amount of time. Still, it's impossible for a boy to not love his father, to not seek his approval, his agreement. I feel a horrible pang of guilt for making Carter believe that I'm worthy of seeking out approval, that I'm caring and affectionate enough to be generous with my time, my energy. I know full well I'm none of those things. After all, I've already thought horrible things about my poor, sweet boy. I'm the one who should be begging for *his* mercy.

Eventually, I watch as other vehicles begin to fill the small parking lot, guests climbing out of their cars and making their way to the double doors leading into the recreation hall. I lurch out of the driver's seat, lock my car, and pocket my keys. Just as I'm shuffling toward the building's front entrance, I notice Kent milling about near the entryway. He appears to be waiting specifically for me, his eyes widening with such intent as I approach him.

"I've told some of the others that you'll be presenting tonight," he tells me. "You're still going to do it, right?"

I hesitate a little. "I don't know if I should. . . ."

"They're eager to see what you've found," Kent says, then pauses and looks around to make sure no one is listening to us. "They tell me that your membership depends entirely upon your presentation tonight."

My stomach sinks further into the carpet of my bowels. *God, that's terrifying to consider,* I think to myself. But do I actually care? Do I genuinely care what these people think about me, about my grief, about my sweet, tender Jonathan? I suppose I must care on some level. Otherwise, I wouldn't still be standing here, picture in hand and prepared to present myself to their scrutiny.

Kent leads me into the church recreation hall, and we fill two of the seats in the large circle arranged at the center of the space. He seems to immediately notice my nervousness as I begin to tap my feet, my hands starting to fidget as well. I try to compose myself, but my heartbeat quickens even more when I observe Void shift into the center of the circle and address the lot of us gathered around him.

"Friends, we have a very special treat this evening," he announces like the ringleader of our small band of misfits, of broken derelicts. "Mr. Simeon Link, our newest recruit, has something very special to share with us. Isn't that so, Simeon . . . ?"

I dislike the way Void regards me when he turns in my direction. His expression looks pained, almost appearing hopeful I might surprise him but also somehow convinced that I will surely fail. He resembles a teacher I once had in elementary school and hated—the frowning mouth, the manicured eyebrows, the look of disgust permanently etched into his expression. I would often be forced to stay after school as punishment for not completing my homework, forced to sit in silence while he graded papers and made little grunts of dissatisfaction while he labored. I haven't thought of that teacher in so long, and yet I find myself immediately considering him as I regard Void glaring at me from the center of the circle.

I rise from where I'm seated, and I unfold the photograph that I have been keeping inside my coat pocket. I haven't even taken off my jacket for fear that I'll be expelled from the room, cast out by the other group members for presenting something so obviously foolish, so awful. Some of the others look at me queerly while I make my way toward the woman stationed at the projector in the rear of the area, near the exit. The projector whirs alive, a pool of light aimed at the screen on the opposite end of the room near the giant wooden figure of Jesus Christ and the oil portrait of the faceless young man. I pass the photograph to the projectionist, and she accepts the offering without comment, sliding the image into the projector. As she does this, the machine throws the printed image onto the screen. My heartbeat quickens as I study the photograph on the giant screen. It feels so much more painful to see it blown up for all to see—its flaws, its imperfections, its shameful secrets. All those horrible things belong to me, after all.

"I visited my local park the other day," I tell the crowd, clearing my throat a little. "I, uh . . . was really inspired when I left last week's meeting. . . . So I wanted to see if I could find any evidence of my sweet Jonathan. . . . And I found this. . . ."

Murmurs filter throughout the crowd as some guests lean across and whisper to one another. Whether they are impressed or unmoved, I am not wholly certain at this point. I decide to keep talking.

"I found myself drawn to this place in the park. This trellis actually," I tell them. "I decided to take a picture. But when I looked at my camera, I thought I saw a face staring back at me . . . Jonathan's face. . . . You can see it there in the corner . . . the dim shape . . . hiding almost. . . ."

I expect a few will rise from their chairs, moving closer toward the screen to scrutinize the picture further the way some of them did at last week's meeting. But that doesn't happen. Instead, the guests remain in their seats, unmoving. Or perhaps uninterested. I search each of their faces for a reaction—a frown of disgust, a pitying grin. I'm met with nothing. Instead, the room becomes eerily silent, until the only noise we can hear is the faint sound of the projector whirring.

In my peripheral vision, I notice Void moving toward me.

"That's all, Simeon?" he says, prompting me.

I swallow nervously, unsure what else I could possibly say. I expected so much more. Or perhaps I didn't actually. Perhaps this was exactly what I anticipated all along—the dreadful apathy, the listless stares of indifference and unconcern. I dreaded this moment, and everything I feared finally came true.

I shrink, curling inward and struggling to speak.

"I—suppose that's all," I say, swiping the photograph from the projector and returning to my chair next to Kent.

I keep my eyes lowered; my attention is forever trained on the floorboards. I wonder if I should glance up, if I should look to see if Kent is still watching me. But I can't bear to look at him now. It pains me to even be seated next to him, knowing I've performed so inadequately, knowing I've disappointed him. This is what I so desperately wanted to avoid.

Void takes to the center of the circle once more and calls another guest forward. I pretend to listen, but my mind is very much elsewhere. All sound around me becomes muted, blurry-sounding even. While he speaks to the small crowd, I unfold the picture and gaze at the image one final time. Then I crumple the paper and push it inside my coat pocket. I could excuse myself now, could pretend I have a stomach cramp and simply leave for the bathroom. But I don't. Instead, I remain seated next to Kent, enduring the agony of the next two hours of presentations, constantly being reminded of my suffering, my despair, my sorrow. After a while, I find my attention drifting to the wooden figure of Jesus Christ set on the nearby wall. I glare at myself in the reflection of those tiny silver balls fixed in his hollow eye sockets. My reflection looks distorted, damaged almost. It gently whispers to me, *You'll never be cured. You'll always be this way.*

Much to my dismay, the meeting continues. I observe in silence as Void takes command of the small crowd, entering the center of the circle and addressing the lot of us. He tells us how one of the members of the group wrote a short play titled *Predator and Prey: A Play in One Act* that serves as a way to better come to terms with his partner's demise. As one of the attendants begins to pass around bound copies of the manuscript, Void glances about the room in search of two volunteers to play the roles of Predator and Prey.

"I'll play Predator," Kent says, lifting his hand in the air.

I shiver a little, noticing Kent eye me in the periphery of my vision with a look of assurance, an unabashed expression of encouragement.

"Simeon," he whispers to me. "This might help you get in their good graces."

I think about folding my arms and sulking. *What do I need to be in their good graces for?* I'm not committed to this group of people. I don't owe them anything. Still, there's a quiet, reserved part of me that desperately wants them to like me, to care for me the way they seem to care for their own. It worries me, making me wonder what else I'll have to do to get on their good side, to appease them and make them truly care for me.

I raise my hand slightly. "I'll play the role of Prey. . . ."

"Excellent," Void exclaims, passing me a copy of the bound manuscript. "You'll need this. . . . Won't you both stand up? I'll read the stage directions. . . ."

My heart flutters a little. I'm not used to speaking in front of people. Even though it's a smaller crowd than last week, it's still daunting to present myself to these strangers—to allow them the honor of picking me apart, to fillet me and dissect all the intricacies of the things I so desperately yearn to keep from others.

I rise from my chair and make my way toward the front of the group of people, Kent following close behind with his script in hand as well. Eventually, we're situated beneath the giant wooden figure of Jesus Christ, who appears to be accepting of our little performance like some celestial audience member, some ancient deity keen to be entertained by the pageantry of such pathetic mortals.

I notice my hands tremble a little while I hold the script. I glance at the page and then look to Kent for a sign of approval. He waves me on, and it's then that we finally begin. . . .

PREDATOR AND PREY: A PLAY IN ONE ACT

PREDATOR:

You said it was him....It was him, wasn't it...?

PREY:

(voice trembles)

Wh-why did you d-do th-that?

PREDATOR:

Was it him?

PREY:

H-how could y-you?

PREDATOR:

WAS IT HIM OR NOT?

PREY:

Silly thing to ask now that he's—

PREDATOR:

Dead.

PREY:

D-don't.

PREDATOR:

What?

PREY:

Th-that w-word. You know.

PREDATOR:

Well?

PREY:

Please.

PREDATOR:

Was it him or not?

PREY:

I told you.

PREDATOR:

He didn't recognize you, Prey.
After only two years?

PREY:

He l-looked the s-same.

PREDATOR:

You said you were going to help.
You could hardly hold the knife.

PREY:

I told you...

PREDATOR:

Useless.

PREY:

I—d-didn't want to.

PREDATOR:

Didn't want to...?

THE BODY ON THE FLOOR STIRS GENTLY.

PREY:

H-he's s-still m-moving.

PREDATOR:

Ignore it.

PREY:

Please!

PREDATOR SMACKS A HAMMER AGAINST THE SIDE OF THE BODY'S HEAD. THERE IS A CRACKING SOUND OF BONE FOLLOWED BY A JELLIED GURGLE AS THE HAMMER'S PULLED FROM THE WET OUTLET.

PREDATOR:

There.

PREY:

Neighbors.

PREDATOR:

It's three in the morning.

PREY:

They'll c-come l-looking f-for him, won't th-they?

PREDATOR:

You think somebody gives a shit about a homeless ex-cult leader trading hand jobs for heroin?

(*A beat*)

Here. Help me lift him.

PREY:

I c-can't.

PREDATOR:

It's already done, Prey.

PREY:

You're trembling. W-wait. Don't move. I s-see my "self"—

PREDATOR:

Don't say it.

PREY:

It's what I wanted. I th-thought I might n-never—recognize my same—anxiety in you.

PREDATOR:

You don't. I'm fine. What I mean is—how are you to progress if I can hardly keep it together?

PREY:
If only sensitivity wasn't an extinct language to you.

PREDATOR:
Just give me a minute, will you? Ignore it.
(claps hands)
Ignore it.
(claps hands)
Ignore it.
(claps hands)

PREY:
Another headache? Is it a bad one?

PREDATOR:
You're saying the letters *e* and *t* again?

PREY:
What?

PREDATOR:
What was that three weeks ago? A game? Something he taught you...?

PREY:
It's a coping mechanism.

PREDATOR:
Who taught him? The Reverend Jim Jones?

PREY:
How d-did you g-get him here?

PREDATOR:
Told him I'd suck his cock.

PREY:
Did you?

PREDATOR:

No. But I would've. If it meant getting him where we wanted him.

PREY:

Is that why you've never touched me?

PREDATOR:

I wouldn't have enjoyed—pleasuring—the bastard. But it was for you.

PREY:

Spare me.

PREDATOR:

You think I'm a queer?

PREY:

I think you've never had the privilege of meeting your—"self." Most people haven't. To them, it's just an obscured reflective film glued to the underbelly of their brain.

PREDATOR:

Doctors shouldn't risk integrity by screwing their patients.

PREY:

Why should it even matter? You're not one.

PREDATOR:

Yet. We had an arrangement. Or need I remind you again?

PREY:

I know the arrangement.

PREDATOR:
Then tell me why we've made absolutely no progress. My candidacy depends on you and a detailed record of your mental rehabilitation.

PREY:
That's a word that belongs in the mouth of a lizard in a suit. I don't know why you use it when there are other—more pleasant ones.

PREDATOR:
You promised, Prey.

PREY:
Ugh. Th-that n-name.

PREDATOR:
It's yours.

PREY:
It's too—unkind.

PREDATOR:
We talked about that. Kindness is the most insensitive of all therapeutic deceptions. Do you want compassion or results?

PREY:
I wish I could give up wanting things from you.

PREDATOR:
Trauma is often latent. You know that. Anxiety from being baptized into a death cult like the Eaters may not become apparent until many

months—even years—after the fact. But what do I say? True therapy is ignorance of the inevitable. Once the issue has been challenged and the unpleasantness tickles you in the sorest place—what do you do? IGNORE IT. Emotions are not real, Prey. They're indefinite. Meaningless outside the confines of our perception. They might as well be numbers.

PREY:

Emotions are the only things I've been able to remember.

PREDATOR:

Things. See, you said it. Acknowledgment followed by disregard of what's not real is the true pathway to successful recovery. Ignorance is fundamental. I swear you'll live in pleasure for those moments of ignorance. That's what real pleasure is after all: relief from the otherwise constant ache.

PREY:

According to your thesis.

PREDATOR:

Six months' worth of research from when we first met. You inspired me.

PREY:

You'd give your test subject that much credit, Predator?

PREDATOR:
What did I say about that name?

PREY:
Why shouldn't I call you that?

PREDATOR:
We had a deal. For Christ's sake, look what I did for you. I'm *wearing* the son of a bitch.

PREY:
I never wanted you to. Least of all, bring him here to my place. You didn't have to kill him.

PREDATOR:
Didn't have to kill him? You said you wanted to have the satisfaction of watching him die after all he did to you. He was a monster. I did it because I—

PREDATOR PAUSES.

PREY:
Yes?

PREDATOR:
I did it because it's what you wanted.

PREY:
I never said that was what I wanted.

PREDATOR:
You had me convinced that we could make progress on your anxiety. Enough of the games.

We can finally get what I—*you and I*—want.

PREY:

Some things can't be given—words. I don't want to...

PREDATOR:

We were to finally address the root of your nervousness. You've shared everything with me except the truth of your fixation on death.

PREY:

Don't say it. I hardly expect you to understand it.

PREDATOR:

You don't expect me to understand it? It's crippled you even more now, Prey. The locks have been changed. I couldn't get a hold of you for nearly a month. You hardly ever leave the bed. If you do, you embarrass yourself. I'd be surprised to find that you were actually going to your classes.

PREY:

It's philosophy. We talk, talk, talk. Pointless talk. I know better now. I don't have a plastic mind anymore. Besides, you said my thesis was "pedestrian."

PREDATOR:

When was the last time you spoke to your parents?

PREY:

I don't need to. They sent me a check for the rent last week. I get by fine now. I—h-have it under c-control.

PREDATOR:

Under control...? They fired you from the shoe store after your hysterics a month ago.

PREY:

A lot has changed in a month. That's an entire life cycle for some things. I don't need you, Predator.

PREDATOR:

Don't need me? How can you not need me? Even if you have made developments, it's because of *this*—because of our progress.

PREY:

We have to clean this up.

PREDATOR:

No. We're not focusing on that now. We're ignoring it. What do I say?

PREY:

Ignore it.

(claps hands)

Ignore it.

(claps hands)

Ignore it.

(claps hands)

PREDATOR:

Very good.

TINY CLAWS SCRATCH AT THE FOOT OF THE BATHROOM DOOR.

PREDATOR:
What's that? The dog?

PREY:
I keep him in the bathroom when I have guests. He scratches when he's hungry.

PREDATOR:
Don't.

PREY:
He's upset.

PREDATOR:
When we're done.

PREY:
I thought we were finished.

PREDATOR:
We're not.

PREY:
I have a gram left. You want some?

PREDATOR:
Prey...

PREY:
I need to smoke it.

PREDATOR:
When we're done. I want you to tell me about it.

PREY:
About what?

PREDATOR:
You know good and well.

PREY:

What would you have me say?

PREDATOR:

There's a great deal to, isn't there?

PREY:

The busy crab has no time to be sad.

PREDATOR:

You ignore what I tell you to ignore. All right?

PREY:

I'm just predisposed to a carnivorous mind. Any good sense gets chewed on.

PREDATOR:

You just don't want to remember.

PREY:

You don't know that.

PREDATOR:

I've lived in those moments with you for six months now. What did he do?

PREY:

He wanted all of us to—transcend—and then return.

PREDATOR:

From death.

PREY:

(nearly retches)

Th-that w-word.

PREDATOR:

And you told him what you saw?

PREY:

Only a few of us did. And once we had and told him what we had seen, he was done with us.

PREDATOR:

What did you see?

PREY:

I already told you. Some things—can't be given words. The mouth—disrespects them.

PREDATOR:

But you have given them words. You told him what you saw.

PREY:

...I lied. I—made it up.

PREDATOR:

You saw something....

PREY:

N-no.

PREDATOR:

It's the foundation upon which your anxiety has been built.

PREY:

You think you're so clever.

PREDATOR:

I want you to tell me.

PREY:

I saw something—real.

PREDATOR:

Yes.

PREY:

What do you care?

PREDATOR:

I'm doing this to help you.

PREY:

You help yourself, Predator.

PREDATOR:

What?

PREY:

A person's not a vending machine. A person cannot give and give and give until there is more on the outside than there is left on the inside. That's when a person dies.

PREDATOR:

It's the final opportunity I have to redeem myself, Prey. I'll be ruined.... Who am I kidding? I'm surprised I was accepted into the program. Most of them probably know anyhow.

PREY:

Know what?

PREDATOR:

That I plagiarized my first doctoral dissertation at another university. Word for word. And when the school uncovered the deception, they expelled me.

PREY:

What?

PREDATOR:

It wasn't until I met you that I—started thinking for myself.

PREY:

You—never told me.

PREDATOR:

That I was a fraud? How could I?

PREY:

You're not.

PREDATOR:

Please.

PREY:

I've wanted to show it to you for quite some time now.

PREY OPENS THE BATHROOM DOOR.

PREDATOR:

(covering his mouth)

That smell...

BLOOD AND OTHER BODILY FLUIDS DRIP FROM THE TOILET, SHOWER, SINK, ETC.

PREY:

He's very tired. His name's Iz. You see, he *is*—because I am not.

THE SMALL CREATURE MEWLS WITH A GUTTURAL GROAN AND EXCITEDLY CLICKS ITS PINCERS.

PREDATOR:

(he sees the creature)

What—what is it?

PREY:

There's one inside you, too. It's when you ignore it that it comes out.... You don't recognize it? I didn't recognize it at first. But he gave me a gift from death.

PREDATOR:

(nearly retches)

Th-that w-ord.

PREY:

He helps me to say it. I change—when I'm near him. My "self" does, that is. Your body and your self are two completely different things. There's an illiteracy of self. It's life's travesty that you can live in your body, but never truly know it.... Your body is the house, you see? Your organs—the tiny rooms inside. But your "self" is—the certainty of that house and the recognition of what it truly is: decaying organic matter. And your "self" adjusts depending on how you identify that.

PREDATOR:

How—are you s-saying these th-things?

THE SMALL CREATURE CONTINUES TO MEWL, SCURRYING ABOUT THE FLOOR.

PREDATOR:
Keep it a-away from m-me.

PREY:
Hear his delight? Don't touch him. You'll be sorry if you do.... I have to keep him healthy just as you keep any body part strong and fit.

PREDATOR:
Wh-where's th-the d-dog?

PREY:
Poor thing was starved. Nothing seemed to please him. Wet fur and the brawn of meat did, though.... He's grown a lot since then. At least we won't have to trouble ourselves with disposing of the body. He hasn't eaten in days....

THE SMALL CREATURE LOCATES THE BODY ON THE FLOOR AND BEGINS TO FEED, MAKING LABORED SOUNDS OF CONSUMPTION. FLUIDS STIR, BONES CRINKLE AS HE FEEDS.

PREDATOR:
How is it—m-moving?

PREY:
Why are you holding the hammer?

PREDATOR:
L-leave.

PREY:
No.

PREDATOR:

C-close the door behind you.

PREY:

I won't let you. I need him.

PREDATOR:

Move aside, Prey. D-do you h-hear m-me?

PREY:

He's more of me than I ever was. That's why I must hold on to him.

PREDATOR:

Out of the way.

PREY:

No, Predator. Don't.

PREDATOR:

Get out!

PREY:

Please!

PREDATOR SMASHES THE HAMMER INTO THE CREATURE'S CARAPACE WITH A WET CRUNCHING SOUND.
THE CREATURE SCREECHES IN AGONY AS PREDATOR STRIKES DOWN AGAIN AND AGAIN.
AFTER A MOMENT OF SILENCE...
PREDATOR LETS THE HAMMER SLIP FROM HIS HANDS.

PREY:

How—could you?

PREDATOR:

I h-had to. I—couldn't let it b-be.

PREY:

What am I to do without him: my anxiety? How can I live until I die in the same house—the same body—and be expected to cope?

PREDATOR:

Wh-when I f-first met y-you, I l-loved h-how b-broken you w-were.... I—did it b-because I l-love you.

PREY:

(startled; blissfully)

That word. You said it....

A GUTTURAL GROANING COMES FROM THE CREATURE.

PREDATOR:

It's st-still a-alive.

PREY:

Wait. Don't move. I see my "self" in you....

PREDATOR:

What?

PREY:

(releases a sigh of relief)

I knew it would happen—if I was patient. I knew that one day I might see my "self" in you. You have my word. I promise to take care of you just as you've taken care of me. The both of you...

PREDATOR CONVULSES, GROANING, WHILE THE CREATURE STIRS IN ITS PLACE ON THE BACK OF HIS HEAD.

PREY:
Another headache, darling? Is it a bad one?

THE CREATURE CLICKS ITS APPENDAGES EXCITEDLY, FUSSING LIKE AN INFANT.

PREDATOR:
(his voice trembles)
Ig-nore it.
(claps hands)
Ig-nore it.
(claps hands)
Ig-nore it.
(claps hands)
Ig-no- it.
(claps hands)
Ig-no- i-
(claps hands)
Igno- i-

The play comes to an end, and there's scattered applause throughout the small crowd. I search their somber-looking faces for a semblance of appreciation or any kind of reaction, for that matter.

Unfortunately, I'm left wanting.

As usual, they seem to accept any kind of offering I'm willing to give with a dull, vacant expression. Almost like what I've donated hasn't been enough and that I'm completely useless.

Kent and I make our way back to our chairs on the opposite end of the circle, and we sit beside each other once more. I can't help but feel a sense of pity for both of us, for baring so much of ourselves only to be met with such a decidedly tepid and half-hearted response. I wince a little, realizing that so much of my life has involved me attempting to please other people, only to be met with anguish and despair when I realize that they simply do not care for me. You cannot force a person to love you, to tend to you no matter how much you yearn for the sympathy of their touch, their courteousness, their kindness. Sometimes I wonder if that's why I mourn Jonathan so much. I wonder if I continue to grieve for him because he loved me unabashedly, and I never had to fight for his attention or thoughtfulness. It was always there. I suppose I foolishly believed that he would always be there, no matter what. Of course, I was horribly mistaken. It's a wretched truth that I wish I could ignore.

I let my car idle for a while, sitting in the driver's seat and thumbing through local news notifications on my phone. Occasionally, I glance up from my scrolling and observe the various group members filtering out of the recreation hall while they make their way toward their vehicles in the parking lot. Sometimes they regard me with inquisitive looks, peering through the windshield and then making muted comments to one another as they traipse in front of my car. The more willful, stubborn part of me wants to raise a middle finger to them, to flip them off and curse them. But I compose myself and merely nod at them, forcing a respectful smile while they pass in front of my vehicle.

I know full well that they do not deserve such courtesy, such consideration, from me. After all, they seem to have already made up their minds about me joining their private group. My lips curl a little, my hands tightening to fists when I think of their disrespect, their discourtesy. If I could, I'd shift the car into gear and slam my foot on the accelerator until I've mowed them down—until they're battered and broken, trapped helplessly beneath the idling wreckage. I soften a little, realizing that these daydreams—these awful, hate-filled fantasies—seem to be spilling into my mind more comfortably as of late. It unsettles me to consider how easy it is to think of something horrible, to dwell upon the carnage, the butchery of others. I wonder why I've been considering such ghoulish things lately, especially without much remorse. But do they deserve any remorse from me after all they've done to reject me? An uncomfortable part of me seems convinced that they do not.

Just as I'm about to exit the parking lot, I notice Kent hastening toward the passenger door of my vehicle. He pulls it open and climbs inside, greeting me with a patronizing look.

"That went well, didn't it?" he asks me, his voice breaking a little.

I throw him a scowl, as if to say, *You can't be serious.* Thankfully, he recognizes my dissatisfaction immediately.

"I suppose it could've been worse," he says. "They've been known to be especially unforgiving to folks they don't trust. . . ."

I lower my head, biting my lip a little. "I think it's obvious they don't trust me."

I can't quite understand why I care so much. After all, I don't necessarily believe in the same things that they do. I cannot continue to pretend to understand their rituals, their customs. Still, there's a very human part of me that yearns to be accepted, to be welcomed, to be understood.

"That's not true," Kent says. "These things take time. You know this."

"I don't know anything about these people," I say softly. "They can't help me. . . . They can't help me bring Jonathan back. . . ."

"Is that what you truly want?" Kent asks.

I roll my eyes at him. "I thought it was obvious. . . ."

"I'm afraid they wouldn't be helpful for that," Kent tells me.

Then he's alarmingly quiet. I wonder if he'll excuse himself, if he'll climb out of the passenger seat and make his way back toward the recreation hall, far away from me. Like everything, everyone else. It's attractive to leave someone, to part company with them and know for certain that you've decimated them by removing yourself from their presence. It hurts to be left, to be the one who's been discarded.

I notice Kent inhale sharply like he's about to say something. Finally, he does:

"But there's someone who could do that for you."

I shake my head. I'm not in the mood to play these guessing games any longer, and I hope Kent senses that.

"There is," Kent says. "There's someone I know of who could help bring Jonathan back to you. . . . For a short period of time at least . . ."

"If it's another fucking support group, I'm not interested," I tell him, tossing my cell phone on the dashboard and crossing my arms.

"No, it's not a support group," he says. "It's—something I've been keeping from you . . . because I wasn't sure if you were serious enough to follow through with it."

I stir in my seat, my eyes narrowing at him. "Follow through with what?"

Kent reaches into his coat pocket and then pulls out a small business card. This one is printed on black paper with the words engraved in bright white lettering. He passes the card to me, and I read it: *Clovis R. Morrow*. There's a mailing address printed below the name, presumably where one might be able to send correspondence.

"Who is this?" I ask him.

"He represents a very special person," Kent tells me. "Have you ever heard of a man named Porcelain Khaw?"

I think for a moment. Yes, it's a name I've certainly read before. In fact, I recognize it immediately. It's the same name I saw on that strange forum I browsed with the story about the young boy being auctioned off for the sake of comfort, for the sake of convenience. The host's name was Porcelain Khaw. I bristle a little, feeling foolish for accepting Kent's explanation without any criticism. It's one thing to read something online, to encounter a name in a hidden forum, a secret better off kept by teenagers and fools. However, it's an entirely different matter for those things—the names from those internet threads, those web-based monsters—to crawl out from the screen and coil around your feet.

"Porcelain has a unique gift," Kent says. "He can help you the same way he helped me. . . ."

"You've visited this person?" I ask, studying the small card again and again, memorizing the curve of each printed letter. "I've heard of him. . . . I read about him online. . . ."

"He—transformed me," Kent says. "I'm not the same person I was before I met with him, before he took all of my sorrow. . . ."

My breath whistles a little when I inhale and then exhale. "What did he do exactly?"

But Kent shakes his head, his eyes lowering. "It's best if you see everything for yourself. . . . I can't promise that he'll agree to see you, of course. But if he does . . ."

"What should I say to him?" I ask.

"Tell him that I sent you," Kent explains. "Tell him that you're eager to follow all instructions. No matter how outlandish, no matter how senseless."

I squint at him again, unsure. "What will he want me to do . . . ?"

"I'm afraid I can't say," Kent tells me. "But it's imperative you follow his every order. Otherwise, it's all pointless. . . ."

Then again, isn't everything?

I shift in my seat, staring at the small black business card for what feels like hours.

"You're certain he could help me?" I ask Kent once more.

"He'll change everything for you," he says. "Write to him and tell him you're ready and willing."

Then Kent grabs hold of the door handle, pulls it tight, and climbs out of the vehicle. He passes another look to me—this one more earnest, more hopeful—and then slams the door shut before making his way back toward the entrance of the church recreation hall. I watch him until he vanishes through the double doors leading into the center. Once he's finally gone, I shove the business card into my pocket and grip both hands around the steering wheel. I ease my foot on the accelerator and gently begin to drift out of the parking lot until I'm speeding down the highway, heading toward home.

While I drive, Kent's voice fills all the empty corners of my mind: *He—transformed me,* I hear him say. *I'm not the same person I was before I met with him, before he took all of my sorrow. . . .*

I press my foot down harder on the gas pedal—an attempt to escape him, to flee from his promises, his meaningless assurances. But he continues to follow me, twisting his way into every spoiled thought, every dimly lit crook where I attempt to hide.

I'm not the same person I was before I met with him, before he took all of my sorrow. . . .

PART THREE

Porcelain

Nothing hurts more than to see the one that you love subjected to mistakes and wrongs.

—*Antichrist* (2009)

Chapter Nine

I think about the first person to hurt another living thing for the sheer pleasure of it. I don't pay much mind to the thought of accidents or flippant chances when it comes to human suffering. Pain is a language often spoken by amateurs and, therefore, seldom understood. I wonder if they knew they were inflicting such agony, such torture on their victim. I wonder if that made them feel proud—if they found a sense of solace in the knowledge that they held such power, such control over another human being, another life-form. It feels good to hurt another living thing sometimes. It feels pleasurable, godlike even.

While I grip the small business card that Kent delivered to me, I can't help but wonder if this person will delight in hurting me as well. *Is this another one of those cannibals I keep thinking about?* I wonder to myself. *Is this the same monstrous being from the story I read about the boy to be covered in jelly?* Yes, I've been musing about him so frequently as of late. It would make sense to find myself faced with a connoisseur of human suffering, an expert in the savoring of pitiful flesh. I'm sure he'd be only too delighted to strip me of my clothing, to peel the skin from me and feast on the gristle buried there, the wellspring of blood flowing just beneath the surface of flesh. Am I nothing more than a hole waiting to be filled, a hollowed container designed for the deposit of someone else's agony, someone else's despair?

Once again, I hear the sound of Kent's voice vibrating inside the walls of my mind:

He—transformed me. . . .

Indeed, I think to myself. Perhaps I need to be transformed. Perhaps I need to be filleted by a skilled surgeon and smartened with makeup and rouge like the grisliest-looking cadaver. But those are just aesthetics, after all. I need something else—something that's capable of taking root in the very brawn of the human soul.

I pace my apartment living room, back and forth from one end of the room to the other. Do I dare send a letter to this man? Do I dare reach out and initiate this? If I do, I'm the only person to blame for my suffering when the time inevitably comes. But what if I'm overreacting, anticipating something far worse than what might actually happen? After all, Kent appears confident and assured every time I see him. It's not like he's been hollowed out with a spade and then left for dead on the side of a highway. Then again, there are many ways to undo a person, to destroy a living thing without actually harming them. Perhaps Kent's wounds are not visible to everyone. Perhaps they're hidden away like all other kinds of ailments, all other sorts of monstrosities that wither in the threat of daylight.

Still, there's a part of me that feels compelled to send a letter to the address printed on this card. I can't quite explain it, but I feel a need to sit down and write a letter. Perhaps I won't mail it. Perhaps I'll toss it in the trash can as soon as I'm finished writing it. But I know I won't feel sated until I follow through with the scenario I've invented in my mind—the inevitable sense of initiation, of beginning the dance and starting to sway to the soundless music.

Before I allow another moment of hesitation, I sit down at the kitchen table with some lined paper in front of me and a fountain pen. Finally, I begin to write. . . .

Letter Written by Simeon Link Addressed to Clovis R. Morrow

May 2, 2025

Dear Mr. Morrow,

I hope you will pardon the forwardness of this letter; however, I have been instructed to write to you. My partner of several years passed away, and I've been suffering a great deal since his unfortunate demise. I find myself lost, unfettered, unable to cope, and, even worse, unable to perform basic tasks I once found fulfilling, gratifying.

A new acquaintance of mine suggested that I contact you directly as he claimed that you might be able to help me more efficiently process my grief, my sorrow. I must admit that I'm not expecting a miracle by any stretch of the imagination. I certainly don't mean to dishonor you or disrespect your talents in any way; however, I find myself completely incapable of possessing the slightest bit of hope when it comes to my future, my overall outlook. Perhaps this is something you might be able to address when we meet? If we meet, that is. I wholeheartedly understand if you're not accepting new clients on behalf of your associate at this time.

Regardless, I sincerely hope you will see this letter as an offering—a clear sign that I will submit myself and obey your instructions, whatever you may suggest.

I look forward to hearing from you.

Best wishes,
Simeon Link

Letter Written by Clovis R. Morrow Addressed to Simeon Link

May 5, 2025

Mr. Link,

Your acquaintance informed me that you might be reaching out, and I have been expecting your letter for quite some time. I must admit, I have been looking forward to coming in contact with you. I believe I am able to assist you and perform the necessary obligations to permit you access to my client.

Enclosed in this letter you will find a checklist of items and protocol to consider before meeting with my client. It is imperative that you read the entire letter thoroughly and understand the contents before agreeing to a consultation. I trust you will contact me directly if you have any further questions. To reach me more speedily, you may contact my private email address: clovis.morrow@[redacted].com.

Regards,

C

Formal Checklist Included in Clovis R. Morrow's Letter

If you are reading this form letter, then you have been selected to meet with the contact I represent for a truly unique in-person experience. In order to gain entry to the private room where you and my client will be left undisturbed for precisely fifteen minutes, you must follow the guidelines carefully explained in this letter.

- *Prior to your one-on-one meeting with my client, you will be asked to send an item of significant importance to the following address:*

    Clovis R. Morrow
    [Mailing address redacted]

    This item may be anything related to your departed loved one. Previous items of sentimental value have run the gamut—from a hairbrush to a framed photograph. One client in particular once sent us a fishbowl containing a live goldfish. Unfortunately, it is not possible for this item to be returned to you after the ritual takes place. This article will be considered a gift, something that my client can utilize during the ritual to better understand your deceased loved one. Regardless, it's of vital importance that this specific article be of great emotional value. If it's not, then the ritual will not be as effective as one might hope.
- *Although we will be unable to return the article you send, we ask that you provide your return address so that we are able to provide you with an invocation for the ceremony. You will be sent a box containing a specific kind of insect—a silver, reflective beetle, to be precise. There will be a hundred or so living beetles in the box that you receive. It's of great*

importance that you care for these small creatures before, during, and after your private session with my client. Regrettably, we are unable to devote too much time to assisting you while you nurture these small creatures. However, most of the maintenance related to their care can be quickly accessed through a Google search. Their conservation is not as complicated as one might imagine. Although it's quite possible to destroy any living thing if you're determined enough.

- *After you receive the box of silver, reflective beetles, you are expected to contact me and inform me of the shipment's arrival. From there, we will discuss the plans to initiate the ritual and commence the private ceremony.*

Now that you've reached the end of this checklist, it's imperative that I relay something quite serious to you. Once you send the article of sentimental value to us, the ritual cannot be avoided. We are not permitted to cease the procedure once the invocation begins. By you sending us this item for us to keep, you are issuing a clear invitation—something that cannot be undone. So, before you send us the item you wish to use during the process, please think carefully if you'd actually like to proceed. There are many things in this world that would probably be far better off if left undisturbed. Yes, of course, my client is sensitive to your grief. Naturally, we wish to help you. But if you are easily skittish and, in any way, doubtful of our unusual process, we ask that you refrain from pursuing this endeavor any further. We will not contact you in any way if you decide against the procedure. I assure you that you will be left alone. However, if you send us the article of value, we will interpret such an action as a formal invitation to begin. In turn, we will see to it that the integrity of the ritual is upheld until the final moment of your private session with my client. I hope this is clear.

We sincerely look forward to hearing from you if you make the choice to respond.

Regards,

C

Instant Messaging Conversation Between <simeonlink_86> and <babyfacexoxo>

[**simeonlink_86** has entered the chat group The Grim Laurels]

[**babyfacexoxo** has entered the chat]

12:07:08 <simeonlink_86> Oh, shit . . . it's you . . .

12:07:25 <babyfacexoxo> I didn't think you'd remember me

12:07:36 <simeonlink_86> How could I forget?

12:07:49 <babyfacexoxo> You're sweet

12:08:01 <simeonlink_86> You're here to jack off?

12:08:14 <babyfacexoxo> Is that the only reason you're on here?

12:08:22 <simeonlink_86> I thought we already went over this . . .

12:08:29 <babyfacexoxo> It's been a while . . .

12:08:39 <simeonlink_86> Yes

12:08:50 <babyfacexoxo> You haven't been on here much . . . I haven't seen you . . .

12:08:59 <simeonlink_86> Been busy . . .

12:09:11 <babyfacexoxo> You went to that group I told you about . . .

12:09:34 <simeonlink_86> How did you know?

12:09:45 <babyfacexoxo> I saw you there . . .

12:09:56 <simeonlink_86> Who are you?

12:10:09 <babyfacexoxo> Still better not tell you

12:10:19 <simeonlink_86> Why not?

12:10:33 <babyfacexoxo> Because what's the fun in that?

12:10:47 <simeonlink_86> It doesn't matter. I'm not going back to those meetings . . .

12:10:59 <babyfacexoxo> They didn't care for you

12:11:10 <simeonlink_86> They made that clear

12:11:29 <babyfacexoxo> But Kent seems to like you

12:11:37 <simeonlink_86> You know him? How?

12:11:50 <babyfacexoxo> He told you something after the meeting the other night . . . What did he say?

12:12:03 <simeonlink_86> How do you know that?

12:12:14 <babyfacexoxo> I saw you and him talking in your car . . . What did he tell you?

12:12:28 <simeonlink_86> I thought you knew everything . . .

12:12:40 <babyfacexoxo> Don't play dumb

12:13:00 <simeonlink_86> He told me about someone who could help me

12:13:12 <babyfacexoxo> And you believe him?

12:13:26 <simeonlink_86> Why shouldn't I?

12:13:37 <babyfacexoxo> I'm sure he says that to every guy he's trying to fuck . . .

12:13:56 <simeonlink_86> We haven't fucked

12:14:09 <babyfacexoxo> Yet . . . What else did he tell you?

12:14:18 <simeonlink_86> To write a letter to someone . . .

12:14:37 <babyfacexoxo> Who?

12:14:52 <simeonlink_86> You don't know anything . . .

12:15:06 <babyfacexoxo> I know enough

12:15:19 <simeonlink_86> Someone named Clovis R. Morrow . . .

12:15:36 <babyfacexoxo> He told you about Porcelain Khaw?

12:15:52 <simeonlink_86> You know him?

12:16:10 <simeonlink_86> Well?

12:16:22 <simeonlink_86> I'm waiting . . .

12:16:39 <babyfacexoxo> Yeah. I know him . . . I know *of* him, I mean . . . Never met him . . .

12:16:44 <simeonlink_86> What do you know exactly?

12:16:57 <babyfacexoxo> I'm not sure if he's real . . . I hope he's not . . .

12:17:11 <simeonlink_86> Why do you say that?

12:17:27 <babyfacexoxo> He's an internet legend . . . One of those creepy ones you find in the darkest parts of websites . . .

12:17:46 <simeonlink_86> And?

12:17:59 <babyfacexoxo> He's mentioned on a few forums, a few blog posts. You have to search hard to find them . . . Some of them have been taken down already . . .

12:18:15 <simeonlink_86> Why?

12:18:28 <babyfacexoxo> Doesn't like his name online . . .

12:18:37 <simeonlink_86> You know that for a fact?

12:18:51 <babyfacexoxo> I don't know much about him

12:19:09 <babyfacexoxo> He scares me

12:19:17 <simeonlink_86> Why?

12:19:39 <babyfacexoxo> Things I've been told . . . Rumors . . . That's probably all they are . . .

12:19:50 <simeonlink_86> Rumors about what?

12:20:07 <babyfacexoxo> What he's like . . . What he does to people . . .

12:20:21 <simeonlink_86> I've heard he helps people . . .

12:20:39 <babyfacexoxo> Maybe

12:20:48 <simeonlink_86> You've heard other things?

12:20:59 <babyfacexoxo> I've heard that he must hurt you in order to help you . . . I suppose all things are like that . . .

12:21:08 <simeonlink_86> How?

12:21:18 <babyfacexoxo> Whatever hurts the most . . .

12:21:33 <simeonlink_86> Is he a monster?

12:21:52 <babyfacexoxo> Perhaps a kind of monster . . . I heard he stole a young boy from a family. Covered the poor thing in red jelly until the boy was eaten alive by flies and gnats.

12:22:03 <babyfacexoxo> I've also heard he's a consumer of souls . . .

12:22:15 <simeonlink_86> That's bullshit . . .

12:22:29 <babyfacexoxo> Is it?

12:23:37 <simeonlink_86> Where the fuck did you hear that?

12:23:44 <babyfacexoxo> Saw it posted on some forum a while ago before it was taken down . . .

12:23:49 <simeonlink_86> Who posted that?

12:23:59 <babyfacexoxo> Someone who had met him . . . Been in the room with him when it happened . . .

12:24:08 <simeonlink_86> When what happened?

12:24:23 <babyfacexoxo> When he took all her sorrow away from her . . . She said it felt wonderful at first. But then she began to crumble apart. Like something had poisoned her, contaminated her . . .

12:24:39 <simeonlink_86> Who was she?

12:24:54 <babyfacexoxo> Someone who had sought him out . . . She brought this on herself . . .

12:25:12 <simeonlink_86> That's what they all say . . .

12:25:27 <babyfacexoxo> When you empty a container, you can fill it with other things . . . Things that can hurt you . . . Makes it easy to possess you . . .

12:25:39 <simeonlink_86> Is that what happened to her?

12:25:55 <babyfacexoxo> I think he emptied her out and filled her with something else . . . Something that destroyed her . . . He possessed her . . .

12:26:09 <simeonlink_86> You don't know for sure . . . You can't believe everything you read on the internet . . .

12:26:28 <babyfacexoxo> No . . . You're right

12:26:47 <simeonlink_86> An empty vessel has no definition, no meaning. It should always be filled with something else . . . Otherwise, it's a waste . . .

12:27:00 <babyfacexoxo> Is that what you think?

12:27:18 <babyfacexoxo> You'd let him empty you out?

12:27:35 <simeonlink_86> If it meant I could bring my husband back . . .

12:27:56 <babyfacexoxo> You'll never get him back . . . When something leaves you, it's gone forever . . .

12:28:07 <simeonlink_86> Just like this . . .

[**simeonlink_86** has left the chat]

[**babyfacexoxo** has left the chat]

Email Addressed to Simeon Link from Evelyn Rhodes

from: Evelyn Rhodes <evelyn_rhodes@[redacted].com>

to: Simeon Link <simeonlink_86@[redacted].com>

date: May 17, 2025

subject: Hello?

Simeon,

I've tried texting and calling a few times, so I feel like emailing you is my last and only option at this point. I apologize in advance for my bluntness; however, I worry that you're avoiding me on purpose. I can't pretend to not notice that you haven't been as attentive with Carter as you have in the past. He asks for you constantly and worries that he won't see you when you make promises to visit. I've spent so many nights trying to calm him, trying to convince him that his father still loves him, still cares for him. I know you do. Even though you may not show it all the time, I know you still love our son.

I don't even know why I'm writing this email. I feel so stupid typing this out and then reading it back to myself. There's a good chance you won't even read it. *Or maybe you will?* Maybe you'll read it through to the end and then toss it in the trash because it doesn't suit you, or perhaps it makes you feel poorly about yourself. I promise I'm not trying to make you feel guilty or make you feel worse about the whole situation. When we were together a few months ago, I was so happy, so filled with joy. At the time, it seemed like you were as well. But now I cannot be so certain of it. I worry that you're pulling away again, and I hate to see it happen once more. I certainly don't expect you to be perfect–to be exemplary in every way so that your integrity is never questioned, your worth is never devalued. To me, you are godlike. You are worth so much more than a one-night stand—a momentary distraction, a temporary diversion. You're none of those things.

More than anything, I want you to tell me when you need help. I want to know when things are becoming difficult, when things get tough, so that I can help you. I can't perform miracles, but I can try to make things better, more bearable. You don't have to be so alone. You don't have to be brave and push people away because you're fearful of being hurt by them. Not every living thing is capable of doing harm to another. Sometimes you have to be more trusting, more openhearted. I know our history is shoddy at best, but I like to imagine that I've been helpful, that I've been a kindhearted and forgiving partner. Of course, I can't pretend to act as though I completely forgive you for everything you put me through—the heartbreak, the despair, the manipulation. I know you did those things to survive. I realize you behaved in such a way because the world told you it wasn't acceptable to be a certain way, to love the way you love. But it's so easy to damage another person when you're trying to hide parts of yourself. Naturally, I can't claim that I haven't been wounded by your deceit, your dishonesty. I feel so stupid saying this, but I still love you no matter what. I still care for you. I treasure the moments we shared together and the life we created—our precious boy, Carter. He loves you, too.

I don't exactly know where I'm going with this email, but I've tried getting in touch with you so many times over the past few weeks, and I worry that you might not want to see me ever again. I think if you told me that you wanted to step away for good, I wouldn't be able to cope. I wouldn't be able to accept it. The truth is this: I still care about you, and I will always care about you. When you're young and foolish, hearts are easily tethered to one another and impossible to break apart. That's how I feel about you, Simeon. I truly believe our hearts–*our souls*–are bound with a precious kind of wire that cannot be severed no matter what. I realize there's a possibility that you don't feel the same way about me, and I can try to learn to accept that. But please don't push me away. When you love someone, you pour yourself into them entirely with the hope that they might refill you one day. Please don't let me go too long without being replenished. I know you didn't ask for any of this, but it's the life we've built together. There's a part of me that hopes you'll come to understand.

As always, you know how to contact me. I trust you'll reach out when you're ready, when you're prepared to finally have a very necessary conversation. I want you to know something: I've never blamed you for the pain I've endured, but I've secretly wished you'd held my hand during it. Please don't pull away when I reach out. It would destroy me.

I hope to hear from you soon.

Sending all my love,
Evelyn

Email Addressed to Evelyn Rhodes from Simeon Link

from: Simeon Link <simeonlink_86@[redacted].com>

to: Evelyn Rhodes <evelyn_rhodes@[redacted].com>

date: May 18, 2025

subject: RE: Hello?

Evelyn,

I realize that I've been difficult to deal with over the past few weeks. I recognize that you've reached out time and time again only to be ignored, only to have your hopes dashed and your pride wounded. For that, I am truly sorry. I know nothing I write here will be able to make up for the fact that I've been a miserable bastard as long as you've known me. But I want you to know that I hope I'll eventually become a better father for Carter. I know he deserves that more than anything. I've been a pathetic excuse for a father, just like my father was to me. Perhaps it's some kind of warped, self-fulfilling prophecy–some horrible kind of inheritance, a terrible birthright.

In your email, you asked me to come forward and let you know when I'm struggling. I suppose I've been too prideful, too afraid, to ask for help. But the truth is that I desperately need help. If I don't reach out to someone, everything might change for me. I don't expect you to work miracles, but I'm short on cash. I owe my landlord for last month's rent, and I'm struggling to make ends meet as we speak without a steady, full-time job. Of course, I've been looking for work since I was asked to leave a few months ago; however, I haven't been as successful as I had hoped.

Although it pains me to ask and makes me feel like such a failure, I was hoping you might be willing to spare some money to get me by until the end of the month. I know I don't deserve your kindness or your sympathy. So I wholeheartedly understand if you must decline. But I want to show you that I'm making an effort to be more vulnerable, to be more revealing, and to ask for assistance when it's needed.

Like I said, I certainly don't expect you to agree to help me. You should absolutely say no if it's not possible at all.

Tell Carter I love him and give him a kiss for me, will you?

Love,
Simeon

Email Addressed to Simeon Link from Evelyn Rhodes

from: Evelyn Rhodes <evelyn_rhodes@[redacted].com>

to: Simeon Link <simeonlink_86@[redacted].com>

date: May 19, 2025

subject: RE: Hello?

I just sent a payment to your bank account.

Let me know if it didn't reach you for whatever reason. I appreciate you telling me how difficult it's been for you lately and how you need help. I want you to know that I'm here for the good and the bad. I want us to remain open, to remain connected the way we should. You already know I don't have much family left in the area, so I try to hold on to as many loved ones as possible. I'm happy to help and make things easier for you. I hope you're never too scared to ask me.

See you this weekend? Carter would love it.

Xoxo,

Evelyn

Email Addressed to Evelyn Rhodes from Simeon Link

from: Simeon Link <simeonlink_86@[redacted].com>

to: Evelyn Rhodes <evelyn_rhodes@[redacted].com>

date: May 19, 2025

subject: RE: Hello?

Evelyn, I don't quite know what to say. Thank you so much for your generosity, your kindness. I won't ever forget this.

Yes, tell Carter I'll see him this weekend. All my love to you both.

Yours,
Simeon

Chapter Ten

I close my email with "yours" even though I don't actually mean it. I cannot pretend to think I belong to Evelyn in any way, shape, or form. I could never belong to her the way she envisioned me, the way she always imagined the two of us and how we might one day end up together. Yes, perhaps it might be true if I were hollowed out and remolded to suit her fancy. But the truth is that two users have nothing truly selfless to offer each other. The only reason we lasted as long as we did was because we had to care for Carter. We had to tend to his needs and pretend we loved each other long enough for him to truly believe it. But it was never true. Yes, I suppose I did love and care for Evelyn once upon a time. But I cannot search myself for those feelings now while I drive late at night, heading toward the private address that was sent to me. It's a part of town I don't venture to too often, and I can't quite find my way without using the GPS installed in my car.

While I drive, the faint silhouettes of small houses flickering past me and a two-lane roadway stretching miles upon miles ahead, I think of Evelyn. I think of how I continue to harm her—to damage her despite her unwavering faith in me, despite all the care and affection she's afforded me year after year, transgression after transgression. I suppose it seems foolish on her part to assume I'll change, to pretend I'm honorable and forthcoming and kind. I am none of those things. I can't bear to think she imagines me as such. I feel a pang of guilt spreading inside my chest, unfurling there, whenever I think of the email I sent—the very informal plea for her to take pity on me, to send me the money to help me get by for the rest of the month. Of course it was all a lie. I needed the cash to pay for my meeting with Porcelain. Mr. Morrow expects it from me upon first entry, after all. Naturally, I don't know exactly what to expect when I make my arrival; however, I find myself filled with such inquisitiveness, such insatiable curiosity to know more, to discover more.

I already mailed Mr. Morrow a copy of the photograph I had taken and shown the Wretches. Of course, he, in turn, mailed me a small box filled with those reflective-looking beetles he had promised in his letter. The box arrived at my doorstep in a small crate without markings, and when I pulled the cardboard box open, the damn things spilled out all over the carpet and began sneaking off toward freedom. I did what I could to spoon them into my hands and then dump them back into the box, but I'm afraid some of them escaped in the process. While I lie awake in bed at night, I often find myself staring at the ceiling and wondering if I'll notice a small, dark shape creeping there—a muted whisper, a kind of melancholy stalking, a pitiful aching to go on existing.

I twist the dial, and the radio hums alive. I search for a station, the speakers hissing while I turn the small knob. Just then, I land on a channel, and a familiar voice greets me. I tilt my head at the sound, wondering if it's even somehow possible. It sounds so much like my voice. But it can't be. I raise the volume, and the voice speaks to me:

I've been taught to never ask about my mother. The only thing I know about her is that she died while giving birth to me. That's the way all creators should perish—a voice silenced during their final declaration, their ultimate gift to the world. It's very strange to think that I was that gift. What became of her corpse, I'll probably never be allowed to know. Such information is guarded from me for the sake of my protection. If I do happen to ask about her, I'm scolded. I'm forced to eat unsavory things that taste like rusted metal or to hold my breath for an impossible length of time until I'm lightheaded and weak. Naturally, my curiosity overpowers me from time to time; however, I know for certain that there will be no secrets revealed, no profound truths exposed even if I'm courageous enough to ask them about her. To me, my mother remains nothing more than a dim, shapeless silhouette—a flicker against a nearby wall, a formless prospect caught in the muted glow of trembling candlelight. I often think of her, even though I never truly knew her. I wonder what her face looked like. I wonder if her cheeks dimpled when she smirked or laughed. I wonder if her voice sounded like mine. I suppose in many ways it's preferable for children to never know the people who created them. To recognize someone—to know something as simple as the spelling of their name—is to possess them, to claim ownership over them. Therefore, sacred things are not meant to be known. A creator's name must never be revealed to its invention. Such a discovery would completely undermine the beauty and the majesty of the actual creator. Even though I yearn to know my mother and what she looked like, I know for certain that it's best I'm never told such things. It's for the sake of the purity of my spirit, my very essence. I don't wish to know my mother's name. It would be an insult to her generosity, her benevolence as the vessel that brought me into this world. Yes, I suppose all creators could be considered "vessels." They carry the weight of the possibility of new existence—soft, tender, and pink. A woman's womb is a precious kind of container—the place where all life begins, where tissue blooms open, and where a new life-form's blood begins to flow freely like a secret mountain spring. The attendants with masks who come to my cell often remind me that I possess the same gift, the same ability to carry life. But part of me cannot believe them. Even though I've been instructed to accept everything they tell me, there's an inquisitive, stubbornly willful part of me that cannot accept such a fantasy. Am I capable of becoming a creator? It makes little sense to me. After all, I'm aware of my name. I'm aware of what the handlers refer to me as. I've been taught that the name of any creator must never be spoken, because it's an offense. I wince sometimes, remembering what my name is and wishing I could somehow drain the reminder from the half-empty pool of my thoughts. If only my ghost could skate along the water's edge, tip my toes beneath the surface, and then shake the memory from my hair. Perhaps then I would be deserving of becoming such a sacred vessel. Perhaps that's why it's taken so long for me. Of course, the attendants who come to tend to me every day are never condescending or impatient. "It will happen when it's supposed to happen." That's what they tell me. But I wonder if they realize it might never happen simply because I know my name. How can a god—yes, even an earthbound god like a creator—recognize its own name? I'm not supposed to know such things. It feels cruel to think that they might have deliberately told me my name so that I wouldn't become something more meaningful while I'm alive. After all, each living thing wants more eventually. Today, perhaps an extra loaf of bread. Tomorrow, the key to open the cell's only door. The only way out . . .

I twist the dial, and the voice clicks off at once. The car is completely silent. The only sound—the engine's growling motor while I'm carried along on some invisible leash guiding me toward my destination. In the quiet dark, I imagine I'm nameless—a soft, pink, and tender thing. Without a name, without a soul to ache.

Just then, I feel something small—impossibly faint, perhaps even a little prickly—crawl across my left hand. I jerk the wheel, and the car swerves slightly until I grab hold again and keep my aim true. I glance down and notice a small reflective beetle—shiny like metal and velvety smooth—scurrying across the passenger seat and then dipping out of sight as it burrows into the cushioning. I shiver, perhaps a little more distrustful for allowing myself to become so upset by the sensation of the tiny creature. Just as it vanishes from my sight, I think about how the awful thing might like to burrow into my skin—how it might prefer to part my flesh and make a home of the hollow opening there, a secret that I'll never share with anyone, a suffering that I must endure alone.

A more distrustful and suspicious part of me wonders if I'll perhaps find Kent waiting for me in the small red house's driveway at the end of the cul-de-sac. After all, he was the one responsible for setting this whole ordeal in motion. I certainly wouldn't be here if it weren't for him and his recommendation. There's a part of me that remains beguiled by Kent, entranced by his charm and his ability to take command of the room no matter the setting. Naturally, I've imagined scenarios where the two of us end up in bed together—tangled in bedsheets, our sweating, naked bodies glued to each other and tethered by the promise of passion. But those fantasies are usually short-lived no matter how much they excite me, no matter how much I seem to delight in the idea of his sexual company. It feels like a betrayal to poor Jonathan, just as my rendezvous with Evelyn was an insult to the integrity of his memory, the value of his very spirit. I suppose it's fair to say that I've already betrayed Jonathan quite a bit since he's passed. I've forever damaged the invisible shrine I've constructed of him inside the theater of my mind. But there's every possibility—however small, however impossibly fragile—that Porcelain Khaw can help me rebuild that betrayed honor, can help me succor the wounds I've opened in Jonathan's beloved memory. I suppose that promise—the phantom of that possibility—keeps me pressing my foot on the gas pedal, forces me to carry onward despite my hesitation, my reluctance.

I finally arrive at the small red house with the gray shingles framed inside a small thicket. The houses are somewhat identical with their steep, pitched roofs and their neatly manicured lawns sweeping toward the road, all seeming to possess the notion of poised, dignified families dwelling here. It's obvious that someone like me might not be welcomed in this place. My indiscretions, my penchants, my interests—all would probably insult the honorable families who reside here, perhaps shock them even. Still, there's something about the small redbrick house—something that whispers to me that I'm at the threshold of something I've been creeping toward since Jonathan died, an inevitable rite, an obligation to endure.

I pull into the empty driveway and throw the car into park as soon as I arrive. My attention drifts toward the house, and I notice how most of the windows are curtained, no light permitted there. Part of me wonders if it might be a sign—a refusal to accept my presence, a rejection of the invitation once sent. Am I truly not welcome in this place? I find myself hesitating more and more, gripping the steering wheel as the car idles and wondering if I should leave. Should I throw the car into gear and peel out of the driveway, tires spinning madly?

Of course, I had every intention to arrive here and see the matter through so that I could finally meet with Porcelain; however, there's an unsettled part of me that wonders if I should actually do this. Even worse, all the horrible things babyfacexoxo told me about him in that chat room begin to play out on a loop in my mind.

I've heard that he must hurt you in order to help you . . .

I shudder, trying to fling the thought away. I've already been hurt, after all. What more damage could possibly be done to me? I've already been emptied out like some jar. There's nothing else Porcelain could take from me.

I've also heard he's a consumer of souls.

The world is full of cannibals—eager desirers of one another's pain and agony. I'm loath to admit it, but even I'm guilty of feeding on the misfortune of others. Even if I were to take this seriously, I know it can't be true. Kent wouldn't have let me come here if he had known this to be accurate. After all, he claimed he had been salvaged by Porcelain. His soul—knitted back together. His heart—permanently freed from the discomfort of such ache, such terrible longing.

I yearn for that, too.

I drag the keys out of the ignition, shove them in my pocket, and pry open the car door. I climb out of the driver's seat and step out, a gentle gust of wind greeting me and circling with such curiosity. I begin to make my way up the narrow brick path weaving across the lawn and leading toward the entrance of the small home. As I approach, I sense a disturbance muffled beyond the door—footsteps, someone scurrying back and forth as if in preparation for my arrival. I draw closer and notice the doorway is framed with two small stone gargoyles—their sharp, pointed horns; their lips curled in an imitation of fury. But the most unsettling part of their appearance isn't their rage-like expressions, but rather the fact that they're both holding identical mirrors aimed at whoever approaches. The glass on both mirrors is spiderwebbed with cracks and warped from the New England weather; however, I immediately catch my reflection while I pass, and I see myself frown as I gaze at my likeness for a moment—my permanent and unchanging expression of misery, of endless despair.

Just as I'm about to reach out and ring the bell, the door opens slowly, and a gaunt-faced gentleman is revealed to me there at the home's threshold. He's somewhat older than I initially expected, but I can't quite make sense of his features as he idles just beyond the dim glow of the porch light. I squint tightly, making every attempt to comprehend him, but sadly I'm left to mere guesswork as he stands there.

"You're Simeon?" he asks me, his voice watery and muffled, almost like he was speaking to me through a damp sheet of parchment paper.

"Yes," I answer, my voice trembling. "Are you—Clovis Morrow?"

"Yes," he replies, and then drags the door open farther with a visible invitation. "Come inside."

I hesitate for a moment. But my feet soon make the decision for me. In a matter of seconds, I'm forced across the threshold, and I'm inside the entryway of the small home. I don't quite know what I expected the interior would look like, but it doesn't really resemble anything I thought of. The walls are bare, undecorated. There's carpet stretching from the foyer to the nearby corridor leading down some dimly lit passage toward a closed doorway. The whole house is still, quiet, and even more peculiar, there's no discernible scent lingering in the air the way most homes possess a kind of sweet, welcoming smell. This place doesn't feel like a home. In fact, it feels more like a penitentiary—a place where things are kept, warehoused, forever locked away.

"You have the amount we agreed upon?" Clovis asks me, holding out his hand.

I pull my wallet from my pocket and thumb through a small wad of bills. When I'm done counting, I pass the money to him, and he counts it a second time. Satisfied, he folds the bills and then pockets them. Then he shows me a small wooden box on the table beside the doorway.

"Put your cell phone in here," he tells me, motioning toward the box.

Even though I probably should, I don't question him. I shove my phone into the pine box, and then he tips the lid closed, casketing it for now.

After he tucks the box away in a nearby cabinet, Clovis turns to me and produces the small photograph I sent him in the mail several weeks ago. Yes, that wretched picture.

"This is the item you'd like to use during your meeting?" he asks me.

But the way in which he asks me sounds more like a judgment rather than a confirmation. I squirm, my cheeks heating red.

"Will this suffice?" I ask him.

"Porcelain thinks so," Clovis says, handing the photograph to me.

I swallow nervously. "Good."

Before I can ask another question, Clovis is already peeling away from me and making his way toward the corridor at the far end of the foyer. I trail after him like a smitten schoolboy. When we reach the passageway's threshold, Clovis turns to me with a look of disapproval, of such condemnation. I hesitate, unsure what to say at first.

"Is something wrong?" I ask.

"This is where I leave you," Clovis tells me. "You're supposed to do the rest of this on your own. . . ."

Of course, I'm not surprised. I expected this. It isn't like Porcelain and I would need a chaperone during our secret rendezvous. However, there's a part of me that's frightened to be alone with him, to be in the room unmonitored, unsupervised.

Anything could happen.

I find myself drifting away from Clovis while he idles there, and very soon, I'm gradually making my way down the narrow stretch of corridor until I finally slow to a halt, noticing something shimmering on the carpet in front of me. I squint, struggling to comprehend what I'm looking at, and it's then I realize what's scuttling at my feet: hundreds of reflective beetles. The tiny creatures scurry about the carpet like tossed gemstones, climbing up the walls and even creeping across the ceiling. I hesitate, worried I'll inadvertently squish some of them while I make my way toward the door at the end of the hall.

Tiptoeing with catlike precision, I continue to make my way down the narrow passage and do all I can to avoid the beetles littering the floor. I dread the possibility of a crunching sound with every step I take, every attempt I issue.

Finally, after what feels like hours of balancing on a tightrope, I arrive at the doorway. My stomach curls, sour-tasting bile surfacing in my throat, as I eye the door handle. It's then that I notice a small beetle crawling across the threshold right in front of me—a muted whisper in silver, a tiny mirror to capture the loveliness of my sadness once again. *Why is it looking directly at me, though? It appears like it wishes to tell me something. . . . A secret?*

After the insect has passed, I grab hold of the handle and push the door until the threshold is sprawling open before me. The large suite waiting for me there is nothing like I might have once expected. The walls—like the ones in the entryway—are completely barren, empty, possessing utter nothingness. There's a large bed arranged in the center of the room, and it's obvious someone has tended to the area in order to make it as comfortable and as appealing as possible with cushions and pillows organized there. Just then, I observe something lurking in the periphery of my vision. I turn slightly, and it's then I notice a man of medium build and dark complexion curled in the far corner of the room. His arms are wrapped around a rusted metal grate fixed to the wall, his wrists tethered behind his back in some cruel act of bondage.

His shirt has been torn off to expose his bare chest. He resembles a man of perfect health, of an admirable physique—rippling abdominals, firm and finely sculpted pectorals, broad shoulders complementing a nearly perfect tapered waist. But despite his obvious bodily perfection, there's something wretched, something utterly loathsome about the poor man. His eyes widen in horror, his mouth hanging open and his skin dappling with beads of sweat. I can't help but think he resembles some kind of poor, soon-to-be-executed sinner from a religious painting. Or even worse, some innocent victim of genocide to be paraded around as a trophy, one of the spoils of an unforgivable war. In fact, there's a part of me that becomes slightly unnerved at the sight as I recall how much the poor, wretched thing resembles an oil painting of an Italian beggar facing a tribunal that Jonathan once obsessed over when we visited the art museum in Chicago. I hesitate at the room's threshold, uncertain if I should step closer toward the man in agony. There's something artificial, decidedly insincere about the way in which his limp body dangles from the metal grate there. It almost appears as though the whole scene—this crude, makeshift crucifixion—has been staged for my satisfaction, my enjoyment. If you could even call it enjoyment, that is.

Eventually, the poor man's eyes rise to meet mine, and he seems to soften slightly with the awareness of another who is similarly afflicted. He appears to thaw, looking at me, chapped lips parting to whisper something I cannot hear at first.

"Please," he mutters. "Untie me. . . ."

I hesitate once more—wondering if I've perhaps misheard him, wondering if I should actually touch the poor, worthless man and thinking that his misfortune could somehow contaminate me, poison me, pollute my very soul. I curse myself for thinking something so foolish. It's what others have thought of me since Jonathan passed away. Why do I think the same thing of others? I suppose all of us are afraid of eventually becoming contaminated.

Without another moment of hesitation, I grab hold of the cords securing his wrists behind his back, and I loosen them until they slip off. Once he's been freed from his captivity, I ease him off the metal grate where he's pinned, and I help him to the floor. He quivers slightly, and I notice his knees buckle, his body almost crashing forward and collapsing under his own weight. Too weak to carry on. I loop an arm around his shoulder, and I guide him toward the bed arranged in the center of the empty suite. He lies down on the bed, and I watch his chest rise and fall for a moment, thanking God that he's still alive despite his obvious distress. I circle the bed and admire him for a moment, thinking how unremarkable and how decidedly plain he looks. Despite the fact that he possesses certain bodily perfections I admire, I can't help but be disappointed by his looks. In fact, he looks so forgettable, so easy to be misremembered and then eventually abandoned to more pressing, more worthwhile thoughts. Even more curious, he slightly resembles the dreadful host from my dream. I shake my head. *It can't possibly be true. The dream wasn't real.* But still, there's a part of me that remains guarded. I'm reluctant to even help him—wondering if it could be true, hoping that I'm wrong.

"Do you need a doctor?" I ask him. "I can send for one. . . ."

But he will not respond to me. Instead, he lies there on the mattress, his breath shallow and ragged.

I'm about to step away and call for Clovis when the man on the bed rises to meet my attention. He swallows hard, gazing at me with an inquisitive, probing look.

"You recall the museum in Chicago?" he asks me. "The painting that Jonathan kept returning to. The one he stood in front of for an hour . . ."

Yes, of course I recall that painting. Naturally, I don't remember the exact details, but the man in front of me certainly reminded me of such a portrait—the terror in his eyes, the despair upon his trembling lips.

"Yes, I remember," I say to him gently, worried that my voice might upset something, might undo the trust I've already earned in the few moments I've been in his presence.

"It was his favorite," the man tells me. "He thought of it often. . . ."

Just then, as I look up, I notice a large mirror hanging over the bed arranged in the center of the empty suite. I see myself reflected there, but curiously enough, I do not see the man captured in the reflection. He's not there. I wave my hand gently and see it mirrored. But even as he stirs there at the edge of the large bed, there is no reflection of him. It's like he's invisible to all reflective surfaces—a wraith, some unkind phantom.

I ease away from him, fear spreading through me until I'm filled with it.

"Are you Porcelain Khaw?" I ask him.

"Yes," he answers.

I appreciate the fact that he does not hesitate to tell me. But I don't know whether that calms me or frightens me even more.

"You can help me see my Jonathan?" I ask, nervous of how he might respond.

He leans forward, extending his hand. "You have the artifact for me?"

I remember the photograph crinkling between my hands. I uncrumple it and then pass the picture to Porcelain, who takes it without comment, without thanks. I watch him study it for a moment, his eyes scanning every corner of the photograph as though he were looking for some fault, some kind of blemish or imperfection. Or rather, perhaps he's looking for an entrance, a portal to pass through, to collect the memory of my sweet, beloved Jonathan.

After a few minutes pass, Porcelain looks at me and orders me to completely undress. I squint at him, wondering if I've misheard what he said.

"You needn't worry," Porcelain tells me. "I won't make fun of the birthmark on your inner thigh."

I curl away from him, shocked that he knows such a thing about me. *How can he possibly know that?* I wonder to myself. But then again, I can't be too astonished. This is what I wanted, after all. I wanted magic. I wanted things that were not remotely possible to suddenly exist within the realm of actuality. Perhaps Porcelain is all of those things combined.

I undo my belt and let my pants slip from my waist. Porcelain watches me while I do this, appraising my every movement, my every gesture. It feels strange to have another man observe me while I undress. Of course, I've been naked with others since Jonathan passed. But those interactions were quick and rough—trembling hands lubed with spit, frowning mouths searching for secrets that will never be told, body parts dewy with sweat. This moment feels more thoughtful, more intimate, in fact. When I pull my shirt off and toss it on the floor, I half expect Porcelain to laugh at me the way other men might be amused by my lack of definition, my absence of muscle. I am no specimen of masculinity. That much is certain. That's why I struggle so terribly to be intimate with others, especially while the lights are still on.

Finally, after much hesitation, I peel off my underwear until I'm completely exposed—my shriveled cock dangling there and curtained by a wasp's nest of pubic hair. I wonder if Porcelain might shrink away at the sight of me completely undressed, utterly exposed. But he does no such thing. Instead, he pries his pants open, and his cock, wilted as well, flops out into the open. We are bare for one another, completely and utterly uninhibited.

Once we are both naked, Porcelain leans back against the pillows and beckons me to join him in the bed. I think twice about it, but there's a part of me that suddenly becomes acutely aware that he senses my indecision. I find myself being dragged toward the mattress by some invisible lasso. Eventually, I'm curled beside him—our naked bodies pressed together, our cocks touching and slowly beginning to arrive at full attention.

"I need you to offer me all of your resistance," he tells me.

I'm not quite sure what he means. After all, I've already taken off all my clothing, and I've climbed into bed with him. I don't quite know what else I could possibly offer him.

"You're resisting me," Porcelain says. "Don't. . . . Let yourself be free. . . ."

He orders me to close my eyes, and I obey. Just then, I sense his hands on my thigh. Then slowly crawling up my leg until they arrive at my waist. I feel his breath heating warm against my face. In a move that surprises me, he presses his mouth against mine, his tongue stabbing me and searching deep inside. I sense myself soften. It's been so long since I've felt this safe, this protected with another man. I would open myself for him—my body, my very soul. I would lie down on my back, grab hold of my ankles and let him slide deep inside me, until he was buried to the hilt and might never crawl out from inside me ever again.

I open my eyes. But I'm not greeted by Porcelain. Starlight flickers at the corners of my vision, so I rub my eyes just to be sure. *It can't possibly be. Is it? Is it actually true?*

Jonathan is staring back at me.

His dark brown eyes, his luscious dyed blond hair, his effervescent smile—all telltale signs of his presence, all things I could never forget no matter how much time we might be sentenced to spend apart.

I exhale sharply, shocked at the sight. I glance around and notice that we're no longer inside Porcelain's suite. Instead, we're lying in bed together at the apartment—the dim glow from the nearby television washing us in pale silver light, the sound of a Gershwin record playing from a distant room, the jasmine scent of Jonathan's expensive cologne that I bought for him for Christmas one year.

"Jonathan," I exhale, stifling some of my shock, my dismay.

He merely smiles at me with an invitation. I say nothing else. Instead, I leap at him—our naked bodies swaddling one another in a precious riddle of twisted limbs that could never quite be solved by another who did not fully comprehend our passion, our love, our devotion. Mouths devouring one another, Jonathan pulls me deeper into his embrace, and I wonder if I might slip farther into him. Our lovemaking had always felt like that—slowly dissolving into each other, melting gradually together like balls of wax until we are entwined, forever interwoven into the very fibers of our flesh. Never to be brought apart.

After what feels like hours of making love and taking turns fucking and sucking each other, Jonathan and I lie in the dim afterglow of our muted passion. Jonathan keeps an arm wrapped around me, and I sink farther into the crook of his armpit—inhaling his musk, savoring his scent. Just then, I sense dampness threatening in the corners of my eyes. I wipe the tears away, hoping Jonathan will not notice. But of course, he does. He was always so observant—perhaps even a little *suspicious*—like that.

"What's wrong?" he asks me.

"Nothing," I tell him, shaking my head.

But he throws me a look of dissatisfaction that I recognize all too well. I swallow, burying myself deeper into his embrace and hoping I might thread myself into his very skin.

"I—just . . . I never thought I'd see you again," I say to him. "I was prepared to live with only your memory for the rest of my life. . . ."

"And that's such a pity, my darling?" he asks me.

I shake my head. "I didn't want to live with only a memory. . . . I wanted *you*. . . . I've always wanted you."

"Sometimes we should be grateful for the memory," Jonathan says. "Our memories are often different from what actually happened. . . ."

But this time, his voice does not sound like his. Instead, it sounds watery, rotted almost.

I tilt my head at him. "Jonathan . . . ?"

“It’s time to go,” he tells me.

But I shake my head, grabbing hold of his face and pressing into his skin just to feel something, to feel *him*.

“I—can’t,” I whisper. “I don’t want to go. . . .”

“Ignore it,” he says.

I sense parts of myself unspooling, wondering if I heard him correctly.

“What did you say?” I ask.

“Ignore it, my love,” he says. *“Ignore it. . . .”*

I search him, desperately trying to comprehend what he means.

But as suddenly as I blink, I open my eyes and find myself returned to Porcelain’s bed inside the empty suite. Porcelain is staring at me with a look of concern, as if I’ve just made some horrible transgression, as if I’ve done something that can now never be undone. His lips part. He’s about to tell me something. But I do not wait for it. Instead, I crumple into his arms and begin to sob, wailing like some poor animal caught in a steel trap and about to be slaughtered by an approaching huntsman.

Porcelain does not say anything to me. He merely holds the back of my head and strokes my hair while I sob, occasionally whispering things to me that I cannot quite comprehend. I’m thankful for his kindness. It’s the first time I’ve been so lovingly touched by another man since Jonathan died. I forgot what the tenderness between two men in love felt like.

Eventually, I find myself being dragged from Porcelain’s embrace and being ferried down the corridor, away from the large, empty suite. I’m careful with my footing, afraid to squish any of the small beetles littering the cramped passageway and guarding Porcelain’s lair the way scarabs might guard a pharaoh's ancient tomb. I don't quite register who's dragging me away until we reach the entryway, and I glance up to notice Clovis idling there with a look of concern.

"You took longer than the time allotted," he barks at me, opening the pine box. He snatches my phone, and then shoves it at me.

"I'm sorry," I say to him, pocketing my cell.

I feel dizzy, weightless almost, as though all of my thoughts had been drained from a secret faucet hidden somewhere deep inside me.

"Is there anything else I need to do?" I ask Clovis, secretly hoping he might assign another task for me to properly complete the ritual. *Anything to stay here, any excuse to mindlessly dawdle in Porcelain's sacred presence.*

But Clovis shakes his head, instead motioning toward the door.

Very soon I'm at the home's threshold, glancing back at him, at the narrow, beetle-infested passageway weaving toward the closed door at the very end of the hall—the room where I was finally reunited with Jonathan, the portal to the sanctity of his memory. It feels almost impossible to look away, to remove myself from this place—this consecrated, hallowed home, this den of absolution, of unending grace and sympathy. How can I possibly turn my back and leave all of this behind?

"Well?" Clovis says, prompting me to leave.

I turn slightly, a bitter chill bracing me. "May I ask you something . . . ?"

Clovis throws a look of distrust at me, a sense of unease spreading across his expression. He appears irritated I would pester him with a question now, but I cannot allow my curiosity to go unsatiated.

"Has he always been like this?" I ask him. "Has he always had this power?"

Clovis turns slightly, almost as though he were upset that I was making the attempt to peer behind the curtain, to shed light upon the facade they've so expertly built, the dark magic they've invoked for the sake of those who are grieving and occupied with the agonizing rot of despair.

"Not always," Clovis tells me, pulling out a cigarette and lighting it. "When I first met him, he was sucking cock for a living. Turning tricks at a hostel in the city. Eating ramen noodles out of Styrofoam containers and getting high when he wasn't getting paid for fucking . . ."

It feels strange to realize that Porcelain had had an entire life before I encountered him this evening—a complex history, a dizzying mythology filled with other souls, other people. It feels especially sour to recognize the fact that Porcelain was once a prostitute, especially since he appeared so sophisticated, so elegant tonight when I first met him. Then again, I suppose the arrangement he's made with Clovis is not too dissimilar from a whore and a pimp. Still, it seems unnatural to think of Porcelain in such a way—to regard him as a usable good, something to be tried out and then discarded once it's no longer of service.

"Has he . . . always had this power?" I ask him.

Clovis shakes his head, displeased. "You ask too many questions."

He blows a wreath of smoke into my face, and I cover my nose, recoiling a bit from him.

"Please," I beg him. "Won't you tell me?"

Clovis sighs, crossing his arms. "He's had this—*power*—for as long as I've known him. . . . Even when he was a red-faced, sullen-looking young man eager to please others, too excited to be used. I never thought such a person could exist. . . . Some people are born to be used, I supposed. Their only purpose in this world is to serve others. . . . He didn't always know how to use the power properly. That skill came slowly, gently over time. . . . He taught me about it. I was just a young boy when I first met him, when he covered me in strawberry jelly and begged me to follow him around everywhere like some loyal dog. . . . I gladly submitted. . . . I would do anything for him. . . ."

I sense myself pale a little, my heartbeat racing. Surely he can't be the young boy from the story I read on that "Dream Warrior" forum. . . . *But what if he is?*

There's something strange about the way in which Clovis speaks of Porcelain—almost like a teenager struggling to remember or describe a loved one who abandoned them when they were smaller and more vulnerable. Even though I assumed Clovis to be the one calling the shots, it feels like Porcelain possesses a significant hold over the poor man—a measly puppet to be paraded, hurt, displayed for the sake of amusement. Does Clovis mind this? I cannot be certain.

"You care for him, don't you?" I ask.

Clovis's attention snaps to me, and he stares at me long enough to make the moment feel uncomfortable and sour.

"I—love him with my entire being," he answers. "I always have . . . always will. . . . How could I not? He still owns me in many ways. . . ."

I think to ask another question, but Clovis appears like he might pull away from me at any moment. I don't want to risk insulting Porcelain while I'm here. Still, I cannot help but wonder if it is a difficult thing, a maddening kind of tension to love a person and know that they will never be able to love you fully and completely in return.

"Will you . . . please thank him for me?" I ask him.

Clovis says nothing. Instead, he stares at me with a vacant kind of expression—the same kind of horrible look of indifference that Porcelain practiced when we were first in bed together.

I shudder a little, hoping Clovis might now offer a small word of comfort, a modicum of consideration. But there's none to be had from him. Perhaps I should have expected this. He doesn't resemble the kind of person who might offer tenderness when it's explicitly needed. Instead, he looks like someone whose only language is violence, the brutality of those who suffer, who come here destitute and in dire need. I suppose that was me not too long ago. I suppose that's still me to some extent.

I pry myself from where I'm standing at the house's threshold, and I begin to make my way down the path toward the driveway where I parked my car. I hear the door slam shut behind me as I walk, but I do not turn back. There's a part of me that, of course, wants to look, wants to see the locked entryway—the shuttered portal to my love, my misery, my despair. But there's a part of me that worries I might be turned to a pillar of salt if I glance back, if I make any attempt to look behind me while I try to move forward, to carry on.

Eventually, I reach my car, and I climb in the driver's seat. I sit still for a moment, wondering if I'm even capable of driving right now. There's still a part of me that feels as though I'm trapped in that suite with Porcelain, cradled in his arms, sobbing hysterically while he strokes my hair and whispers affirmations to soothe my restless spirit.

Just as I'm about to push the keys into the ignition, my cell phone begins to hum. I glance at the screen and notice it's an incoming call from Kent. I slide my finger across the screen and hold the phone to my ear.

"Hey."

"Has it happened yet?" Kent asks me, his voice greeting me on the other end of the line.

I whimper a little, completely involuntarily. Whether it's from the excitement or the memory of what's transpired, I cannot be wholly certain.

"I just left," I tell him.

"How was it?"

I swallow nervously, unsure what to say. Naturally, I know full well he knows the extent of Porcelain's powers and the things one must do in order to complete the ritual; however, there's something about the aftermath, the moments following the ritual that feel so private, so decidedly intimate. I feel grotesque to divulge them.

"It was amazing," I tell him, trying to play coy and be as calm as possible.

"Of course it was," he says. "I knew you two would get along famously. . . . Did you—see Jonathan?"

I sense tears beading in the corners of my eyes, my fingers trembling while I hold the phone to my ear.

"I—held him," I say to Kent, my voice breaking apart. "It felt like how it used to be. . . . The two of us . . ."

"How do you feel?" he asks me.

I hesitate, unsure how to properly answer. In fact, I don't quite know how I feel. It felt euphoric to idle in Jonathan's presence once more—to inhale his scent, to taste his sweat, to fuck him mercilessly. But now that it's over, everything else feels so hollow, so decidedly muted and dull. When I was with Jonathan, everything surrounding me seemed to vibrate in Technicolor. But now everything appears so dimmed, so colorless and dismal.

"I don't really know," I tell him, hoping he might understand what I mean.

He stammers on the other end of the line, uncertain.

"I want to do it again," I say to Kent. "I need to see him again. . . ."

There's a long beat of silence, like Kent isn't quite sure what I've said, what I've actually confessed.

If Porcelain is a kind of drug—stimulant, treatment, *whatever*—then I want to be consumed, I yearn to be destroyed by all the wonders, all the enchantments he can possibly show me.

Chapter Eleven

When you're gay, the whole world wants to annihilate you. In fact, it takes pleasure in doing so.

There's something inherently dangerous about existing as a queer person—dwelling comfortably outside the confines of what it means to be normal, typical—about coupling with the same sex, and, even worse, being prideful about what should instead be shamed, what should be punished. I think of this often, especially during late-night drives around town when I feel particularly restless, when I cannot find peace even in my sleep. I sense myself overwhelmed with the thought that others wish me dead, others want me executed for the atrocity of my preferences. Even our own bodies betray us, unable to accommodate our perversions—how they eventually fruit with disease, how they rupture as if it were adequate punishment for our transgressions against the natural order of things.

As I drive home from the outskirts of town where I met with Porcelain, I find myself truly thinking about myself—my sexuality in particular. For me, it's always felt as though I've existed as a nuisance, something to be squished or snuffed out because of my perversions, my carnal crimes against nature. It seems strange that I might think like this, that I might be so self-loathing and despise so much of my identity. It's not as if my parents were vehemently against my coming out as a gay man. In fact, my father told me he had always suspected it and was glad that I had finally confessed the truth to him. Of course, he would hint from time to time that my life might be easier if I wasn't gay; however, I couldn't argue that I disagreed with him. I knew exactly what he meant. The truth is—I know my circumstances would be so different if I had continued to pretend to be straight, if I had pretended to prefer the companionship of women as opposed to my natural affection toward men. It often feels as though the world wishes to devour me. Or perhaps, at the very least, devour parts of me, so that I'm crippled, so that I'm incapable of existing as a content, free, and joyful spirit. The world would rather destroy us than let us be free.

Just as I'm about to exit the highway and pull onto the street where my apartment building is located, a memory thuds into my mind and shrieks to be noticed, to be remembered. It's something I had forgotten about. I don't quite know how or why I had neglected the memory for so long; however, the recollection seems to pulse with urgency, vibrating in my thoughts like it had been ladled there by some invisible force—something that desperately wanted me to remember this otherwise forgotten moment. It's a memory of Jonathan and of a young man we once met at a bar. Jonathan struck up a conversation with the man, probably smitten with the tightness of his T-shirt or the fact that he was wearing a baseball cap embroidered with the name of some female pop star Jonathan had once admired. We talked for hours at the bar, buying one another drinks and exchanging stories of life in the city.

Before long, we were headed back to our apartment with the young man in tow—our personal prize for the evening, our fuckable reward. The memory of the night crisps and sizzles hot in my mind, shrinking and blackening like a shred of paper held over an open flame. When I'm about to give up on remembering anything else, I recall the sight of Jonathan spread out on his back and the young man from the bar mounting him. I had curled myself into the far corner of the bedroom, watching everything with an open mouth from an armchair near the television set. I recall how I observed Jonathan while he was being fucked by the young man—his whole body tensing at every pulse, his soft whimpers while he stroked his own cock. Then I remember something else I had forgotten—how my eyes and Jonathan's met. He looked directly at me, the young man grabbing hold of his throat and squeezing tight while he pushed more of himself inside my beloved Jonathan. Our eye contact held only for a few moments. But in that time, Jonathan whispered something to me. Something I had completely forgotten.

"Ignore it," he said gently. *"Ignore it. . . . Ignore it. . . ."*

I struggle to remember more, but nothing else makes its presence known to me. I can't seem to think of anything while I grip the steering wheel, aiming the car from the highway and ambling down the exit ramp onto a side street.

I shake my head, wondering how I could have forgotten such a thing. I'm afraid I can't be certain. In the moment, I recall being excited, being fully erect at the sight of another man making love to my husband. But now, even more distanced from the event, I wonder if that excitement has been replaced with a feeling of sadness, of incurable pity. Not only for me, but for Jonathan as well. Of course, he wanted to fuck that young man. He yearned for him, begged me to allow it. I agreed, naturally. *But why did he want to fuck that young man so desperately? Why did he want to share our marriage bed with another person? Had he grown tired of me? Was he feeling particularly restless or ravenous that evening?* These are questions I'll never be able to answer unless I meet with Porcelain again.

I sense myself shudder at such a realization, understanding the simple fact that Porcelain holds so much power over me, over the memory of my sweet Jonathan.

It isn't long before I arrive at my apartment building's parking garage. I steer the car through the double bay doors and aim for an empty parking spot located near the stairwell. My mind races even as the car slows. Naturally, I think of Jonathan. *Ignore it?* I wonder if I could possibly be misremembering the night, if I've somehow added other elements from different recollections. *Am I even remembering Jonathan correctly? Or is there a point when the memory of a loved one begins to shrivel and rust, all facets of their identity dissolving away to be forgotten?*

I park the car and sit in the driver's seat for a few minutes. The radio hisses an old Irving Berlin song at me, and I twist the dial, turning the volume down so I can think properly. I wince, alone with my thoughts, and I sense a pang of worry stab me in the center of my chest like a small needle. It's something I didn't consider before, and it causes me to shudder when I really and truly consider it.

Monogamy doesn't exist. It's a deception invented by men and women that gay people are incapable of properly imitating. This is a thought that comes to me time and time again, especially when I'm asked to visit Carter at the park with Evelyn. She calls me early in the morning and asks if I might be willing to join them in the park before school starts. I feel a pang of guilt for not checking in with her more regularly, even though I promised her I would. I feel even worse for making these hollow, formless assurances to poor, sweet Carter and breaking those guarantees almost every chance I get.

It seems as though I yearn for him to loathe me, to despise me and the life I've chosen over him and his mother. But, for whatever reason, he will not hate me. Instead, he seems to crave my attention, often shouting at me to watch him while he skates on the ramp or when he performs a trick in midair. Still, as I watch him skate on the board we purchased for him last Christmas, I'm filled with the horrible thought: committed, untainted love between two people cannot and will never truly exist. It's impossible to love solely one person—to claim them as yours, to belong to them in a way that makes you content to not seek out others for similar companionship.

I glance at Evelyn while she scrolls on her phone, adjusting her sunglasses and dodging some of the sunlight trickling through the thin canopy of trees overhead. I think of whether or not monogamy might have been truly possible with her some time ago. Perhaps it's easier for men and women to commit themselves fully to each other. It's different when you're queer, especially for gay men. A blow job is more like a handshake as opposed to some sacred sexual act between committed partners. Of course, anal sex might be reserved for a more trusted, more dependable partner. Regardless, it's so easy to submit yourself to someone else for the sake of pleasure, for a few moments of relief.

As I observe Carter while he skates across the half-pipe, I wonder if I've fucked up my life to the point where nothing is salvageable. Perhaps I've reached the end of the road. Perhaps there's nothing left for me after this. Even though I truly loved Jonathan and built my whole world around him, I wonder if it was the right choice. *Was I a monster for leaving Evelyn with a brand-new baby boy to take care of? Did I make a mistake that can never be undone?* If I had suppressed my urges, my more carnal desires, I might not be wasting away, tirelessly mourning the memory of a man who I have already begun to forget. It's strange to admit, but after meeting with Porcelain, I've come to realize that there are so many things about Jonathan that I do not remember. Whether or not I've chosen to banish those memories from my mind for my own safety, for my own preservation, I cannot be absolutely certain.

"Parent-teacher conferences at school are next week," Evelyn says to me, wrenching me from the fetid swamp of my contemplations. "Would you like to join?"

I hesitate a little. It's the first time she's asked me to attend. Probably not because she didn't want me there previously, but rather because she wasn't certain if I even cared.

"You want me to come?" I ask her, just to be totally certain.

"Of course," she tells me. "I've always wanted you to be there. . . . I just wasn't sure if—"

"I know," I say, cutting her off. I don't want her to confirm what I've always suspected—the monster I've become over time. "I'd love to come. . . ."

Evelyn smiles a little, seeming to soften, as if not only impressed, but comforted by my promise as well. Just then, I feel a little tremor aching in the very center of my chest—a horrible reminder that I'm a cheater, that I'm an expert when it comes to breaking promises and hurting loved ones.

My attention drifts away from Evelyn, and I find myself gazing at Carter while he skates from one end of the elevated platform to the other. I notice Evelyn check her wristwatch and then make a comment about how they're going to be late for breakfast with her parents at a nearby diner. I pray she doesn't ask me to join them for that visit. Evelyn's parents have hated my guts since I first came out, since I broke their daughter's heart and abandoned her for the company of other men. I'm sure Evelyn knows this and wouldn't ask me to join. But still, there's a part of her that seems so excited, so overjoyed to rekindle the relationship we once shared. I wouldn't put it past her to ask me.

"Carter, come on," she shouts to our son. "We're going to be late. Nanny and Poppy are waiting for us. . . ."

Carter's attention snaps to us, and I suddenly shudder when I notice something strange about his eyes. I can't quite tell if it's because of the sunlight reflecting off the jungle gym equipment, but the boy's eyes look shiny and almost mirrorlike. I wince, ambling forward and struggling to block out more of the light so I can see my son properly. His eyes are like identical silver orbs—the very same glittering pieces of metal I saw in that awful wooden figure of Christ in the recreation hall. I swallow nervously, wondering if my mind is playing tricks on me, if I've been tricked by the light.

"What is it, Dad?" Carter asks me, removing his helmet and brushing the hair from his face. His reflective eyes slowly open and close like a mechanical device.

I shake my head, hoping to fling the horrible sight from my vision—Carter's open mouth in constant question, my bemused reflection caught forever in his sparkly, mirrorlike eyes.

Evelyn seems to sense my distress almost immediately. She tugs on my shirtsleeve.

"Is everything okay?" she asks me. "Something wrong?"

I inch closer toward the apron of artificial greenery where the skateboard area begins, and I sense Carter shrinking farther and farther away as I begin to approach.

I blink again, and, without warning, Carter's eyes are normal once more. They are no longer the glossy and reflective little bits of glass I once feared. I sense myself heave with a semblance of relief, the bile slowly retreating down into the back of my throat.

"Simeon," Evelyn says to me, tugging on my sleeve once more. "What is it? Is there something wrong?"

"No," I say quietly, even though I don't entirely believe myself. "Nothing's wrong. . . ."

For the first time ever in my life, I wonder if I can truly trust the people I love, the ones who are supposed to care for me.

I wait a few days before calling Kent on the phone. I don't want to seem too eager even though I am, even though I'm desperate to reconnect with Porcelain in any way possible. Naturally, I wonder if I can actually trust Kent, if I can truly depend upon him in my time of need. But my desire, my unbearable ache to meet with Porcelain again, outweighs any semblance of indecision or apprehension about contacting him. Unfortunately, I can already hear Kent becoming disinterested with me—his tone softening with a queer kind of indifference, his responses becoming more and more lethargic-sounding. I know for certain that he's growing tired of me, that we're perhaps well past the expiration date for our relationship, our connection. Still, I continue to press him.

"Well, what do you think?" I ask him again and again—hoping his tone might change, praying that he might sound more interested, more invested in everything I've done.

"I don't know if Clovis will go for it," he tells me. "Most people only go to Porcelain once and that's it. He's never mentioned a repeat visitor. . . ."

"You think it's out of the question?" I ask him.

Kent sighs heavily. I can tell he's becoming frustrated, vexed by the very thought of continuing this talk of Porcelain Khaw.

"Try it and see what happens," he says. "It's a pity it didn't work the first time. . . ."

When we hang up, I realize that he's right—it *is* a pity that the whole ordeal didn't take root the very first time I connected with Porcelain. Then again, I certainly wouldn't be returning to him if I felt uninspired, unmotivated to come to terms with my memories of Jonathan. In fact, perhaps our first time together was almost too perfect. Perhaps we achieved something that very few clients experience while in his presence. Naturally, it was euphoric to rekindle the spark that Jonathan and I once shared—to make love to him, to taste him, to savor him. Then again, so much of our lovemaking felt so new and exciting, almost like I were coupling with a stranger. It's then I wonder if Porcelain's essence is present at all during those rituals, if he's able to peer in on our private lovemaking. *Was I enraptured with the memory of Jonathan? Or rather, was I excited to make love to something as alluring, as intoxicating as Porcelain Khaw?*

At the moment, I cannot be certain.

I flick my fingers across my phone screen, and I thumb my way to Clovis's cell number listed in my contacts. I press down on the number and hold the phone to my ear, waiting for a response. Finally, after what feels like hours, he answers.

"Yes . . . ?"

"It's Simeon," I tell him. "I hope I'm not calling at a bad time. . . ."

Clovis grunts.

"I won't be coy or pretend that I'm calling about something else when I'm not," I say to him. "I'd like to see Porcelain again. . . . Whenever he's available . . ."

There's a long pause on the other end of the line, almost as though Clovis is struggling to think of a way to respond.

"The ritual only takes place one time," he says. "You didn't get your fill when you were last here?"

"Yes, I know," I respond. "I was hoping you might make an exception for me. Especially if I'm willing to pay extra . . ."

"It may not work a second time," he tells me, exhaling heavily. "You should know that."

"I don't care. . . . I want to try it. Surely you're okay with that? I won't ask for the money back if it doesn't work. . . ."

Clovis's breath shudders while he breathes hard into the receiver.

"Come tomorrow night," he tells me. "Bring another item of sentimental value. . . ."

Before I can respond to tell him that I'll be there, the line disconnects. I set my phone aside, get undressed, and then slip into the bathroom to take my morning shower. When I idle in front of the washroom mirror, I'm reminded of something I had forgotten—a memory I once shared with Jonathan. I recall how we once took an art class at the local university. Jonathan was always so much more gifted, so much more skilled in artistry than I ever was. I was a poor imitation—a soulless, inexpressive effigy—whenever it came to creating original pieces, inventive artwork. Still, there's a memory I cannot shake while I gaze at my naked body in the mirror.

I recall the class instructor once told us about how certain things are reflected closely to one another, especially in nature. For instance, when you look at a painting of a lakefront cottage framed in front of a sunset, you'll notice how the small building is reflected almost immediately in the nearby water. That, of course, made me think more of Jonathan—how easy it once was for me to imitate his eccentricities, his very personality. So much of my personality, my entire being was comprised of things I observed from Jonathan, little peculiarities I could mimic. But now that he's gone, I sense that reflection growing dimmer each and every day. The two of us are no longer standing on some distant shore, our reflections flickering at us on the water's iridescent surface. It's impossible to reflect something, *someone*, when you're so far apart. Because of that, is it impossible to truly love someone who you might never see again? I ache to see myself reflected in Jonathan—to exist close enough to see pieces of myself bleeding into his character, his very temperament. God, I wish we were a painting—a moment caught in time, a love captured on canvas and immortal.

While I idle there in front of the bathroom mirror, I think of Porcelain and realize how he's become a sort of fun-house mirror for both me and Jonathan—a portal for us to comfortably view each other.

While I laze in bed with Jonathan—Porcelain's spirit, his essence, his energy loitering somewhere on the periphery of our dimly lit bedroom—I can't help but think of how making love is one of the few times when I truly feel like a man. Jonathan always preferred me to be more dominant, while he accepted a more submissive, quieter role in our lovemaking sessions. At first, I had felt so out of sorts, so out of place ass-fucking him and treating him like some object to be ravaged, defiled, and then abandoned. But that's what he adored. He cherished the more aggressive, the more animalistic forms of lovemaking where pain was a common language, and refusal to obey meant punishment, the exquisite thrill of agony.

The truth is this—*I don't often feel like a man.* I feel like some kind of gruesome pastiche, some horrible joke on the pathway toward true masculinity. Whether it was my upbringing in rural Connecticut or my introduction to gay life in my late thirties, I remain totally uncertain. There's something about Jonathan that makes me feel feral, that causes me to tremor and awakens some kind of longing, yearning deep inside me—the kind of lust that defines a true man.

I slip farther into his embrace, gripping hold of his broad shoulders. His skin is damp, wet like he was freshly showered. I guide my curious tongue along his neck, and I taste the rankness of his sweat, the dew of his masculinity. Together, we are feral beasts—impossible to be captured, inevitable that we eventually destroy each other with our passion, our force.

While I idle there, I realize I don't quite recall how we arrived in our bed in the first place. Our lovemaking seemed to have erased so much of my memory, my recollection of the evening before I undressed, before I teased him with the prospect of physical intimacy before finally making good on such a promise. But as I struggle to remember, I soon recall how I delivered one of Jonathan's combs to Porcelain earlier this same night—how he regarded the artifact with such reverence and closed his eyes, breathing deep and inhaling what little he could of Jonathan's curdled memory. Then it wasn't long before I was face-to-face with my precious Jonathan once more, drowning in his embrace, suckling from him like a newborn as though my very life force depended upon him, his passion, his sustenance.

"Do you remember one of the first times we made love?" I ask Jonathan.

I sense his shriveled cock pressing limply against my thigh, rubbing me. I sniff the air, our bodily odors circulating there with a horrible foulness that arouses me and makes me quiver all at once.

"Which time?" he asks.

"When I made us reenact one of my favorite paintings," I say, tracing a line across his firm chest from one stiffened nipple to the other.

Jonathan laughs, amused. "Caravaggio, wasn't it . . . ?"

"*David with the Head of Goliath,*" I reply.

I sigh, recalling the very night when I asked him to humor me—to situate his chin on the edge of the small table arranged in the corner of our hotel room so that he appeared like he was some disembodied head. I recall how I stripped completely naked and then dressed myself in white linens from the nearby closet, swiping the hair dryer from the bathroom to use as my sword.

"You asked if you could behead me," Jonathan says, pecking me on the cheek with a small kiss. "To make everything look more authentic."

"You said I looked handsome in the robes I wore," I remind him.

"You mean the cheap hotel bedsheets?" he asks, giggling.

I press against him. Harder this time, hoping he senses my erection stabbing his belly button a little. He doesn't seem to react to it. Instead, he rakes his head back against the pillows and stretches his arms, exposing the hair in both of his pits. I do everything I can to prevent myself from burying my face there, inhaling his musk.

"You said it was a perfect night," I tell him.

I glance at Jonathan and notice that he's softened considerably, looking almost wilted somehow. His eyelids lower; his mouth pulls downward in an obvious frown that seems like an insult to his beauty, his poise. I suddenly guard myself, worried that he might say something that will undo the dream we've been allowed only because of Porcelain.

"I said a lot of things when we were together," he tells me, his voice hollow and rotted almost.

I peel apart from him, wondering what I could possibly say. I've imagined the two of us together for so long, it feels unnatural to say something that doesn't feel scripted or meticulously prepared in some way.

"Why do you keep coming back to me?" he asks.

I'm surprised he would ask something so callous, so cruel. *Is this him talking, or is it Porcelain?*

"Because I love you," I tell him, stirring with such discomfort. "Isn't it obvious?"

But Jonathan shakes his head. "You come here with everything prepared. Everything you want to say—so carefully rehearsed . . . What's the point of any of it?"

I sense myself shudder slightly. Of course, I don't want to admit that he's right, but there's a part of me that must understand what he's saying. What's the good of any of this if I'm not allowed to lower my guard, to let myself simply be the way we once were? Why must everything be so perfect in his presence? *The answer is simple,* I think to myself. *I want him to love me more than he did when he was alive.*

"When you loved me, were you merely reflecting bits of me

because we were so close?" I ask him, surprised at myself for asking something so impulsive, so unprepared. "Was it like a kind of reflection you knew that I desperately wanted to see?"

Jonathan stirs, sitting up in bed and dragging the sheets off him until he's exposed.

"Is that something you truly want me to answer?" he asks.

I do not hesitate. I nod.

Jonathan inhales sharply and then exhales, preparing for something unpleasant. *Yes, indeed,* I think to myself. *Something truly unpleasant is on the way.*

"I'm afraid you're misremembering me," he says. "I never talked like this. You mention things we did that I do not remember. . . . I cannot remember them, because they never happened. . . ."

I sense tears threatening to curl in the corners of my eyes.

"That's not true," I say to him. "They happened. . . . You said those things to me. . . ."

But Jonathan still doesn't appear convinced. He drags himself out of bed, pulling farther away from me, and then begins to pace the floor like some sort of captured beast.

"Have you ever heard of something called a reverse haunting?" he asks me.

I shake my head.

"It's when the living won't let the dead rest," he says. "There are no such things as ghosts, Simeon. . . . You're the one keeping me alive. You're the one haunting *me*. . . ."

I clear my throat, my esophagus burning like ash and feeling as though it might seal shut.

"That's not true," I say, shaking my head in some kind of feeble attempt to hurl the accusation out of my mind.

Jonathan's expression appears to sour. He throws me a horrible scowl that feels as though it might rot me from the inside out.

"Ignore it," he tells me gently. *"Ignore it. Ignore it. . . ."*

But before I can respond, I'm suddenly delivered back to Porcelain's suite—the large bed framed in the center of the room, the mirror on the ceiling. I recognize Porcelain at once. He quivers a little when he notices me, severed from his trance, and I can't help but notice a small dark line of blood creeping from one of his nostrils.

"You're hurt," I tell him, pointing at his nose.

He dabs a finger there, wiping some of the blood away. Not all of it, of course. There are still some remnants lingering there, and he resembles some kind of predator who has just fed, just savored a fresh kill.

"I want to go again," I say to him. "Please?"

But Porcelain waves me away like a lover who's already been drained and satisfied.

"Not tonight," he tells me. "I'm spent. . . ."

I swallow nervously. "Soon, though . . . ?"

Porcelain does not answer me. Instead, he turns over on his side and begins to sleep. I watch him for a moment like a nervous mother observing a dozing infant before I dress quickly and then sneak out of the room, sprinting down the hallway littered with beetles and finally out the front door.

There's something that troubles me terribly while I undress in front of the bathroom mirror in my apartment—a horrible, nagging thought that won't be silenced no matter how much I strain to overwhelm the idea, to drag it screaming from the gutter of my mind and pinch it between my fingers until it's squished. *Have I actually misremembered moments I thought I had once experienced with Jonathan? Is he telling me the truth? Or rather, am I instead forced to endure a replica, a crude imitation of Jonathan fed through the mind of Porcelain Khaw?* It's concerning to be met with the possibility that you might not be remembering the person you once loved with correctness, with absolute authenticity. *Has my mind been playing tricks on me?*

I idle in front of the washroom mirror, gazing at my naked body—the lines forming around my mouth, the small marks wrinkling near the corners of my eyes. When I twist the sink faucet, the water sputters cold and then hardens with heat. I splash a handful of water into my face—as if it were a last resort, as if it were the only thing that could possibly wake me up from this nightmare. But it does nothing to calm me, to stir me from my miserable state.

Fuck, I think to myself while my stomach spirals itself into impossible little knots. There's every possibility that Porcelain Khaw is reflecting inaccuracies at me when I'm with him—horrible misinterpretations of Jonathan filtered through the lens of his mind, the many people he's already attempted to help. There's every risk that he's become polluted, that he's been burdened with so much sorrow, so much heartache that it's somehow warped his abilities. Perhaps he's only able to reflect my fears, my worries. I find myself softening when I think of that possibility. That's somehow easier to stomach. Still, there's also a decent chance that Porcelain is reflecting the truth to me—something I've always desperately yearned to avoid.

We reflect what we are near.

Just as I'm about to creep into the shower stall, I sense a dull ache heating in the pit of my stomach. My legs begin to quiver, and I worry I'll lose my balance, so I grab hold of the sink to properly brace myself. The pain continues to throb behind my belly button, and it seems to thrum harder and harder the more I struggle to ignore it. In fact, the agony becomes so unbearable that I wonder if I'll faint—if my knees will give out and I'll be sent crashing to the tiled floor before all goes black. *Who will find me?* I wonder to myself. *Will anyone come looking for me?* That's the trouble with living on your own. It's a prison sentence of isolation that could be ended at any moment for any minor transgression.

The pain in my belly button feels as though it's spreading, curling, coiling deeper inside me—like a small child's hand raking itself through my guts, my very innards. I gaze down at my belly button and notice a dark line of red drooling from the small opening and crawling farther down toward my nest of pubic hair. I push my index finger inside my navel, and the hole feels slick, greased and oily with a trail of blood. While I push my finger deeper inside me, I sense something curled at the end of the narrow passage. Something sharp. *What is it? What can it be?* Its edges are serrated and uneven, crude almost. I push my thumb and index finger into the hole this time and pinch the tiny object corkscrewed at the end of the belly button's cramped passage.

When I finally pull the object out and gaze at it, I nearly don't believe what I'm seeing, what I'm holding between my fingers—a small broken piece of reflective glass. One side is blank; the other is smooth and mirrorlike. I wipe the beads of blood dewing on the shard of glass and pull it closer toward me, expecting to see my horrified reflection captured there and mocking me with a look of bewilderment, of blind terror. But I don't. Instead, I see Jonathan's face staring at me. It takes me a moment, but it's not long before I realize that it's of a memory I had forgotten—a memory of one of the last nights we spent together before he left me.

"What would you do if we had a baby together?" I asked him.

He regarded me with such puzzlement, his eyebrows furrowing and his lip pulling down.

"A baby?" he asked me. "What makes you think we'd be good enough to raise a child?"

"You don't want to have a baby with me?" I pressed him, trying to corner him.

He thought for a moment, the silence and stillness lingering over the room nearly destroying me.

"I suppose we could name him Spot," he said, smiling.

"Why Spot?" I asked, apprehensive to fully understand his reason.

"Because he would be a dark stain on the both of us," Jonathan said. "A dark stain on me. Something I would eventually regret . . . Just like you . . ."

I hesitated, his words tipping daggers deeper and deeper into the hollow spaces he had already opened between my shoulder blades—the invisible blood welling up in strange little patterns he might have use for if he were attempting to tell the future.

"You regret me?" I asked, my voice quivering.

"Perhaps I should call you Spot," he said, swiping a jacket from the coatrack beside our apartment door. "You certainly have the face for it."

I watched him while he shoved both arms into his sleeves and scrambled to dip his feet into his winter boots.

"Where are you going?" I asked him.

"Out, *Spot*," Jonathan said. "You don't know by now?"

"Why do you keep leaving at night?"

He turned to me, his eyes narrowing to mere slits.

"You want me to say it, don't you, *Spot*?" Jonathan asked.

"Stop calling me that," I said to him, my voice brittle and thin.

"Because I like to forget about you," he said to me. Ever so gently. Like he was reciting items from his shopping list. "I like to head out at night. Walk around the city. Pretend we're not together . . . I like to forget I'm married to you. . . ."

I closed my eyes, hoping to shut off the tears I could already sense that were forming there behind my eyelids.

"Why?" I asked him.

"You ask me this all the time, *Spot*," he said to me. "I tell you the same things day after day. . . . You know what you do? *Ignore it. Ignore it. Ignore it. . . .*"

"That's not true," I said to him.

But just then, the memory dims from the shard of splintered glass I'm holding—a bright light flickering for an instant and then the mirrorlike surface going dark. It's not long before I'm left standing there, staring at my own reflection.

I can't bear the thought of being left alone tonight—being isolated with my thoughts, left to idle here in my misery, my despair. I toss the piece of glass into the sink, and I hear it clink softly before skating around the bowl and then tinkling down the drain, disappearing from my sight. I rush into the bedroom, and I grab my cell phone on the nightstand. I thumb through my list of contacts until I arrive at Evelyn's name. I hold down on her number and call her phone. The line begins to buzz softly. Finally, she picks up.

"Yes . . . ?"

"Can you come over tonight?" I ask her.

She hesitates a little. I can sense her astonishment even when I can't actually see her.

"Is something wrong?" she says, the sound of her breath heating the mouthpiece.

"Please," I beg her. "Please come. . . ."

An hour or so passes, and my door alarm buzzes. I make my way from the bedroom into the living area, sprinting toward the entryway. I pull the door open, and Evelyn, her face flushed with color, greets me at the threshold. Part of me wondered if she might bring Carter with her, but I'm relieved to find she's arrived unaccompanied. As much as it pains me to admit, I do not wish to see my son right now.

"Simeon," she sighs, passing across the threshold and moving farther into the apartment. "What's the matter? You sounded hurt on the phone. . . ."

I close the door and follow her into the kitchen. She looks around the empty room, almost disturbed to find that nobody else is present with me.

"There's nobody here," she says so matter-of-factly.

What exactly did she expect? I wonder to myself.

"Why would anybody else be here?" I ask.

"I don't know," she says, pushing her car keys into her handbag. "It sounded like you were here with someone. . . . Like something was wrong. . . ."

"I don't feel well," I mutter, leaning against the kitchen door frame for support.

Evelyn seems to recognize my uneasiness and immediately comes to my side, propping me up with one arm and looping the other arm around my shoulder.

"You look pale," she says, guiding me into the living room and eventually depositing me on the nearby sofa. "Did you eat something bad?"

"Haven't eaten in a while," I tell her.

She presses her hand against my forehead and then pulls away at once, surprised.

"You feel feverish," she says.

"I didn't call you over to act like my mother," I tell her, waving her away and hoping she'll retreat some.

Evelyn squints at me, obviously unsure what to say at first.

"Why did you call for me?" she asks.

I swallow. I can sense my throat closing around the words. "I wanted to know something . . . from someone I trust. . . ."

Evelyn sits on the sofa beside me. She appears to thaw slightly, visibly pleased with the idea that I trust her, that I would lean on her for such comfort, such care.

"Yes . . . ?"

"Do you think Jonathan loved me?" I ask her.

I notice how immediately her face begins to whiten, her lips pulling downward and her eyebrows furrowing with such concern.

"What?" she asks me.

"I need to know from someone else," I tell her. "My memory can't be trusted anymore. . . . Do you think Jonathan actually loved me? Do you think he wanted to build a life with me?"

But before I can ask another question, Evelyn wrenches herself from where she's seated on the sofa and crosses her arms.

"Jesus Christ," she exhales. "That's why you called me? I came all the way across town just to talk about Jonathan?"

I sense parts of myself bending, twisting with shame. I lower my eyes. "I didn't think you minded talking about Jonathan. . . ."

"You think I find pleasure in talking about the man who stole you from me?" she asks.

"He didn't steal me away. I went willingly," I tell her, straightening from where I'm lying. "Besides, I thought you were over what happened between us. . . ."

"You think it's so easy to forget?" she asks me. "I wish I could. . . ."

I draw in a deep breath. I know I've hurt Evelyn. I know I've already destroyed any chance for peace between the two of us. But I can't let my memory of Jonathan dim any further. It's the only thing that's keeping me alive, keeping me tethered together.

"I need to know what you think," I tell her. "Do you think he actually loved me?"

"That's the only reason you called for me?" she asks, her voice quivering with the inevitable possibility of such despair, such heartache.

I'm still not quite sure why she might be so upset, so despondent, to visit and answer a fairly simple question.

"Why else would you think I'd call for you?" I ask.

It's then that I notice tears webbing in the corners of her eyes, a deluge about to erupt and sweep the both of us away.

"I—thought you wanted to tell me something," she says softly.

It's then I understand the horrible truth of what she means, what she's after.

"You thought I was going to call you over here to tell you something?" I ask. "What? That I love you?"

Evelyn turns away from me, her cheeks heating bright red with a familiar look of humiliation.

"You know that wouldn't be true," I tell her. "I still care about you. . . . But it's not something that could be called love. . . ."

Evelyn smears the dampness from her eyes with an index finger.

"What about Carter?" she asks.

"What about him?"

"Do you love him?" she says to me.

"How can you ask me that?" I ask. "Of course, I love him. . . ."

She stares at me for a moment, silence filling the space between us.

"But you could never love me," she says, her voice quivering a little. "Why?"

I don't answer her for a moment. What's there to say? What could I possibly tell her that she doesn't already know?

"Am I nothing more than a *spot* on your memory?" she asks me. "Is that what I am?"

I notice how her hands are tightening, curling into fists like she's about to make good use of them on me.

"That's not true," I tell her, hoping that what little comfort I'm willing to offer might be enough for her.

Of course, it's not.

"Tell me," she says. "Why won't you love me?"

But there's nothing I can say. There's no explanation I can possibly offer that might make sense to her right now—that might make sense to someone so blinded, so irreparably broken and desperate to receive love from another. I sense my lips parting slightly, words clogging in the pit of my throat. All the wrong words, naturally. None of them are correct. None of them would soothe her, would relax her the way she needs to be calmed.

"I just don't," I finally tell her. "You can't make another person love you. . . . Surely you must know that. . . ."

Evelyn stares at me for a moment, her eyes mechanically opening and closing like that of a child's doll when a cord on her back is pulled. After a while, she gathers her things and makes her way toward the entryway. I call after her, trailing close behind. But nothing I say can possibly stop her now. She slips out through the door and slams it shut right in my face. It's what I deserve after all the pain I've caused her, after all. In fact, I deserve much worse than that. Much worse, indeed.

I idle for a few moments in the entryway, gazing at the empty room waiting to swallow me whole—the emptiness I've invented, the desolation I've created from loving too much or not enough, the vacancy I've earned from a life misspent.

Email Addressed to Clovis R. Morrow from Simeon Link

from: Simeon Link <simeonlink_86@[redacted].com>

to: Clovis R. Morrow <clovis.morrow@[redacted].com>

date: August 2, 2025

subject: Meeting soon

Clovis,

I need to schedule another meeting with Porcelain as soon as possible. Please let me know availability. Tonight?

Best,

Simeon

Email Addressed to Simeon Link from Clovis R. Morrow

from: Clovis R. Morrow <clovis.morrow@[redacted].com>

to: Simeon Link <simeonlink_86@[redacted].com>

date: August 2, 2025

subject: RE: Meeting soon

Simeon,

I'm not sure if it's feasible (or even worthwhile) to arrange a third meeting with Porcelain. I would caution you against attempting to make further contact, for your own safety.

Regards,

C

Email Addressed to Clovis R. Morrow from Simeon Link

from: Simeon Link <simeonlink_86@[redacted].com>

to: Clovis R. Morrow <clovis.morrow@[redacted].com>

date: August 2, 2025

subject: RE: Meeting soon

I'm coming over tonight. You can expect me to arrive there at eight o'clock. I will not accept "no" as an answer.

Chapter Twelve

I arrive at the small bungalow around eight o'clock, and I half expect to find Clovis greeting me at the end of the driveway with a look of disapproval, with arms crossed and an invitation forever revoked. No such thing occurs. Instead, I'm left to my own devices, finding my way as I drift toward the house and then eventually throw the gear into park. I scramble out of the driver's seat and do not hesitate before making my way up the path leading toward the front door. Once again, I observe the small statues of gargoyles guarding the home's threshold—denizens of another world, purveyors of brutality and eager to judge all trespassers, all who might arrive unannounced. I slam my fist against the door and wait a few moments. I wonder if I'll hear approaching footsteps. But I'm left there to wait. Seconds turn to minutes, and very soon I come to the awful realization that nobody is going to answer the door. I twist the handle and lean against the frame, pushing the door open. I'm surprised, of course. I imagined Clovis might greet me there with a stern lecture, with all sorts of condemnations and criticisms worthy of a child who disobeyed their captor.

I ease across the threshold and close the door behind me, moving farther and farther into the entryway. Calling out for Clovis, I'm met with only silence in return. The whole house around me seems to soften, thawing with warmth the way a giant beast might settle when presented with the sacred offering of nourishment. *Am I something to be fed to some invisible deity, some gibbering monstrosity?* I can't be saddled with those meaningless questions right now.

Just then, I hear the sound of someone—*something?*—stirring inside the washroom located adjacent to where I'm standing. The bathroom door is open slightly, and a light has been left on inside the room, so I figure someone must be in there. Naturally, this isn't the time for pleasantries, and normally I might wait for Clovis—or whoever's in there—to come out, to reveal himself to me. But I feel especially unsettled. Or perhaps I feel indifferent to his privacy right now. His comfort doesn't matter to me. I tiptoe across the entryway and lean against the door until it eases open, and I'm left standing there at the small, windowless room's threshold. The washroom is just as unfriendly-looking, just as unappealing and unattractive as the rest of the household. In fact, it leads me to wonder if this is merely one of a few places that Clovis brings Porcelain to meet with his clients. The more I dwell here, the more I explore, the more I realize that this place feels like a transient sort of place. A place without an identity, a godless creature without a proper name.

I peer farther into the bathroom and find no decorations in the space. There's a rusted-looking toilet situated in the corner of the room near the heater. There's a large mirror over the washroom sink; however, there are no visible toiletries or things for guests to clean themselves with. It feels like a room where I am not allowed. I turn slightly, and it's then that I notice a large portrait hanging on the stretch of wall hidden behind where the door swings open. The oil painting is of both Porcelain and Clovis, their features somewhat exaggerated and embellished to make them appear more menacing, crueler even. In the portrait, Porcelain is situated on a large chair, and his legs are spread open with an obvious invitation. He's dressed entirely in white like some angelic cherub, like some impressive dignitary from a celestial court. Behind him, Clovis leers over his shoulder with the same disapproving scowl of a parent or guardian.

I notice something especially unusual about the way the artist has drawn their eyes in the painting. Their eyes are silvery, reflective almost, and hollow-looking, as though they have been carved out and replaced with tiny bits of metal. At the bottom of the portrait, there's some graffiti scrawled there. I squint, drawing closer, and I read what's been written in the corner: *Fucking cannibals.* I tilt my head slightly and lean nearer to read the inscription of the artist's name, but the paint there has been worn away.

Just then, I notice the edge of a small photograph sticking out from behind the ornate portrait frame. I squint, struggling to look closer. With my thumb and index finger, I grab hold of the photograph's edge and pull it out until it's freed. I hold the small picture in my hands, my eyes going over the image again and again. The blurry picture is of an empty park bench, pink flowers arranged on both sides. There's an inscription scrawled in permanent marker at the bottom of the photo. It reads *Charlotte "Charli" O'Connell, Member of the Wretches—August 2022.* I sense my heartbeat quicken, my blood racing when I read the word "Wretches." *It can't be,* I think to myself. *An image from their private club? Are there others? Indeed, there must be others.*

My breath becoming shallower, I grab hold of the large picture frame against the wall, and I start to pull. The frame, though ornate and flecked with what appears to be genuine gold, is much lighter than I anticipated. The damn thing comes off the wall in a few seconds, and hidden on the frame's back side are dozens—*no, there must be hundreds*—of photographs of inanimate objects with people's names and dates written in chicken scratch at the bottom of each image. I do a double take, wondering if I recognize one of the photographs pinned at the bottom of the large frame's edge. It's the very same photo I saw in Mr. Whittaker's office—the picture of the grove of trees, the supposed picture of his dead wife. I wonder if I'll vomit at the horrible recognition. *How many have there been before me? Even worse to consider, where are they now?* I shake my head in disbelief, eyes scanning images of furniture, plants, kitchen cutlery—all different kinds of objects. Each photo taken with such care and nuance, as if begging the viewer to understand that there's something hidden inside this photo, there's meaning here. If there is, I'm afraid I cannot recognize it. I see no human faces in any of these objects. Instead, I sense a quiet desperation—an unshakable urgency for this magic to be true.

I run down the narrow passageway littered with small reflective beetles, until I finally come upon the door at the end of the hall. I think about knocking first, about warning Porcelain that I've arrived, that I've come to take more from him. But does Porcelain actually deserve such decency? Is Porcelain worthy of such formality? I don't think so. More and more, I can't help but think of Porcelain as some wretched prostitute, some miserable panhandler on the cramped streets of a foreign city deceiving tourists with decaying rituals of magic and woeful showmanship.

I push the door open and step inside the suite. Immediately I notice Porcelain milling about in the corner of the room. He's facing the wall, his back greeting me as soon as I enter the small room.

"Clovis told you not to come," he says to me, his voice flat and without feeling. "Why did you disobey him?"

I inch farther into the suite. "Clovis doesn't understand how badly I need this. . . ."

"What do you need exactly?" Porcelain asks, turning to face me. "Haven't I offered you enough?"

"You've offered more questions than explanations," I tell him. "You could at least try to possess enough decency to provide some answers. . . ."

Porcelain titters, amused. "What would you know about decency?"

I swallow nervously, realizing I'm not getting anywhere with Porcelain. He seems so much more obstinate, so much more difficult to get a sense of his feelings. I reach into my pocket and pull out a large golden hairpin in the shape of a butterfly.

"I brought this for you," I tell him. "Something Jonathan once bought at a market . . . I thought maybe you could . . ."

But my voice trails off, unsure. There's a part of me that must recognize the simple fact that Jonathan's spirit—*his essence*—no longer wishes to see me, to be haunted by me. That's exactly what I'm doing: *I'm haunting him.* I'm unspooling the moth-eaten threads of his spirit bit by bit each time I send for him, each time I attempt to make contact with his ghost. Perhaps I am destroying him. Perhaps that's why I am misremembering moments we shared together—I am devouring my own memory of dear, sweet Jonathan.

"I thought maybe you could bring him back to me one last time," I say to Porcelain. "I need to say goodbye."

But Porcelain shakes his head. "You've already said enough to him."

I sense my stomach tightening into a knot. "Is that what he thinks? Or is that what you think?"

I'm surprised at myself for pushing such a challenge toward him, for calling his bluff. But I know in my heart I must see Jonathan once more. One last time. And that will be it. I won't seek out Porcelain ever again. I won't crave Jonathan's tenderness, his sympathy. I'll finally be able to let him rest. But I just need one more moment with him.

"The answer is no," Porcelain tells me, turning away.

I move closer toward him while he dawdles in the far corner of the room like a petulant toddler who was sent away for a time-out.

"You could refuse me?" I ask him. "After all we've shared together?"

"I shared," Porcelain says. "You took. . . . That's all you do. . . ."

"Weren't you willing to give?" I ask. "Isn't that what you're capable of doing?"

"Try doing it day after day after day," he says gently, his breath whistling.

I sense my hand curling into a fist. I feel such a need, such a desire to hurt something, someone. I don't quite know where exactly this desire, this need came from, but it shocks me all the same.

"You're turning me down?" I ask him, trying to disguise my shock with sincerity, with hurt.

But Porcelain won't answer me.

I don't realize what I'm doing until I'm lurching toward him, reaching out to touch his shoulder. As soon as I touch his arm, Porcelain swivels around with a power that shocks me, nearly knocks me over, and he charges at me with a hand against my throat until I'm pinned against the nearby wall.

"Don't fucking touch me," he shouts at me, gripping hold of my throat and squeezing tight.

What happens next is a blur, and I find myself lost in a stupor, eventually awakened—snapped to reality—when a burst of blood splatters me in the face. Porcelain's blood. His mouth hangs open, a dark line of red trickling from the corner of his chapped lips. It's then that I realize the horrible truth: I'm holding the golden hairpin, its needle-thin point skewering Porcelain's throat and stirring there gently. Porcelain regards me with such surprise coupled with obvious dismay. *How could you?* His eyes seem to beg me for an answer. I'm afraid I have no explanation to divulge while I hold the hairpin there for a moment. Realizing the horror of what I've done, I drag the pin from the hole I've opened in his neck, and blood shoots out, spattering the nearby wall.

"Wait," I whisper, as if I could somehow undo what I've done, as if I could salvage his body and mend the wound I've so carelessly opened in my fit of rage.

But it's too late for such enchantments, such fanciful forms of magic. Porcelain's mouth opens and closes, trying to say something. Perhaps he's calling for help. Perhaps he's seeking absolution from a lesser god. I can't be certain, and I remain guessing even as he leans forward, crumpling into my arms. More of his blood drenches me, dyeing my clothing dark red. I try to hold him, but he's too heavy, and eventually he slips from my grasp and crashes against the floor with a stomach-turning thud.

I kneel beside him and flip him over to face me, observing while a steady stream of his blood leaks across the carpet like a late-night tide. For a moment, I see my reflection in the pool of blood spreading farther and farther across the floor like the very last remaining bits of his shadow. I grab hold of Porcelain's trembling hand and squeeze it tight.

"I'm sorry," I tell him. "I didn't mean to . . ."

Porcelain seizes. He coughs, blood spattering me in the face when he gazes at me.

"Do what you've always done," he says weakly. *"Ignore it. Ignore it. Ignore it. . . ."*

But I shake my head, grabbing his hand and holding tighter. "I don't want to ignore it. . . . I want to know if he loved me. . . . If he actually cared. . . ."

Porcelain's whole body shudders like he's in the throes of some uncontrollable convulsion. When he finally calms, he gazes at me with a look of such tenderness, of such pity.

"He's inside me," Porcelain says.

"Who?"

"Your Jonathan," he tells me, lifting his shirt and exposing his quarter-sized belly button. *"Open me up further. . . . Come find him. . . ."*

I look down and notice how the edges of Porcelain's belly button are scabbed black and cauterized as if burned, as though a blowtorch had been held there for an extended period of time by some kind of sadist, some sort of bloodthirsty marauder. The opening is small and yet also large enough to fit a slim finger or two inside. I do what he tells me to do—I ease my index finger inside Porcelain's navel, and I sense him wincing, shifting. Not from pain, though. From excitement. I hear how he coos, how he mewls like a kitten—delighted to receive me there, eager for me to spread the edges of his freshly greased hole farther and farther apart. I feel my emerald ring—the very thing Jonathan once gifted me, a token of his affection, a symbol of love and death—slip off my finger and disappear inside like it had been sucked up by some ancient vacuum.

As I push myself farther inside him, I sense the passage of his belly button dilating under the force of my pressure. The opening feels rubbery, slick, recently oiled with his blood. It isn't long before I can fit my entire right hand inside his opening, more of me spilling into him until I sense parts of myself becoming viscous, syrupy—easy to slip inside. I feel compelled to claw my way deeper inside him, as though I were acutely aware of some invisible prize or trophy awaiting me, as though I had been commanded to push myself farther inside him by some soundless voice—the voice of an ageless deity, some powerful cosmic essence longing to be fed.

A consumer of souls.

The edges of Porcelain's belly button furrow, wrinkling apart and rippling until it's large enough to fit my entire head into the opening. I do not hesitate this time. Although I might be frightened, might be nervous to delve deeper into Porcelain's body, I find parts of myself thawing with what could only be described as momentary pleasure. I feel as though I'm being cradled, gently swept away on a fast-moving current that will send me out to an infinite sea—a place where I can search for Jonathan until I drown.

I have become the wretched, incurable thing that now looks out from behind Porcelain's eyes. I am the curiosity lingering in the weighted breath of every question forced upon a meek, unassuming visitor who might never return. I am the sadness existing in the wordless questions, the muted condolences, the pitiful touch. I am nothing more than a blemish on Porcelain's very soul. *Am I a ghost? Am I something that yearns to be remembered, a thing that aches to be recalled by someone else?* No one will ever come for me. That much is certain.

I am now very much a permanent relic of Porcelain's assortment of curiosities—a spirit not so dissimilar from the tiny, reflective ones that Kent once spoke of. In fact, I wonder if he knew all this was going to happen to me. I'm sure he did on some level. He had to have known what might happen if he sent me here, if he encouraged my obsession with Porcelain and his strange magical powers. Yes, perhaps he was the one I encountered in those chat rooms. Of course, it's likely I'll never know the true answer.

For now, I am a wretch, a blighted thing to be tucked away in some unspoiled corner of the soul, pushed to one side so that I don't disturb or damage the other nearby organs. In fact, there are times when I wonder if I am slowly mutating, if I am becoming a functioning structure inside Porcelain's body—something that could never be removed, something that would destroy him if it were ever excised. There are times when I feel soft and fleshy, easy to squish. It feels nauseating to realize that you're living for someone else, for the care and upkeep of another living organism, like I was some sort of parasite, some kind of ravenous, insatiable bloodsucker. Then again, haven't I always been those things? Haven't I always been desperate to use others, to drain them of all their love and affection so long as it's convenient for me?

Perhaps it was Porcelain who made me realize and come to terms with what I truly am—a leech, a kind of cannibal who's eager to assimilate and devour the goodwill of all others around me. I find myself sulking very often now, recognizing how miserable I've been and wishing I could do something to alter my fate, to make it so that I had one more chance with those who loved me, truly and unmistakably loved me.

Maybe the only good fortune I've inherited since being consumed, since being swallowed whole, is the fact that there are others existing inside the cramped fishbowl of Porcelain's spirit—others who sought similar answers and were met with riddles that could never be solved. *At least I am not alone here,* I think to myself. Sometimes we converse with one another and recall the moments we endured when we were once fully human. It feels strange and also sad to think of our lives as over now, our existence completely dependent on our host. There are others trapped in here who can hardly speak. Instead, they sob quietly and beg for release, plead with Porcelain for a semblance of mercy, a stroke of pity that he might release them, that he might cast them out and let them be free. He ignores their pleas, of course. Still, there are some who are imprisoned with me inside this puzzle, this forever undulating sculpture of muscle and sinew, who are somewhat pleasant despite the awful circumstances.

There's a middle-aged woman in particular I quite enjoy talking to. She tells me her name is Genevieve.

I always thought that was such a pretty name.

HAUNTED

If I lay at your feet and yelped like a dog, would you still step over me?

—*Possession* (1981)

One of the thoughts that upsets me day after day while I exist here is the memory of my sweet, precious Carter. I should have loved him more. I should have cared for him more fiercely. Although fatherhood probably never suited me and I was ill equipped for the role, I should have offered that boy more affection, more sensitivity and tenderness. Of course, I already know how much I've hurt Evelyn—how I've irreparably wounded her, cast her out like some damaged piece of pottery. I should have loved her more earnestly as well. She deserved so much better.

While I idle in the filthy sewers of Porcelain's essence, I come to the awful realization that I wasted so much time, so much energy, pining for a love, a person, who could never return the intensity of my love to the fullest extent. Although Jonathan was a sweet, caring man, I cannot help but wonder if I squandered so much time yearning for him and neglected so many of my other responsibilities. Yes, it's obvious now while I stir in the murky depths of Porcelain's soul.

I curse myself for abandoning Evelyn and Carter so thoughtlessly, so cruelly. *How can they ever forgive me for what I've done to them?* I should have loved them more fiercely. . . .

I peer out from behind Porcelain's eyes and notice Clovis as he enters the suite, shutting the door and locking it behind him. He holds a small, folded piece of paper in his hand. There's a part of me that wonders if Clovis might be able to observe me, might be able to serve as witness to my suffering—my silhouette dimmed beyond the transparent curtain of Porcelain's left eye, my presence stirring there and aching to be noticed. He doesn't seem to react when he approaches Porcelain, even though I shout to him, praying that he might recognize me.

"A letter arrived this morning," he tells Porcelain. "A prospective client . . . A woman named Evelyn Rhodes . . ."

I feel myself tense at the very mention of her name. *It can't be,* I think to myself. *Can it really be Evelyn?*

"She comes highly recommended," Clovis says.

"She won't be much of a problem?" Porcelain asks, straightening.

"I suppose we never can truly tell until they're here in the room," Clovis replies, unfolding the letter. "Shall I read you what she wrote?"

Porcelain merely gestures for Clovis to begin.

Clovis slides on a pair of reading glasses, tipping them at the end of his nose and squinting when he regards the paper. He begins to read:

Dear Mr. Morrow,

I hope you will pardon the forwardness of this letter, and I sincerely hope that I'm not intruding upon your privacy by contacting you. I realize that you must be incredibly busy, so I'll try to dispense with the formalities as much as possible.

A new acquaintance of mine informed me that you represent a certain individual who might be able to assist me. I hope I'm not being too forward.

I'm afraid I've been mourning the presence of my ex-husband—a man who told me time and time again that he did not love me, did not care for me nor the life we had created together. Naturally, I feel foolish wasting so much time, so much of my energy on someone who proved his disloyalty again and again; however, I find it nearly impossible to release him, to banish him from the confines of my mind. It's not that he haunts me still, but rather that I've chosen to haunt him. I've elected to spend my precious time thinking of him, pining for his spirit, his tenderness, his care. I worry that I'll split apart if I continue to carry on like this, to continue wasting so much of my energy, my spirit.

I've come to the hideous realization that there are people in my life that I'll never truly comprehend. Of course, this may not be a terribly painful revelation for some who remain guarded and not so easily trusting. But I hardly expected I would need to remain guarded with my own child, my own son. It's taken me an extraordinary amount of time to recognize the fact that my child, Carter, has had dealings with unsavory people online. He's plotted and planned certain events, certain attacks, against people he did not trust.

Most notably, his father.

It's almost too disgusting to confess, but my son has made every attempt to undo the resolve of his poor father, to irrevocably destroy him. I came to this discovery after checking our internet browser history and after reviewing so many correspondences with others in an online community known as the Grim Laurels. Even more disturbing: my child's username—babyfacexoxo.

It's too hideous to even think about—to consider the actuality of a young, sixteen-year-old boy setting out to destroy his father, to dismantle a grown man in every which way and render him as unusable goods. My ex-husband certainly was not a perfect man; however, in the eyes of our child, he was monstrous and vile. Carter mentioned on many forums how destroying his father would be a kind of "mercy killing"—a sort of "coup de grâce." How he rationalized this, I will never truly comprehend. I didn't think he knew such words. It frightens me terribly. It makes me worried about my child, fearful of what he might do to me if I ever displease him, if I ever become as loathsome and vile as Simeon was in his eyes.

Of course, you might not believe any of this. It's too ridiculous, too outrageous, to even attempt to credit as true. But my son is not who he appears to be. Even worse, I fear he's done something irreversible to my ex-husband by coordinating so many parties in an effort to get rid of him. I worry that I'm somewhat responsible for my child's actions—for allowing him to sign up for social media accounts at an early age and permitting him to have unrestricted access to the internet while I wasn't supervising. His designs to destroy his father undoubtedly came from his own mind, but I certainly aided him in the process. I, in turn, caused the destruction of my beloved Simeon.

I realize it's probably futile, but I'm hopeful that you may be able to help me. I'm still processing the hideous truth that my son is not as innocent, not as charming and kind, as he pretends to be.

I'm hopeful that by paying you and your associate a visit, the memory of my ex-husband will become less painful—less of a gruesome reminder that we are inevitable subjects to the scheming of others. I hope that I have not intruded too much on your valuable time. I sincerely look forward to hearing from you.

Best wishes,
Evelyn Rhodes

Finally, Clovis pulls his attention away from the sheet of paper and glances at Porcelain, expecting a response, anticipating a word, a signal, a sign—anything.

I sense myself tremor. Carter. It doesn't feel real or possible. I know I wasn't the father he deserved; however, I truly wonder if I was such a poor excuse for a parent that it seemed right to him to attempt to destroy me. I tremble, realizing all the things I said to him in that chat room—my own child. If it's possible, I feel even more disgusting for having shamed myself in front of my son.

Naturally, I also feel pity for poor Evelyn—for all I've done to her, for all the misery I've caused, for leaving her in the middle of a sentence. *But what am I to do now?* I'm left to languish here, to remain a trinket of Porcelain's private collection—a benign cyst attached to one of his vital organs. If only there were a way to reach out to her, to prevent her from coming here, to make her reconsider everything before she becomes the same sort of relic warehoused forever inside Porcelain's gruesome depository. I must do something to save her.

"What shall I do with this one?" Clovis asks him.

Porcelain hesitates for a moment. I can taste his indecision, the panic of his uncertainty. It's sweet, candied almost.

"Send for her," he finally tells him. "I'll wait. . . ."

After Clovis leaves the room, I sense Porcelain softening a little—his joints aching, his heart quickening in anticipation of a new rendezvous, a new client to impress with all his wonders.

"I'll wait with you," I whisper to him in the way we've become able to communicate with each other while I laze inside the bulb of his eye.

But he shakes his head, his eyelids narrowing to mere slits as though he were making every attempt to squeeze me from there—to expel me, to send me out through a single teardrop. *Is he going to—Why now?*

"You can't stay any longer," he tells me in his mind. *"I've no more use for you. . . ."*

"Use for me?" I ask him. *"What's to become of me?"*

"I can't keep you inside me," he says, swallowing again and again. *"There are certain souls I'm not able to keep, not allowed to fully possess. . . ."*

I sense what remains of myself thawing until I'm completely dissolved and then dripping into the pit of his throat. It's warm and soft there.

He starts to heave, pushing me out like bile slowly rising. Even though I've become impossibly small—probably the size of a thimble—he struggles to push me from the bed of his tongue—to evict me, to birth me again. Finally, after an arduous labor, I crawl from his mouth, and I'm delivered inside a ball of warm phlegm to the spongy carpet, where I rest for a moment before composing myself, before recognizing the horrible truth of what I've become. I have more legs than I can adequately recall. My casing is shiny, reflective, almost like a showroom mirror.

I find myself settling there for a moment, realizing how everything around me is so much larger than when I was human. I can't help but feel insignificant, so inferior. *Why has he done this to me? Was this part of his plan all along?* I scurry along the baseboard until I arrive in the far corner of the suite, where I imagine I'm safe for the time being.

Just then, the door to Porcelain's room opens, and I observe as Evelyn enters the room. She's thinner than I recall. Probably hasn't been eating much lately. Her face is flushed, her hands trembling. I watch in silence as Porcelain greets her the same way he greets most of his new arrivals—with a look of indifference, of such disdainful apathy.

"You brought an item for me?" he asks her coldly.

Evelyn winces, snapping awake from her trance. She reaches into her handbag and pulls out a printed photograph. I can't quite tell exactly what it is from where I am, but I think I recognize what she's brought him. It's the picture I took in the park of the trellis—the photograph of my beloved Jonathan's face.

"Simeon loved this picture," she tells Porcelain. "Always carried it with him . . ."

Porcelain accepts the offering, glances at it, and then tosses it on the nearby nightstand.

"Very good," he mutters to her. "Shall we begin?"

Evelyn observes while Porcelain drifts back toward the bed, sitting there at the very end of the mattress and spreading his legs open with an obvious request.

I notice how she trembles a little. "How?" she asks him.

Even as a lowly insect, I feel such pity for poor Evelyn—for making her come here, for manipulating her and the sweet child we created together who I know full well I will never see again. It's then I begin to make my way up the empty wall adjacent to the suite's bed, my set of feet carrying me as fast as I can scurry.

"There are many ways for this to begin," Porcelain tells her. "But I'm afraid you won't like any of them."

I observe how Evelyn convulses a little, shivering.

"Why is that?" she asks.

Porcelain leans forward a little. "Because you're going to have to suffer," he says to her with such delight, such excitement to be the one inscribing her very destruction.

I crawl along the partition arranged beside the bed. I am impossibly small and almost too delicate to appreciate fully if it weren't for my silvery reflective shell in the shape of a small gemstone. I hope that Evelyn notices me, that she might acknowledge the loathsome insect that I've become. *But what can she do to help me?* Of course, I can't pretend to imagine she'd be able to do anything to undo Porcelain's enchantment. Still, I ache for her attention. *Don't ignore me, Evelyn,* I quietly beg her. *Please. Don't ignore me. . . .*

Perhaps she may not be able to help me; however, I must do everything I can to save her, to spare her the same fate I've been sentenced to endure. I must get her to notice me, to recognize the awful truth of the miserable wretch I've become. *Please, Evelyn,* I think to myself. *Please understand what can happen to you if you're foolish enough to cross this threshold.* My selflessness surprises me, in fact. It's been eons since I've thought of anyone besides myself. I'd give anything to help her, to spare her the affliction, the misery that Porcelain will undoubtedly put her through. It won't be long before she'll be consumed and then spat out upon the carpet—a vile, lowly creature forever sentenced to squat and scurry around his feet like a worthless, pathetic thing.

When it happens to her, I wonder if she'll finally despise me, if she'll finally loathe me as she should have all this time. *Why didn't you stop him?* she might ask me. *Why didn't you prevent all this senseless horror from happening?* Naturally, I will have nothing to say. There are no explanations to be rehearsed for when that dreaded moment finally arrives. I've already failed her and our son. Carter will be left without love, without the tenderness and care of a proper guardian. His parents—immortal bugs on display and under the care of some depraved, ageless entity, some kind of all-devouring, ungodly force. Even though he betrayed me and devoted so much of his life to organizing my downfall, I still love him. I still yearn for my precious boy to be loved by others.

There's a brief moment when I wonder if Evelyn will finally turn, if she'll tilt her head at me and gaze at the small beetle creeping there, leering at her from the partition. But she does no such thing. Instead, Evelyn moves closer toward Porcelain, who's still waiting for her at the edge of the bed with his horrifying invitation—a dark tide dragging her farther and farther away from me, until I can see her no more.

Further Reading, Viewing, and Listening

While creating the surreal, erotically charged world of *Wretch*, I consumed a great deal of excellent media—from literature to film to music. Here are some gems I discovered during the writing process of crafting this novel. *(Please note, the titles listed below are curated in no particular order.)*

Books:

- *The Discomfort of Evening* by Lucas Rijneveld
- *The Country Will Bring Us No Peace* by Matthieu Simard
- *The Stepdaughter* by Caroline Blackwood
- *The Dumb House* by John Burnside
- *The Marbled Swarm* by Dennis Cooper
- *Nothing But the Rain* by Naomi Salman

Film:

- *Singapore Sling* (1990) Directed by Nikos Nikolaidis
- *The War Zone* (1999) Directed by Tim Roth
- *Nekromantik* (1988) Directed by Jörg Buttgereit
- *Uncle Cyril* (or *The Damned House of Hajn*) (1989) Directed by Jirí Svoboda
- *Morgiana* (1972) Directed by Juraj Herz

Music:

- *Mayhem* / Lady Gaga ("Disease," "Perfect Celebrity," "Zombieboy")
- *PREY//IV* / Alice Glass ("Baby Teeth")
- *OVERSOUL* / Kerli ("The Art of Being Alone")
- *Girl with No Face* / Allie X ("Weird World," "Black Eye")

ACKNOWLEDGMENTS

This novel would not exist without the grace and insight of my editor, Tim O'Connell. Tim and I first connected in 2021 right around the release of my novella *Things Have Gotten Worse Since We Last Spoke.* Since then, he's remained a dedicated fan and supporter of my work. I extend all my gratitude and love to Tim for trusting in my artistic vision. More importantly, I sincerely thank him for guiding me and helping me create something truly remarkable with this novel. Also, I send my eternal gratitude to Caroline Tew and Joe Monti of Saga Press.

I would be remiss if I did not thank my wonderful and equally supportive literary agent, Priya Doraswamy. Priya is another key reason as to why this book exists in the first place.

Throughout the creation of this novel, I listened to one musical artist in particular: Porcelain Black. If you're a fan of dark industrial pop music, I highly recommend listening to her scrapped album, *Mannequin Factory.* Highlighted songs are as follows:

"Mannequin Factory"

"Swallow My Bullet"

"Mama Forgive Me"

"Pretty Little Psycho"

"Stealing Candy from a Baby"

I also read a considerable amount of dark fiction from three authors while writing this book. These authors are Clive Barker, Dennis Cooper, and Chuck Palahniuk. To me, these authors represent the Holy Trinity of transgressive queer fiction. I love them with my whole being and I sincerely thank them for offering their gifts, their talents to the world. *Wretch* would not be able to exist without them.